Bits

Of

Anarchy

Also by the author in reading order:

Destiny: Union Station
Date Night on Union Station
Alien Night on Union Station
High Priest on Union Station
Spy Night on Union Station
Carnival on Union Station
Wanderers on Union Station
Vacation on Union Station
Guest Night on Union Station
Word Night on Union Station
Party Night on Union Station
Review Night on Union Station
Family Night on Union Station
Book Night on Union Station
LARP Night on Union Station
Career Night on Union Station
Last Night on Union Station
Independent Living
Soup Night on Union Station
Assisted Living
Freelance on the Galactic Tunnel Network
Con Living
Empire Night on Union Station
Space Living
Traders on the Galactic Tunnel Network
Orphans on the Galactic Tunnel Network
Swap Night on Union Station
Slow Living
Artists on the Galactic Tunnel Network
History Night on Union Station

Bits

Of

Anarchy

Book One of EarthCent Metaverse

Foner Books

ISBN 978-1-948691-37-6

Hardwick, Massachusetts

One

Mouser blinked when the overhead lighting in his workshop came on at full brightness. He returned the soldering iron to its holder, placed the antique circuit board in a silvery antistatic bag, and swiveled on his faux-antique workbench stool to see who had entered.

"Sorry to interrupt, but it's important," said the visitor. She was in her early thirties and dressed in a conservative business suit, making her an anomaly among the planet's residents. "It can't wait until the next Rules Committee meeting."

"I forgot to stop for lunch and now I'm hungry," the older man said, patting his paunch. "How about we discuss it over pizza?"

"There's no room in the budget," Rayne replied

"For a vending machine pizza? Remind me again why I signed up for the Rules Committee."

"You didn't sign up. We pulled your name out of a digital hat and the drawing was fixed. No, it's better you stay seated," she added, settling herself on the ancient leather couch that was stained with the spilled drinks of excited role players from thousands of gaming sessions. "We're broke."

"You're the treasurer," Mouser said. "Offer everybody a discount if they prepay for the next year's air supply or up the fee on this weekend's hack-a-thon."

"I'm not talking about being short of pizza money for an informal meeting," Rayne told him. "I had to rob the royalty accounts to make the planetary lease payment this morning. If we had a government on Bits, it would be falling as we speak."

"You have access to the royalty accounts? I thought that the programming teams were completely independent."

"I didn't use the word 'rob' for the sake of exaggeration."

"Oh." Mouser got up and went to the small fridge. "Soda?"

"How can you drink soda at a time like this? When everybody finds out what I did they're going to throw me out an airlock."

"The atmosphere is thin, but it won't kill you, at least not right away," Mouser said, bringing her an imported aluminum can of grape soda. "Breathe slow and come around to the spaceport entrance and I'll let you back in. Besides, I remember something like this happening around twenty years ago. We all tightened our belts for a few months, and when the tithes caught up, the Rules Committee paid back the money they borrowed."

"You're not getting it." Rayne pulled back the tab on her soda can and took a long sip. "Our income has been on a slow downward slope ever since the Gem Empire collapsed, and things really started falling off the cliff after the Traitors left three years ago. We've blown through the rainy day fund, the solar flare fund, and the apocalypse fund. Even if everybody agreed to double the tithe, there's just not enough royalties and paying work coming in to save up for the next lease payment, not to mention importing the essentials like—" she took another sip, "—canned soda from Earth."

"I thought that the Hortens leased us the planet on a per-head basis," Mouser said. "Didn't our payment take a big drop when we lost ten percent of our population to Flower?"

"If you add the retirees to Earth and the people leaving for open worlds or Stryx stations in the last decade, our payment has dropped by almost twenty percent, but the problem is on the income side."

"Why? I've got a backlog of repairs that will last longer than I do, and everybody I know is working all of the time."

"They're playing games all of the time. It's not the same thing."

"It's beta testing," Mouser protested. "You wouldn't want the programming teams shipping buggy products and destroying our reputation."

"Sales are shrinking," Rayne said, putting her can down on the low coffee table that was covered with ring stains. She began ticking off facts on her fingers. "The only Gem buying updates to Cloner these days are the ones who were on the wrong side of their revolution, and they've been losing interest ever since the New Gem Empire started bringing back males."

"Did I ever tell you about the time I was working ground control and the head of EarthCent Intelligence visited with a young Stryx to warn us about the collapse of the Gem Empire?"

"Many times, and stop trying to change the subject," the treasurer said, looking at her fingers and trying to remember where she had left off. "The charity jobs we used to get from aliens to do low-level coding for gadgets or to add human-compatible interfaces to equipment for contract workers has dried up. It turns out the Traitors were the ones with the contacts to bring that work in."

"We lost some pretty good salespeople in that group," Mouser said. "Your ex—"

"But most importantly," Rayne cut him off, pinching the tip of the ring finger of her left hand between the thumb and forefinger of the right while brandishing it at him, "sales of in-game enhancements for our retro first-person shooter games are down by half from five years ago, and the launch of Magellanic Clouds Marines laid a big, fat, goose egg."

"That bad?"

"They haven't told anybody yet, but it sold less than a half-million copies, and that includes deep discounts on the presales. Our existing customer base is aging out and new gamers are all getting into that live-action stuff or playing alien titles. The only business that's growing at all is creating apps for the smartphone market on Earth, and that only exists because the cellular network was designated a protected heritage technology."

Mouser crushed his empty soda can and tossed it towards the plastic barrel for aluminum recycling where it joined the other near misses on the floor. "So how long do we have?" he asked quietly.

"I don't know," Rayne said, and her shoulders sagged. "The dome's life-support equipment is all overdue for maintenance, but that's nothing new, and we get our power and hot water from the geothermal wells. When is the next container ship expected?"

"Not for another five months. Did the exporters back on Earth get paid for the last batch?"

"Nobody is dumb enough to ship twenty million creds worth of groceries a few hundred light years without getting paid upfront. I thought you knew that was all handled through Thark escrow accounts."

"I wasn't thinking," Mouser said. "So I guess we need to call an emergency meeting of the Rules Committee."

"Won't do any good unless you have a solution to cram down their throats," Rayne said. "Twelve people who don't have a clue what to do next are no better than two. Besides, they'll probably all resign as soon as we tell them."

"Then why did you come to me?"

"Because I've spent every Tuesday night on this couch playing your Phoenician Trader beta for the last couple of years, and the decade before that was one unending dungeon crawl. You're the best gamemaster on Bits."

Mouser put both of his hands on top of his head with the fingers interlaced as if he was trying to prevent his skull from exploding. "No good deed goes unpunished."

"It's true," Rayne insisted. "I can't say two words to Shadow outside of this room without getting into a fight. Delphi pretends she doesn't know me when she's not in character, and don't even get me started on Hercules. Our round ship would have sunk in the ancient Mediterranean three thousand years ago if you weren't so good at managing players."

"Phoenician Trader is still in development so I get to modify the rules when they don't work. I can't ask the exporters on Earth to ship food on credit or tell our alien landlord not to come around in another year looking for the next planetary lease payment. Whatever we do, everybody is going to have to agree on it."

"Bits is an anarchy. The last thing everybody here agreed on was the tithe, and that was before I was born."

"Technically, we agreed to the tithe before we left Earth," Mouser corrected her. "The only thing we've even come close to agreeing on since then was offering our empty dome space to anybody with an interest in gaming. How much revenue is that bringing in?"

"Are you kidding?" Rayne asked in disbelief. "Have you seen any foreigners wandering around looking lost? The only takers have been a few thousand ex-Gem military who got tired of associating with our pirate friends and heard about the rentals from them. And they all made a deal with the landlord to restart the terraforming work rather than paying the head tax. Now, if I had a budget to advertise for immigrants in the Galactic Free Press…"

An obnoxious alarm bell began clanging over Mouser's workbench and he spun on his stool to slap the silencer button. Then he grabbed an old-fashioned microphone that could have been ripped directly from an early twentieth-century radio studio, pressed the button on the base, and growled, "What?"

"Jewel of the New Gem Empire requesting clearance for landing," a stilted voice that was obviously produced by translation technology announced from the speaker of an antique radio cabinet that was probably worth more than everything else in the workshop put together.

"You're not expected and Bits is a safe zone for Old Empire Gem," Mouser said. "Parking for unscheduled visitors is fifty—" he caught sight of Rayne leaning into his field of vision and desperately jabbing her finger towards the ceiling, "five hundred creds."

"You want fifty-five hundred creds to land on this botched terraforming job of a planet?" the artificial voice asked incredulously.

"Just five hundred. I have a little stutter."

"Jewel is an armed cruiser. I'll take out your weapons systems before I'll pay that—what?" There was a silence while somebody filled in the ship's captain on Bit's lack of defenses. "We're landing and we're not paying. Jewel out."

"I tried," Mouser told the disappointed treasurer. "We better go meet them at the airlock and find out what's going on."

"I'll notify our Gem tenants." Rayne tapped to life the screen of her wrist communicator, which was really a small smartphone held in place on her forearm by a wide Velcro strap. "Looks like they already know," she said a minute later. "The main chat room for Cloner looks like comms traffic from a battlefield. And they've decided to make their stand in our museum."

"That's where all the heavy weapons they've sold us over the years are kept, but there's zero chance we're being invaded."

"Why do you say that?"

"Rather than requesting permission for landing, the ship would have come down stealthed and troops would have broken through the airlocks before we knew they were here," Mouser said. "And the revolution was more than twenty years ago. If the winning Gem had been motivated to go after their sisters they would have done it by now."

"It did seem a bit odd that they'd come here when we only have a few thousand Gem in residence and almost never see them," Rayne said, following Mouser into the corridor. The main airlock exiting on the old tarmac was just a dozen steps away. "But what could they—" she stopped short when the most handsome man she had ever seen in her life entered the dome without a hair out of place.

"Mouser. Rayne," the new arrival greeted them as he stepped out of the airlock with an inhumanly perfect smile. "How's the old party holding up? Still raiding dungeons together?"

"Dewey?" Mouser shook his head from side to side as if he couldn't believe his eyes. "Is that you?"

"I decided that if I was going to spend the creds to pass as human, I may as well be good-looking," the artificial person said. "I do miss my old shelving attachment, but I spend less than a quarter of my time in the library these days, and then I'm usually at the front desk rather than working the stacks."

"What were you doing on a Gem warship?"

"Hitching a ride," Dewey said. "They dropped me without stopping and now they're off to go put the fear of the New Empire into a particularly thick-headed bunch of pirates. Somebody owes somebody a favor and they'll be back to pick me up next week."

"They're gone," Rayne confirmed after glancing down at the text flowing across her smartphone screen. "I can't believe it's you, Dewey. How long has it been?"

"Five years, more or less. You see how I've learned not to answer temporal questions down to the picosecond?"

"I'm impressed. Did you come back to Bits for a vacation? You said when you were leaving that if you never saw the place again it would be too soon."

"I was a young artificial intelligence who learned that his existence was purely a matter of accident and that his creators were disappointed they couldn't put him to work as a glorified database system to index all of the information on the planet," Dewey said. "I'll get right to the point and tell you I'm here on business as Flower's emissary. Who's the current chair of the Rules Committee?"

Mouser pointed at his own chest. "I got drafted. Let's go back to my workshop and talk. We're starting to draw a crowd."

"Nothing to see here," Rayne told the people who were leaning out of offices and workshops. "The Gem came, they saw, they vamoosed."

"Who's the hunk?" a teenage girl asked.

"Dewey is artificial intelligence and he's younger than you are," Mouser told the girl in a quiet aside before raising his voice. "Official Rules Committee business. Get out of our way or I'll start delegating."

The small crowd of curiosity seekers melted back into the doorways from which they had emerged.

"I see that the citizenry is as eager as ever to participate in their civic duties," Dewey commented. "I've visited around half of the sovereign human communities in the galaxy since I joined Flower and Bits must be the worst governed of the bunch."

"We aren't governed, that's the whole point of anarchy," Rayne reminded him. "And I don't know if I even want to talk with somebody who consorts with Traitors."

"Traitors?" Dewey tilted his head as if he was having trouble processing her words and needed to slide a new memory into place. "Is that what you're calling the twenty thousand Bitters who were smart enough to join Flower a couple of years after I did? I've worked with them on a number of projects and they're having the time of their lives."

"What a twenty-thousand-year-old Dollnick artificial intelligence is doing babysitting a bunch of human rejects is beyond me," Mouser grumbled as he led the way into his workshop. "And I always thought that Flower was a silly name for an alien colony ship."

"Flower could turn Bits into a ball of molten rock without straining her secondary pile. She chose the name because it's non-threatening."

The artificial person dusted some unidentifiable crumbs off the couch before taking his seat, and Rayne plopped down at the other end. Mouser grabbed a bag of potato chips from a large stainless steel cabinet labeled 'Hazardous waste' and settled into the overstuffed chair on the other side of the coffee table. The two humans exchanged a look and waited for their guest to speak first.

"You're broke," Dewey said.

"How did you know?" Rayne asked.

"And given that you must have left Flower days, if not weeks ago, how did you find out before I did?" Mouser added.

"Flower hosts a group of alien intelligence agents under an arrangement I'm not at liberty to detail, but the point is, we have our sources of information," Dewey said. "Your planetary lease payment to the Hortens is overdue and there's not enough money in the Bits treasury to pay. I'm here to offer you a way out."

The treasurer began to open her mouth to contradict the artificial person but Mouser spoke right over her. "You're right," he said, shooting a warning look at Rayne. "We're broke, and if we can't come up with the payment in a hurry, the Hortens are likely to evict us. So what can you and your rogue Dollnick friend do about it?"

"Flower is not a rogue, and I can offer you two options," Dewey said. "Our schedule is much tighter now that we've added four stops a year at Earth Two to ferry colonists and supervise the final stages of the terraforming, but Flower still has one open discretionary stop every other circuit. She's willing to come here to take you all on board."

"With the Traitors?" Rayne asked, her voice rising. "Never."

"They are fully employed, making more money than they ever did here, and there's enough work for the rest of you and a few million more. The games they play and the hacking they do in their free time is up to them. If you want to continue your ridiculous schism over archaic programming languages and platform technology on board Flower, you'll be free to do so."

"Easy, Rayne," Mouser murmured to the treasurer before she could explode in indignation. He tossed her the bag of chips, perhaps to keep her hands busy so she wouldn't go for the artificial person's throat. "What's the second option?"

"Remote work," Dewey said. "Flower Entertainment has been experimenting with Live Action Role Playing. We have two studios on board and Flower aspires to hosting a tournament for the professional LARPing league. But our game developers—"

"Traitors," Rayne interjected through a mouthful of potato chips.

"—are too busy with other projects to create a whole new role-playing franchise," the artificial person continued, as if the interruption had never happened. "Flower has a rather unique take on the LARPing market. She wants to create a new segment that can be enjoyed by members of the tunnel network species of all ages and played across a full spectrum of platforms, from board games right up through the immersive virtual reality environment with hologram-wrapped bots providing the non-player characters."

"Your boss wants to hire us to create a game franchise?" Mouser's eyes narrowed as he stared across the table. "And you just happen to be showing up here with the offer when you knew we were going broke?"

"Anarchists make for notoriously unreliable employees," Dewey said. "Flower wouldn't have been interested in hiring you if she didn't know you were desperate. I vouched for Bits personally, and she's been impressed by the expatriates you insist on calling traitors."

"What do you mean by all ages?" Rayne demanded. "I've seen holo recordings of professional LARPing league tournaments and they're usually a multi-species bloodbath. Are you saying that Flower wants some kind of kiddie version where adventurers go on quests that culminate in politely asking the dungeon boss to hand over the loot?"

"We've done a great deal of market research and Flower has decided that our best chance of breaking into the business is to provide a unique LARPing scenario. The aliens have a lead of millions of years in producing holographic games involving swords and sorcery, and you probably know that genuine Verlock mages are in high demand with the professional teams." Dewey unsealed the magnetic strip of the messenger bag slung over his shoulder, rummaged around inside, and pulled out two rolls of parchment bound with ribbons. "But before I continue, you'll have to sign non-disclosure agreements."

"Nothing doing," Rayne said, crossing her arms across her chest. "And for your information, we already—"

"I want to hear the rest of this," Mouser cut her off again, accepting a scroll from Dewey and pulling the end of the ribbon to untie the bow. "Besides, non-disclosure agreements are only valid in the jurisdiction—what's that for?" he asked the artificial person, who was now offering a wicked-looking dagger laying flat on his palm.

"Flower wasn't born yesterday," Dewey said. "The non-disclosure agreements were created by a Terregram mage and you have to sign in blood. The enforcement mechanism is built-in so you'll be unable to disclose what I'm about to tell you unless you take the job. After that, only the people who have signed NDAs can know who is behind the project."

"I'm not signing anything in blood," Rayne said, though now she actually looked intrigued. "Besides, I thought Terregram mages were just an alien ghost story."

"There's one living on Union Station and working in the fashion industry. You might have seen her product line featured in the professional LARPing league recordings you've watched."

"Baa's Bags? Do you mean they're real multi-dimensional bags of holding? I thought Baa was a clever marketing ploy and the bags only worked in the virtual reality setup."

Dewey reached in his messenger pouch again and brought out a small woman's purse emblazoned with three feathers that he placed on the coffee table. "This goes to the Rules Committee treasurer if we come to an agreement."

"That's me," Rayne declared, grabbing for the bag. Before her fingers closed, she pulled back her hand as if it had been burned. "I became treasurer before you left Bits and I'll bet you already knew that Mouser was the current chairman as well. How did you arrive when we happened to be together?"

"That part was pure chance, but I would have had Mouser ping you in any case," Dewey said. "I put my reputation on the line talking Flower into giving Bits a chance. I wouldn't have done that if our intelligence hadn't made clear that the two of you were in charge. I haven't forgotten who provided most of the parts for my old body."

"And the blood contract is absolutely necessary?" Mouser asked.

"Just a prick, and smear it in the little circle at the bottom," Dewey said.

The chairman of the Rules Committee complied and the scroll disintegrated before their eyes. Mouser sat back suddenly, burped, and pounded his chest with one fist.

"Are you alright?" Rayne asked.

"I guess that's the first time in my life I've been exposed to an alien enchantment. I think it went down the wrong tube."

"You didn't even read it first."

"What's the point?" Mouser asked. "It's not like a Terregram mage would leave room in a magical contract for editorial changes, and we're up against the wall here. If you don't want to do it, come back later and I'll explain as much as I'm allowed."

"I have scrolls for all of the senior team," Dewey said, pulling more out of the messenger bag as if it contained a bottomless supply. "There's no segment of the tunnel network economy that attracts more espionage than entertainment. For the size of the investment we're talking, Flower can't take any chances."

"How did you sign a blood contract when you don't have any blood?" Rayne asked the artificial person.

"I'm one of Flower's trusted confidants," Dewey told her, looking immodestly pleased with himself. He retrieved the dagger and pinched the tip between his thumb and forefinger, creating a brief glow. "There, it's been sterilized," he said, handing it to the treasurer.

"This better be worth it," Rayne muttered, pricking her left index finger and pressing the drop of blood in the circle at the bottom of the parchment. The scroll vanished and she coughed twice. "Did that go inside me?"

"Baa isn't known for explaining her methods," Dewey said. He reached in the messenger bag pouch, brought out an alien device that had one large button on the top, and pressed it. "That will take care of any electronic eaves-dropping, in addition to putting an end to the primitive attacks I've been ignoring ever since the local hackers noticed that I was online." He shook his head in disgust. "Has anybody been taken in by a phishing message in the last century?"

"Sorry about that," Mouser said. "You know some hackers can't resist a challenge. Now, what's the big secret we can't share on pain of whatever those scrolls will do to us if we spill the beans?"

"You won't be able to spill the beans, that's the whole point of a magical non-disclosure agreement," Dewey said. He shifted to sitting catty-corner on the couch so he could watch both of the Rules Committee members at the same time. "As I said, Flower Entertainment has been doing market research on the LARPing space for some time now. Rather than the medieval fantasy tropes that have become so popular, we've settled on Earth's history just before the Stryx opening as the template for a game."

"That sounds—uninteresting," Mouser said.

"I know that you have copies of the old Internet metaverse in your archives which includes surprisingly detailed mapping data of Earth down to street level views from urban areas. That will save a tremendous amount of time when creating the immersive environment. It's also a period of your history that fascinates many of the aliens, so—"

"How can you expect us to create a fantasy role-playing game based on Earth's Internet Age?" Rayne interrupted. "It was all computers and service jobs. Anybody on the streets with a sword would have been arrested."

"Give Flower a little credit," Dewey said. "The game will present an alternative history, one where everybody on Earth has magic and it's the lifeblood of the economy."

"You want us to replace money with magic?" Mouser asked. "That would change quite a bit."

"Magic and money can exist side by side if you wish. The point is that magic has permeated society, either as a recent introduction or something that existed since time immemorial—it's up to you. You create the history, you set the rules for the universe, you design the game."

Two

"It's a crazy idea," Rayne declared as soon as Dewey finished explaining the details and excused himself to give the two Rules Committee members time to talk. She sat on the couch, clutching the three-feather purse by Baa's Bags that the artificial person had intentionally forgotten behind. "And what does he expect us to do with two hours?"

"Brainstorm," Mouser said. "That's what we're good at. I texted the other members of our group and we'll hash out a path forward when they get here."

"Just like that? The prodigal son comes home dangling a few million creds from the AI of an alien colony ship that took in our rejects and you're ready to call it a done deal?"

"We need the money, creating games is what half of us do for a living, and I can't help the gamemaster side of my brain from spinning off into the possibilities. Taking an economic system like Earth's before the Stryx opening and introducing magic will be like shooting fish in a barrel. I'll have to brush up on my twenty-first-century history, but—"

"That's it," Rayne interrupted. "Dewey must have told Flower about you. Then the two of them dreamed up this scheme to get us on board since they knew you were Rules Committee chair."

"I'm not that important," Mouser said with a laugh. "Neither are you when it comes down to it. Sure, we can accept Flower's deal and get the first payment, but if the artists, composers, coders, and writers don't join in, we'll never see the second payment. You heard Dewey. The idea is a vertically integrated gameverse like the top alien franchises. We can start with cards or dice to work out the gameplay, but Flower is in it for the full immersion LARPing."

"I don't think it's that easy to port a game from paper to holograms and bots, and nobody on Bits would know for sure because we've never done it. There's nowhere near enough processing power on the planet to run a LARPing studio even if we had the bots and the holographic projectors."

"I think we're going to have to trust Flower and Dewey to handle the final conversion. But we can create the franchise, do the board game and a screen-based MMORPG version for networks, and of course, test all of the gameplay."

"I haven't seen you this excited since the Romans sent a galley after our round ship and it got sucked under by a whirlpool," Rayne said.

"Which you and Hercules conjured up by praying to your patron gods," Mouser reminded her. "I'm an overweight sixty-two-year-old hacker whose greatest accomplishment in life is a game in permanent beta that's been played by exactly nine people. This is a chance to be in on the creation of something that could be played by billions of aliens and outlive us all."

"What could outlive us all?" a petite girl in her late teens asked from just inside the door.

"Delphi. I didn't hear you come in."

"You never do," Delphi said. "I have stealth levels that are so high that I can't even see them on my character sheet."

"Dewey didn't say anything about character sheets," Rayne said. "Are we even going to have them? It's all implicit in the professional LARPing league. Your levels just reflect your capabilities and the artificial intelligence acting as the gamemaster adjusts everything on the fly."

"What's so important to drag me away from my synthesizer?" the nineteen-year-old asked. "I was working on the score for the new level the devs are adding to *Abandoned Mine*."

"The one that's full of zombie miners? I thought you said you just speed up the soundtrack by two percent for every new level."

"There's more to it than that," Delphi told her. "I talk it down because it's not real music composition either."

"Here," Mouser said, handing the girl a scroll and the sterilized dagger. "It needs a drop of blood in the circle before we can tell you anything."

"It's not written in English."

"It's an enchanted NDA written by a real Terregram mage," Rayne said. "Dewey brought it."

"Cool." The girl didn't hesitate any longer, pricking her finger and smearing a drop of blood in the circle. She had a brief fit of coughing when the scroll disappeared but it didn't seem to bother her. "What's the big secret?"

"We're broke, but everybody is going to find out about that soon enough. I had to steal funds from the royalty accounts to make the planetary lease payment, though we haven't told Dewey that because he's here to negotiate our bailout. In return, Flower Entertainment wants to hire us to create a gaming franchise based on a pre-opening Earth with magic."

"I'm in," Delphi said. "I love the music from that period. *Totalitarian Trollops* is my favorite girl band of all time."

"Just like that? Don't you know that Flower took in the Traitors?"

"Enough already, Rayne. Everybody knows that you and your ex had been on the road to break-up city for years." The door slid open again, but if Delphi noticed, she didn't let it stop her. "My mom told me that if Gorgeous George hadn't left, one of you probably would have killed the other by now. Besides, I might have joined up with Flower myself if not for Mouser's game night and my mom."

"Gorgeous was always a few bits short of a byte when it came to impulse control," the large newcomer said, dropping onto the couch between the two women. "Are we getting in an extra session? My team leader texted us this morning that the royalty account is empty. I'm out of a job and I have plenty of time."

"You're sitting on my skirt, Herc," Delphi said in irritation. "We aren't here to play. You're unemployed because Rayne emptied the royalty accounts to make the planetary lease payment."

"Wouldn't want to be in your shoes," Hercules told the treasurer. "If you want to hire me for protection, I'm available."

"Bits being broke is almost a side issue," Mouser said, leaning forward earnestly. "The point is that I drink too much soda."

"What?"

"That's not what I meant to say. I'm out of shape."

"Is something wrong, Mouser?" Rayne asked, bounding to her feet. "Do you feel a sudden numbness in your face or on one side of your body? Are you having trouble seeing?"

"It's not a stroke," the chairman of the Rules Committee told her irritably. "I'm just trying to explain to Hercules about potato chips."

"It must be the scroll enchantment," Delphi said with a flash of insight. "We can't say anything about our trip to the zoo until Hercules signs one."

"What's wrong with you people?" the muscular man demanded. "Have you all been smoking Kraaken Red?"

"Here," Mouser said, extending a scroll to Hercules. "It's an enchanted non-disclosure agreement and I guess that's about all it will let me say about it. You have to prick a finger and put a drop of blood in the circle."

"You just said we aren't here to play."

"It's real," Rayne said, though she sounded a bit distant as if she was still thinking about Delphi's bringing her ex-husband into the discussion. "The secret project is about peanut butter."

Hercules looked up from the indecipherable contract just in time for Delphi to hand him the dagger. "What was that about peanut butter?"

"Wipe it off first," Delphi told him. "And somehow the enchantment is making us substitute words when we try to talk about the rubber ducks. See what I mean?"

"You're all going to end up in rubber rooms," Hercules muttered. He wiped the blade on his pants, pricked his finger, and pressed it to the circle on the scroll, which promptly disintegrated. "Now what?" he asked with a cough.

"We wait for Shadow," Mouser said. "He should have been here already."

"I am here already," a sepulchral voice announced from behind the workbench. "My stealth makes Delphi's stealth look like a pink elephant in a tutu."

"Stop screwing around and get over here to sign the NDA," Delphi said.

A skinny young man wearing an active camouflage poncho that must have cost him a month's earnings came out from behind the workbench where he'd blended in with the wall. "I came in right behind you so I already know the score," Shadow gloated. "Seems like whoever created those magical scrolls wasn't so smart after all."

"Whoever?" Delphi asked. "What exactly did you hear?"

"Everything. I know that—" The young man paused and looked puzzled. "I'm sure I heard you talking about, what was it?"

"Blood in the circle," Mouser said, handing over the last of the scrolls Dewey had left with him.

Shadow used his costume dagger to prick a finger, anointed the scroll, and managed to suppress the cough as the magic entered his body. "So is it a special raid? Did we make the finals?"

"This isn't about gaming," Rayne told him. "Well, it is and it isn't. Bits is broke and I hacked the royalty accounts to make the planetary lease payment on time. Dewey showed up an hour ago on a New Empire Gem warship and offered us a contract working for Flower, who wants us to create a new gameverse for the tunnel network version of Live Action Role Playing. We're talking a full development deal with artwork, music, dialogue, the works."

"There isn't enough processing power on the planet to run a LARPing studio, and even if there was, it's the kind of modern gaming that our parents and grandparents agreed never to accept on Bits. That's the reason your ex and all those others left to join Flower three years ago."

"Ancient history," Rayne told him. "What part of 'broke' don't you understand? Thanks to my robbing everybody, we made the lease payment, but programming work has been drying up, and our in-game enhancements and new releases haven't been selling."

"Anarchy only works as long as somebody pays the bills," Mouser added. "There's no point in putting anything to a vote because at least half of the population will be against doing whatever is necessary just on general principle. Dewey's deal falls into the category of offers we can't refuse, and Flower knows that, or she wouldn't have gone to the effort of sending him. The only thing we can accomplish by holding out at this point is to look more pathetic when we finally accept."

"That doesn't change the LARPing issue," Shadow said stubbornly. "Even if we wanted to do the job, we don't have the hardware or the capability. That's the kind of programming that only artificial intelligence can manage."

"Flower doesn't want us to build and manage a LARPing studio," Rayne told him. "She wants us to create the world, design the rules, come up with quests—it will be just like creating any new role-playing game."

"Then let her pay us for using one of our existing franchises."

"She doesn't want an existing franchise. Flower wants to do something disruptive, and at the same time, make it hard for the aliens to copy the idea before she can lock up being the premier brand in the market space."

"You're giving me a headache," Hercules said. "Just pretend for a minute that I'm a big dumb barbarian tank and explain it like you're giving me my marching orders."

"Anything we can do, the aliens can do better," Mouser said. "Sure, the tunnel network has rules protecting some types of intellectual property—" he noted the big man's comic wince, "—that protect some types of ideas that have been fully worked out, like rules to a game if they're exact copies. But there is one thing that we know more about than any of the aliens, even the ones who were spying on us, and that's what it was like living on Earth in the twenty-first century."

"Before the Stryx forced the governments to open the planet and brought us onto the galactic tunnel network," Shadow said, nodding his head. "By that time, everybody on Earth was saving all of their data in the cloud, and we have exabytes of old backups that you old guys brought to Bits."

"But there weren't any dragons running around Earth a century ago, much less elves, sorcerers, orcs, or goblins," Hercules objected. "How are we going to create a game about a world that ran on fast food and call centers? Send people on quests for lost packages? Give them teleportation scrolls that move them to the front of the line at the food bank?"

"I like that one," Rayne said with a laugh, "but we're going to change Earth to a magic-centric economy."

"Like it costs one mana to ride a bus and five for a hamburger?" Hercules considered the idea for a moment. "That could be interesting. Does everybody generate mana at the same rate, or can you get stronger by building your wisdom stats? How about computers? Do they still exist, and would they run on magic if they did?"

"Magic instead of electricity?" Mouser asked. "You know, that might just work. When Earth got caught up in cryptocurrencies, there was a while when electricity and money were practically interchangeable."

"And maybe magic could be distributed over the power grid or the world wide web," Delphi said. "You know, instead of storing your excess mana in a talisman or something, you could save it—"

"—in a magical bank," Rayne jumped in. "And you could borrow mana if you didn't have enough for some spell, or loan it to wizards who were capable of channeling large amounts, but they would have to pay mana interest."

"Or pledge their souls," Shadow put in. "There have got to be high stakes if it's going to keep anybody playing beyond the 'interesting concept' honeymoon."

"But why us?" Delphi asked. "Sure, we've been playing together for a couple of years, but Rayne and Mouser are the only ones on the Rules Committee. The rest of us are just hourly help."

"Unemployed hourly help," Hercules said.

"Because we work well as a team, and Rayne and I are stuck in charge because Dewey knows us and Flower trusts him," Mouser said. "We can't count on everybody to join together to save Bits, that's not how anarchies work. But if we dole out Flower's money and keep her identity a secret for now, I'm betting the work is addictive enough that nobody will walk away when the truth comes out."

"All of the artists I know would go crazy for a chance to do a fantasy version of twenty-first-century Earth," Delphi said. "I just don't know how well it will translate to motion holograms."

"We won't need to worry about that part for now," Mouser told them. "Dewey said Flower wants a vertically integrated franchise, one that starts with board games or playing cards. As soon as the rules are in place, we'll get the programmers started on a screen-based MMORPG version for the legacy gaming crowd among human expats and the networked crowd back on Earth."

"I know that the Stryx designated three heritage technologies for Earth that couldn't be replaced with alien imports," Hercules said. "Two of them were the Internet and smartphones, but what was the third?"

"GPS, the Global Positioning System that works off of satellites. The smartphones on Earth all use it, and replacing satellites has kept the aerospace industry from disappearing completely. Bits did the programming for an upgrade a few years ago."

"So let me get this straight," Shadow said. "Dewey is going to hand over the money for Rayne to pay back what she stole from the royalty accounts and then we're going to start working on a new gameverse and lie to everybody about who's footing the bills?"

"We're lying to Dewey and Flower too if that's any consolation," Rayne told him. "Dewey thinks that we still owe the planetary lease installment, and if we tell him otherwise, he may shrink our down payment for accepting the job. Mouser figures we're better off getting the maximum upfront."

"We should start by coming up with a name that describes the concept," Shadow said, and then noticed the Rules Committee members shaking their heads. "What?"

"Flower reserved the naming rights for herself, though she may accept what we come up with if it will resonate with the aliens in translation. Dewey said something about focus groups."

"But everything else is up to us?"

"It's up to us to work out the gameplay, at least until the first major review," Mouser told them. "Dewey said that Flower is so busy with other commitments that she's giving us a long leash. We'll need to include some family-friendly elements, but while the kids are home learning magic, the adults can be out doing whatever."

"So the fate of Bits is riding on a game the five of us come up with?" Hercules asked. "That doesn't seem fair to everybody else. Why don't we make it a competition?"

"I'm fine with the principle, but I don't want to be sitting here in a month reading through a bunch of half-cocked ideas for games that have been force-fitted to the twenty-first century."

"With magic spread on top," Shadow added.

"There have to be a dozen product teams that are desperate for work," Delphi said. "Will you have enough money to employ them to come up with their own concepts and prototypes? Then we can choose one, or merge the best ideas."

Rayne nodded thoughtfully. "There's going to be plenty of money. I was worried about not being able to spread it around fast enough to keep more people from deciding to abandon Bits. Setting up a competition between teams makes more sense than spamming cash for make-work."

"Then we should get going on that as soon as possible," Mouser said. "Hercules, Delphi. The idea came from the two of you, so you're in charge of vetting the teams that don't have work before sending them on to Rayne to talk money. Start with the producer for each team because they'll prioritize finance and sell the idea to their people even if the director isn't on board with the artistic side of things."

"But don't push too hard on the fact that they need our money or they'll just feel cornered," the treasurer added. "Maybe you could do good-cop, bad-cop."

"They're all going to want to take their existing game engine and just substitute in a pre-opening Earth with magic. Make sure everybody takes a few days for brainstorming, starts role-playing some scenarios, and see how it goes. The worst thing that can happen is Flower doesn't accept our ideas, and then we're no worse off than we are right now."

"Better off, because I won't have been thrown out an airlock," Rayne added.

"I'll start making the rounds as soon as I get out of here and figure out which teams are on their last legs," Hercules said. "But I don't want to schedule any meetings until we know that Dewey has accepted our proposal and the funds are in your hands. It's just the failing game teams you're interested in?"

"I don't want the money going to people who are currently getting by for work. The idea is to add Flower's money to our economy, not displace existing income or start a competition for the best programmers. There will be plenty of time for that when we get beyond the initial stages."

"You might want to allow some of those teams that don't normally work on fantasy games to hire on magic system experts," Shadow said. "I play everything that comes out for competition testing in the weekend tournaments and half of the games are pure action or SciFi."

"Good point," Mouser said. "Make sure to let the producers know that we'll pay for subcontractors at the standard rate.

Delphi half raised a hand as if she was attending a lecture. "I get that art and storylines could be shared when you get past the coffee-table level, but how do you translate from a human gamemaster working with a handful of players to a Massively Multiplayer Online Role Playing Game or an alien artificial intelligence running a professional LARPing studio?"

"I'm pretty focused on tabletop games and hand-helds myself. I was planning to stick with what I know, let the professionals work on the MMORPG version, and leave it for Flower Entertainment to repurpose our content for a high-tech LARP."

"Delphi has a point," Rayne said slowly. "We all want to believe this makes sense because we need the work. But when you think about it, Dewey showing up here with a long-shot proposal for a new gameverse feels like half a story."

"You think our people who joined Flower two years ago are behind it?" Hercules asked. "I've heard that they're well paid, but we still outnumber them seven to one, and I doubt they could afford to subsidize us for any amount of time even if they wanted to."

Mouser arched his back in the easy chair so he could get his hand into his pocket and pull out his smartphone.

"What are you doing?" Rayne asked.

"Texting Dewey. I don't think he'd lie in response to a direct question, and he probably kept his old Bits number even after swapping bodies." Mouser snorted when the return message showed up a moment later. "He's been waiting outside for us to invite him in."

The artificial person entered, greeted Hercules, Shadow, and Delphi by name, and took a seat on Mouser's workbench stool. "Do we have a deal?" he asked.

"Some of us are a little suspicious why Flower is willing to hand over millions of creds on what will obviously be a gamble," Rayne replied. "We want to know what strings are attached."

"I was waiting for you to ask," Dewey said. "It's come to the attention of certain parties that your museum contains items that would be better off elsewhere."

"Are you talking about the old computers or the alien weapons?"

"The alien weapons, of course. I took the liberty of making a quick visit to the museum to refresh my memory while you were talking. I have a list of items that we'll need to move out to the tarmac so I can take them with me when the ship returns to pick me up. I can help with the carrying if that's an issue."

"But we need the museum to model weapons for games," Shadow protested. "One of our most successful—"

"You have three-dimensional image captures of the external appearances," Dewey interrupted. "This request is non-negotiable."

"Does this have something to do with the other species?" Mouser asked suspiciously.

"I'm not at liberty to disclose that information."

"The game developers will never accept it. Everybody loves the museum."

"Tell them that you're selling the weapons in order to make the planetary lease payment, but if everybody chips in to raise the money, you can keep them," Dewey said. "I believe I can predict the results of that offer with certainty."

Three

Sarah trailed around the apartment after her mother while Rayne haphazardly packed some clothes and other necessities in an old box. "Where are we going?" the ten-year-old asked.

"Not we, just me," Rayne said. "You're staying here with grandma."

"But *why*?"

"I have an emergency at work and I won't be able to come home for a few days. You keep up with your programming lessons and your creative writing group."

Sarah stopped tugging at her mother's sleeve and instead positioned herself in front of the door, crossing her arms across her narrow chest in a fair imitation of her grandmother. "You don't have an office, you work from home. Where are you going?"

"To stay in Mouser's workshop, but you can't tell anybody," Rayne said. "Everybody on Bits is mad at me, or they will be when they find out that I borrowed from the royalty accounts."

"Do you need money? I have almost eight creds saved."

Rayne set down the box, cupped her daughter's head in her hands, and kissed her on the forehead. "Thank you, Pumpkin, but it's all taken care of. I just have to stay out of sight for a few days. It will be a vacation for you and grandma. Where is she?"

"Grandma is at the *Empire in Chains* tournament," Sarah said. "She told me she'd be back for lunch so I guess she doesn't plan to do very well."

"It's a senior tournament. They have bathroom breaks once an hour and they freeze everything for forty-five minutes at lunch." Rayne glanced at her smartphone. "She'll be back soon, but I really have to get going. If anybody other than grandma asks, tell them I left to visit the Free Republic with the Gem ship that brought Dewey and I'll be back in a week when they return to pick him up."

"You're going to see the pirates?" the girl asked excitedly. "Can I come?"

Rayne picked up the box and tried to get around her daughter. "The Gem already left, I just don't want anybody looking for me. Think of it as a new role-playing game where your mother is a queen in hiding and you can't tell anybody where I am."

"That makes me a princess!" Sarah yielded the right of way, but she wasn't completely buying her mother's story. "Are you sure you don't need my money?"

"I'm sure." The door slid open and Rayne stuck her head out just enough to check both directions before stepping out of the apartment. "I picked up our week's allotment of frozen vegetables from storage last night so there's no excuse for you and grandma not to cook. I'll see you in a few days."

After the door slid shut, Sarah went directly into the kitchen, climbed up on the counter, and retrieved a package of imported chocolate chip cookies from the top shelf. She just had time to sit down on the couch and activate the retro-gaming console before a seventy-year-old woman wearing a bright orange *Empire in Chains* T-shirt entered the apartment and confiscated the cookies.

"You'll ruin your lunch," Sarah's grandmother said. "What do you want me to make you?"

"Cookies."

"How about a powdered egg omelet?"

"Yuck. Peanut butter and jelly?"

"I suppose we may as well use up the bread before it gets stale."

"Mom was here," Sarah said, popping up again and following her grandmother into the kitchen. "She grabbed some clothes and stuff and then she went to hide in Mouser's workshop. She said to tell everybody she left with the Gem."

"Then that's what we'll do. I was the Rules Committee treasurer for over thirty years before your mother took over and it's a thankless job."

"Then why did you make Mom take it?"

"I didn't make Rayne take the job," June said, removing the jelly jar from the fridge. "We discussed all of the possibilities and decided that it was the best option."

"Will I have to become treasurer after Mom?"

"That will be up to what you and your mother decide if she still has the job herself twenty years from now. Do you want to slice the bread?"

"Can I?" The ten-year-old fumbled through the utensils drawer to find the long bread knife with the serrated blade while her grandmother removed the loaf of Bits Bakery bread from the breadbox and set it on the thick plastic cutting board.

"Try to get four even slices and leave the heel," June suggested.

Sarah concentrated intently as she cut the first two slices, but she looked up halfway through the third and asked, "Where is Mom going to eat?"

"Mouser keeps some food in his workshop and there's a whole row of vending machines in that corridor because it's easy to fill them from the outside cold storage."

"But Mom is always telling me not to eat vending machine pizza from Earth. She says it may have been frozen for years."

"Half of the population of Bits is fed by vending machines, and the quality has gone way up since Drazen Foods started exporting frozen produce from Earth," June told her granddaughter. "We don't grow much of our own here, so flash-frozen food from Earth is as fresh as it gets. Before we had a bakery, all of our bread came frozen as well."

"But *why*?" Sarah asked as she carefully cut the fourth slice of bread the same width as the previous three, leaving a thick heel. "Don't the other human colonies grow their own food?"

"You know that Bits is special. It's one of just three worlds in the whole universe that's entirely under human control, even though we lease it from the Hortens. Our families came here to preserve the hacking and gaming lifestyle that began to disappear from Earth as soon as the Stryx brought us onto the tunnel network."

"Why did they take Earth's computers away?"

"They didn't," June said, smearing a slice of bread with peanut butter. She added a single large dollop of jam the way her granddaughter liked it before putting the second slice of bread on top and squishing it down. "It's just that the aliens all had computer technology so far in advance of our own that it may as well be magic. You can program their machines just by talking to them, and the galaxy is full of artificial intelligences that can write code better than any biological could ever hope."

"Aren't you going to have any jelly on yours?"

"I don't need the extra sugar. The peanut butter has plenty."

June took the pitcher out of the fridge and poured them each a glass of milk that had been mixed up from powder at breakfast. Then the pair sat down at the kitchen table where the family ate all of their meals.

"Do you know why mom has to hide from everybody?" Sarah asked after swallowing the first mouthful.

"For doing the right thing. There are times that people need somebody to make the hard decisions for them. Your mother always puts the good of the community first."

"Is that why my dad left?"

June took almost half a minute to chew her bite of the sandwich before replying. "Your mother and father were very much in love when they had you. Do you remember the time that I brought home a tub of ice cream and you ate it all?"

"I'm sorry," Sarah mumbled through a mouthful of peanut butter and jelly. "I didn't mean to. I just couldn't stop."

"And it gave you such a headache that you've never asked for ice cream again. It was like that with your parents."

"They ate all of your ice cream too?"

"At first, they couldn't get enough of each other, but once they got past that hunger, they could barely stand to be in the same room," her grandmother explained. "It happens sometimes with grownups, and it's hard in a small place like Bits where there's nowhere to go and everything you see reminds you of the other person."

"But if Daddy loved me, why didn't he stay?"

"It was too painful for him and your mother," June said. "George isn't a bad man, he just wasn't the right man for my daughter. It was difficult for him to join Flower knowing it might be years before he could see you again. Don't you get a video message from him every time a ship brings a data dump?"

"He's working for Flower Studios doing anime and he tells me the story for every episode he works on," Sarah confirmed. "When they finish the season, he's going to send it to me so I can binge watch the whole thing."

"Don't let your mother see it. You know how she feels about anime."

"She used to love anime before she heard what my dad is doing for work."

June took a sip of her reconstituted milk and made a face. "Don't you have your creative writing group today? What time do you have to be there?"

"Daniela will come to get me when her mother is ready, it depends on when the baby goes to sleep," the girl said. "I have programming exercises to do until she comes."

"It didn't look like you were getting ready to do programming exercises when I came in."

"That's because I hadn't had lunch yet," Sarah explained.

"You have a lot of answers for a ten-year-old," her grandmother said. They finished eating at the same time and she moved the plates to a dishpan. "What do you want to have for dinner?"

"Cookies."

"Can I trust you to stay out of the cabinet after I leave?"

Sarah frowned. "That's not fair, making it a trust thing."

"So what should I do?" her grandmother asked.

"Hide them? I'll go in the other room and count to a hundred."

The girl ran out of the kitchen without waiting for an agreement and June sighed. She took the package of chocolate chip cookies down from the cabinet, thought about putting them in the freezer, and then returned them to their normal place.

"All set," she called out. "But you can't spend more than a minute looking."

Sarah went directly to the freezer, rummaged through the contents, and then checked the microwave oven and the combination clothes washer and drier on the other side of the sink. She scowled at her grandmother, tried the cabinet under the sink with the mixing bowls and cleaning supplies, and triumphantly pulled a package of cookies from the back.

"Oh, dear," her grandmother said. "I didn't realize that your mother had bought two packages. Let me see how big the cookies are."

The girl carefully opened the package and brought out a single cookie that wasn't much larger than a programmable Stryx cred, though it was several times as thick.

"You can have four," June said, "and I want to see you deep into your coding practice before I have to leave."

Sarah extracted three more cookies, resealed the package with the locking strip, and moved to put it back under the sink.

"I'll take care of that," her grandmother said. "You get started and I'll finish cleaning up." As soon as the girl left the kitchen, June swapped the unopened package of cookies with the opened one, putting the former in the spot under the sink where Sarah had discovered the latter. "Now I've lost track of who I'm trying to fool," she said to herself with a wry smile. Then she washed the dishes manually and moved them to the drying rack.

"Is it true that computers only understand ones and zeros?" Sarah asked her grandmother when June emerged from the kitchen.

"Computers don't understand anything because they aren't sentient. It's only when a smart girl like you writes code that tells the computer how to combine and compare those ones and zeros that the computer can do anything."

"But why don't I *see* them?"

"Because you're coding in assembly language, which is already the next level up. Didn't your mother explain how it works?"

"You know that Mom isn't that into programming."

"She was a difficult child," June said, taking a seat on the couch next to her granddaughter. "The ones and zeros that the processor works with are controlled by what we call machine language. There's an ancient computer in the museum where you can enter instructions two bytes at a time by setting switches up or down, where each switch is one bit. But writing programs in machine language is a slow and cumbersome process for most people, and you have to remember all of the Hex—I'm losing you."

"I like Base-16 math," Sarah contradicted her. "Only babies count on their fingers."

"That's an interesting way of looking at it. When you write code in assembly language, the assembler translates it to machine language and maps all of the memory locations—do you know about memory?"

"Sort of."

"It's a good thing I moved back in last month, I can see we have some catching up to do. When I saw you programming in F-sharp I just assumed you already knew assembly."

"Our coding teacher says that it's important to learn low-level languages if you want to understand what high-level languages are doing," Sarah said. "I don't think my Dad believed that."

"No, he was a Modernist," June agreed. "That's the other reason he left for Flower. And there are plenty more hackers remaining on Bits who also believe we should stop clinging to the past, but they keep quiet about it because they don't want to leave."

"How many? Like half?"

"Not that many, I think, but most of us probably fall somewhere between the two extremes. I think that eventually, the Modernists will win by default because there's not enough work in the old programming languages and operating systems to keep us going anymore."

"I don't see any change."

"That's because you're ten," June said with a smile and pinched her granddaughter's cheek. "And the changes have been taking place on Earth, not here. As alien businesses open back home, the people who work for them end up learning new technology, and then there's less demand for what we do. Plus you have to keep in mind that over half of humanity has moved away from Earth."

"But *why*?"

"For better economic opportunities and to see something of the galaxy. Things were very depressed when I was growing up, and if your grandfather hadn't talked me into moving to Bits, I probably would have signed a contract to go work on an alien world. I recently received a letter from a childhood friend who did just that around the same time that I left Earth and she's returned there to retire. The pension she receives from the Dollnicks allowed her to buy a lovely property in the country, along with a condominium in the city, plus she can afford to visit her children off-world at least once a year."

"Are you and Mom poor?" Sarah asked suspiciously. "I have eight creds."

"You're a very good saver," June praised her. "We aren't poor, but after your grandfather left us, I lived alone for a decade. We won't go hungry, thanks to the tithe, but we aren't what you'd call wealthy."

"If I get a job, can Mom come home?"

"Your mother earns a decent salary from the Rules Committee, and her taking a short vacation has nothing to do with our family finances. And my friend reminded me in the letter that I still own some land in the country near where she purchased hers. The government stopped taking rural property for back taxes because it was too much work and everybody stopped paying."

"What are taxes?" Sarah wanted to know.

"I have to get back to the tournament, Sweetie, but we'll pick it up later." June kissed her granddaughter on the forehead and added, "Do your coding and enjoy your creative writing group."

After her grandmother left, the girl fought an epic battle against the siren song of the cookies. Eventually, she lost herself in debugging a subroutine that was supposed to choose the next move in a game of checkers but kept freezing when a piece became a king. She figured it out just seconds before the door chimed.

"Come in," she called without looking.

A woman who she didn't recognize stormed into the apartment, glanced at the little girl, and made a visible effort to control herself. "Is your mother here?"

"She went with the Gem to visit the pirates," Sarah said, her fingers crossed behind her back. "You can leave a message on the wallboard if you want."

The visitor checked the large touch-screen next to the door where the last message read, 'Make sure grandma takes her vitamins and I'll see you next week.'

"I'll be back," the woman hissed and managed to leave without exactly storming out.

"That was weird," Sarah said to herself. She played a quick round of checkers, easily defeating her program, and realized for the first time that there was more to artificial intelligence than making legal moves. The door chimed again. "Come in."

"You come out," her friend Daniela said from the open door. "The baby finally fell asleep so my mom's ready to teach."

The two girls ended up racing each other down the corridor, dodging around everybody who had forgotten what it was like being ten years old and out of the house with your best friend. They were breathless when they arrived at Daniela's apartment. Three older boys were already there, having received notifications on their smartphones.

"It looks like we're one short," Daniela's mother said when they all gathered in the small living room. "Whose turn was it to read today?"

"Sheila's," the missing girl's twin brother said. "She didn't feel good."

"Does that mean she didn't do her homework?"

Peter shrugged. "Our grandparents started talking about retiring to Earth and she's really sad."

"Oh, I guess I heard that they were leaving Bits. Something about inheriting a house, I think."

"From my grandfather's older brother, who didn't have any children," Peter said. "It's supposed to be a huge house, and they invited all of us to come with them."

"You're leaving too?" one of the boy's friends asked.

"Mom likes her job working on operating systems for smartphones and Dad's in charge of the artwork for a new release of his group's game, so we aren't going anywhere for now."

Daniela's mother nodded. "All right. Does anybody else have something prepared that they want to read, or should I introduce a new subject?"

"Why do you always want us to read out loud when it's creative *writing*?" Sarah asked, putting particular stress on the last word.

"I could as easily ask why you always question everything, but I happen to have the answer for this one," the teacher said with a smile. "Authors who work alone can easily go for weeks or months without showing anybody else their drafts in progress, but the kind of work we do here on Bits requires cooperation between the writers, the artists, the musicians, and the coders. It's rare to be the only writer on a game, and I once managed a project that had fourteen of us all writing at the same time."

"But how can an author write a whole book alone when it takes a team of writers just to do a game?"

"In part, because if you took all of the dialogue, descriptions, history, and rules of a game, it would add up to a whole series of books. But the more important fact is that developing games is a business that follows a tight schedule. The rest of the team can't wait five years for a single writer to produce all of the necessary content, and a good deal of every game writer's time is spent in meetings with those artists, musicians, and coders who need to know how the story is progressing in order to do their work."

"Oh." Sarah swept her phone to life and said, "I have something I can read if you want."

"We're always happy to hear what your imagination is up to," Daniela's mother said. The boys let out a collective groan, but secretly they were relieved that it wasn't them.

Four

Mouser returned to his workshop, hung the supplemental oxygen mask on the peg just inside the door, and struggled out of the straps of a ballistic nylon backpack that looked like it had been standard issue to some army on Earth two centuries earlier. Then he sank into the chair across from the couch to wrestle off his outside boots.

"Were there any problems?" Rayne asked.

"Just a few loudmouths, but they didn't dare get close to the ship with those Gem marines lined up. I don't know if Dewey planned the whole thing himself or if he was acting for somebody else, maybe even the Stryx, but I think he got everything he wanted."

"I was never that comfortable having some of those alien weapons in the museum anyway. There were at least three space mines from extinct species that none of our visitors ever identified, so how could we know whether or not they were still dangerous?"

"Well, they're gone now," Mouser said, pulling off the second boot. "Dewey left us with the ceremonial swords, axes, and spears, practically all of the projectile weapons, and most of the energy rifles and plasma guns provided the power sources were toasted. The artists and physics-engine wonks who spent the most time in the museum are moping around like kids who had their toys taken away, but giving up the weapons added credence to our cover story about the source of the money."

"All I care about is that Dewey released the funds to the Rules Committee and I was able to repay the royalty accounts," Rayne said. "I haven't been home to see my daughter in a week, though she and my mom are probably treating it like a vacation. And thank you for letting me hide out here. I know you like working alone and I feel bad about messing up your schedule. The way you've been moving out all of your junk I was beginning to think you expected me to stay forever."

"I'm outsourcing," Mouser explained. "This new game is going to demand all of my time so I've been parceling out my backlog of repair jobs to the other techs on Bits who can handle the work. I may even have patched up some old feuds in the bargain."

"You really are going all-in, aren't you? Even with the creds in hand, I can't quite convince myself that it's a legitimate job. Maybe the Stryx hired Flower and Dewey to clean up our museum and the whole rest of the story is just blowing smoke."

"I trust Dewey, and I asked him plenty of questions over the course of the week. He claims that since opening her LARPing studio, Flower has become something of a gaming fanatic. She keeps buying dedicated hardware to upgrade the holographic rendering and free up processing capacity for her role as gamemaster, but the population on board is growing so fast that she's spreading herself thin."

"It's weird thinking of a twenty-thousand-year-old alien artificial intelligence as being overburdened," Rayne said as she folded up the blanket that had turned the couch into a bed. "If I was artificial intelligence, I'd spend all of my time earning creds to buy more capacity, or maybe manufacture my own hardware. You'd think her whole ship would be solid computer by now."

"Doesn't work that way," Mouser told her, sailing his boots in the general direction of the door with poorly aimed throws. "The Stryx may have unlocked the key to infinite scalability, but the rest of the artificial intelligence in the universe runs into hard limits due to density and latency issues, whatever their underlying technology. Most of them specialize long before that time in the theory that quality trumps quantity."

"It doesn't sound like Flower has specialized."

"She operates a colony ship and you have to be a generalist for a job like that." He relaxed back in the chair and asked in a casual tone, "So, are you going to tell me?"

"Tell you what?" Rayne asked.

"How you hacked the royalty accounts. I thought they used the same encryption as the Horten pirates."

The treasurer sighed and came to a quick decision. "Have you ever wondered why I took over the treasurer job when my mother retired?"

"I just assumed being suckers for punishment ran in your genes," Mouser said. "Are you trying to tell me you have magical hacking powers?"

"In a sense," Rayne said with a smile. "I've been binge reading Earth's history this last week and I learned they used to run worldwide lotteries that sold billions of tickets. If the pot kept rolling over, the grand prize could go as high as ten billion eBucks. Do you know what mathematicians say about winning a lottery like that?"

"It's proof that the person who wins is living in a simulation, but mathematicians say that about everything with ridiculous odds." Mouser thought for a moment and frowned. "You mean you guessed all of the passwords?"

"Getting colder," Rayne told him as she packed the blanket in the box that held the clothes and toiletries she'd brought from her apartment a week earlier.

"You ran a simulation that guessed the passwords? No, that wouldn't change the odds."

"Colder."

"We're both living in a simulation now?" Mouser ventured.

"Warmer. Try thinking about Bits as if you were an outsider. What is it about us that makes all the other species believe that we're nuts?"

"It's not the gaming obsession, plenty of aliens have that. I've talked with a couple of the Old Empire Gem refugees over the years and they think we're insane for importing all of our food rather than synthesizing it here. And the pirates who stop in don't understand why we don't move back to Earth now that it's half empty and the air quality has improved so much."

"Come on, there have even been stories about this in the Galactic Free Press. What's the *single* factor that sums up our society for the rest of the galaxy?"

"You mean our insistence on preserving the old programming languages and operating systems? We must be the only planet on the tunnel network where everybody works on their own computer and..." Mouser's eyes went wide and he trailed off when he finally understood what she was getting at.

"It really is that simple," Rayne said with a grin. "Everybody on Bits doesn't have their own antique computer. They forget that we're all working on an obsolete Frunge factory controller simulating hundreds of thousands of processors. Guess who has the root password for that system?"

"Don't ever let anybody else hear you breathe a word of that."

"I'm not an idiot, but you asked, and it's a relief to finally talk about it with someone whose name isn't 'Mom'. Even the men in our family never knew."

"That's probably wise since they'd insist on using the superpower for evil." Mouser looked around his workshop. "The others should be here in a few minutes. Did you pack your toothbrush?"

"I gathered up everything while you were outside with Dewey," Rayne said. "Did you make much progress with your basic world-building this week?"

"I used all of the time when I normally would have been crouched over the workbench trying to reflow the solder on some old surface-mount chip with a heat gun. Where did I leave my notebook?"

"Computer?"

"Spiral bound. I went old-school on this one."

"I thought it didn't get any more old-school than notebook computers," Rayne said with a laugh. "I wouldn't be surprised if you have the last one in working condition on Bits."

Mouser grinned and reached into the old military surplus backpack he'd set down next to the chair. "Speaking of antiques," he said, pulling out a colorful retail package, "have you ever tried one of these?"

"A virtual reality headset?" She leaned forward and took the device. "It's still in the bubble pack! I mean, we have a couple in the hardware graveyard, but I've never seen a working one. The technology went obsolete right after the Stryx opened Earth and cheap holographic projectors from the aliens flooded the market. Where did you get it?"

"A surprise parting gift from Dewey. The Gem ship left a container load of them out on the tarmac for us, thousands of units. They were abandoned in some warehouse on Earth and Flower picked them up cheap at auction the last time she stopped there."

Rayne puzzled over the clear plastic bubble encasing the visor and grew increasingly frustrated as she scanned the print visible through the flat section on the back for instructions on getting it open. "Is the packaging supposed to be child-proof or something? I don't see how it comes off."

"Just a sec," Mouser said. He pushed to his feet and went over to the workbench. "Unless you want to risk cutting off a finger playing with a knife, scissors are the best bet. On the bright side, the headsets are probably good for a millennium in that packaging, as long as they're kept out of direct sunlight."

"Hey, I bet these weren't some random parting gift. Dewey and Flower knew there was no way we would be able to set up a real LARPing studio here for product development."

"Poor man's virtual reality," Mouser confirmed, handing her a pair of heavy-duty scissors. "And be careful not to slice yourself on the plastic as you pull it open. I've always found the best bet with bubble pack is to cut around the product until it practically falls open. Try not to cut through the cord."

"A cord, how quaint," Rayne said. She spent the next minute carefully turning the package as she cut around the bulky visor and hand controllers, almost like she was creating a chain of paper dolls. "It's surprisingly light for the size."

"It wouldn't be much fun trying to play games with a heavy weight stuck on your face. Maybe the point of the cord is to save on battery mass. Put it on and I'll plug you in."

"You really have an obsolete Earth power—why am I asking?" she interrupted herself. The soft padding around the eyecups of the visor seemed to mold to her face as she adjusted the plastic straps over her head. "I can't see anything, and the room just got a lot quieter."

"The headphones are the difference between a headset visor and just putting screens in front of your eyes," Mouser said loudly while he located the free end of the ancient USB cable. He identified the connector shape as the final 7.0 version and plugged it into the universal Earth power supply he'd built for his legacy game repair business. "I haven't read the specs on the data feed yet so this is just power to activate the demo mode," he warned her. "I can't believe the batteries for those hand controllers still have a charge but the status LEDs are lit. Maybe they draw power over wireless from the headset."

"Woaaa!" Rayne gripped the controllers and her legs straightened out under the coffee table as if she was plunging down the steepest rollercoaster drop in the world and trying to brace herself. "This is insane."

"How's the audio?" Mouser asked. "I can't hear any sound leakage from the headphones."

"This is beyond insane," Rayne said loudly, leaning way over to one side.

"You can't hear me, can you?"

"It's *way* past beyond insane. It's like—immersive. You're not going to believe the audio. I think the headset is doing something to trick my inner ears into agreeing with the motion my eyes are seeing."

"So I'll just try the other set I brought in," Mouser said to himself. He picked up the scissors from the coffee table, retrieved a second visor from his backpack, and did a much cruder job of getting it out of the packaging than Rayne had. The cord wasn't long enough to reach his homemade power supply from his easy chair so he went to stand closer to the workbench. "Even with the weight considerations, you'd think that a cord this long would be a serious trip-and-fall hazard for virtual gamers," he muttered as he plugged it in.

"You've got to try this," Rayne called out, but she didn't show any signs of being ready to remove the visor. She was on her feet by this point, brandishing an arm in front of her body as if wielding a weightless sword. "Die, you scumbags. Ha!"

Mouser adjusted the strap that ran over the top of the skull to keep the visor from slipping down and tapped the activation button. Ten seconds later, he tore off the headset and ran for the toilet, moving surprisingly fast for an overweight man in his sixties.

"Slash, parry, stab," Rayne cried as she fought an invisible enemy. "I can't believe how good I'm doing at—oh." She let her hands fall to her sides when she realized the demo mode was playing a canned fight scene without reference to her athletic contributions, and a minute later, she removed the visor. "Mouser? Do you want to try it? Mouser?"

"What's that," Shadow asked, causing Rayne to jump. "Can I play?"

"Stop sneaking up on people." She passed him the headset and the hand controllers. "I just reached the end of the demo, so hit the power and it will probably restart at the beginning." Rayne looked over as Mouser returned from the bathroom, a sour look on his face. "I just promised Shadow so you'll have to wait."

"I had my turn," Mouser said, pointing at the visor he'd torn off and dropped on the floor behind the coffee table. "Instant motion sickness. I guess virtual reality roller coasters aren't my thing."

"You're probably too old to start. That was far more immersive than I would have imagined. I really felt the motion." She picked up the visor that Mouser had discarded and began to examine it closely. "Do you think—"

"I want these," Shadow interrupted loudly, throwing a punch in the air which might have connected with Rayne if she hadn't moved around the other side of the table. His next punch got tangled in the visor's cord, pulling it out of the power supply. A minute later he stopped fighting. "What happened?"

"You pulled out the power cord, and the fact you kept going for a minute after that tells me there's a permanent battery that picked up a bit of charge while Rayne ran the demo," Mouser told him. "We've got a few thousand headsets sitting in a container on the tarmac so there are more than enough for the Golden Rule. I wonder if Flower replaced all of the batteries and resealed the bubble pack?"

"I'll bet our people who moved to Flower told her we have a rule that prohibits introducing new legacy peripherals to Bits unless you have enough for everybody at a tournament," Shadow said. "I've seen a visor option in the menu for some of the old games but I thought it would be the same as looking at a screen. That was wild."

"It made Mouser sick," Rayne told him. "And I was about to say that I get the feeling we're being led somewhere by the nose."

"More like the eyes and the ears. But where?"

"Think about it. Dewey shows up with a bailout offer we can't refuse, relieves us of the possibly active weapons of mass destruction in our museum, and then we get a container of virtual reality headsets that meet the Bits definition of legacy technology as a parting gift. These visors are practically the missing link between two-dimensional screens and holographic projectors."

"So you think Flower is trying to drag us out of the twenty-first century the better to put us to work on her Live Action Role Playing project," Mouser surmised. "You may be right, but we still need the money."

"The art group is going to love these," Shadow said. "It will be cool playing some of the old games with visors, but think about how useful they'll be for creating 3D environments. Instead of simulating them with screens, the designers will be able to move around inside."

"But we could have done that and more with cheap Horten holoprojectors if we didn't boycott the technology," Rayne pointed out. "I think that Flower is in league with the Traitors to change Bits."

"Is this about Gorgeous George leaving you?"

Rayne threw the visor at the young man's head, but his gamer reactions made the catch easy.

"Hey, none of that," Mouser said, getting between the two. "Shadow, apologize to Rayne. You're too young to be making comments about her divorce."

"Sorry," Shadow said, and seeing the look on Rayne's face, he wished he hadn't said anything. "People talk. It just came out."

"That doesn't mean I want to hear it," Rayne said, heading for the workbench to get a tissue to blow her nose. "And you're right that we didn't have a choice, Mouser. I suppose I should stop looking for hidden strings attached and just get on with the work. What do you need me to do?"

"Three things," Mouser said decisively. "First, you hold the purse strings for Flower's project, so I'm counting on you to watch the budget and maybe do a little creative accounting to set something aside for a rainy day rather than spending all of the money on salaries. Second, I'll be ready to start beta testing some of my gameplay ideas by the weekend, and it will save a lot of time if I can do that with you and our usual group. Lastly, I need a bright school-age girl to work with and I want you to loan me Sarah at some point."

"What about your grandchildren?"

"Too young. Derik just turned eight, but boys that age can't sit still for long, and to be honest, I think he would get tired of pretend-magic in a hurry. The girls are four and one, but your Sarah must be around nine?"

"She just turned ten," Rayne told him before blowing her nose.

"So it's the perfect age to help me build a magic system that makes sense to children," Mouser said.

"Are you going to try to design the whole game yourself?" Shadow asked.

"We're planning on a dozen parallel teams working on alternative scenarios as soon as Rayne sets up the payroll. We should probably create a mechanism for keeping all of the teams aware of the rules and the history that each is experimenting with so we don't end up with too many direct contradictions."

"Here's your notebook," Rayne said, handing the five-subject binder to Mouser. "It was under the tissue box. Where did you get it, anyway?"

"I found a crate of them in the museum when I went through with Dewey," Mouser said. "I think I may be allergic to paper because I keep sneezing." He sat back down in his overstuffed chair and opened the notebook. "Are the two of you going to stand through the meeting?"

"What about the others?" Shadow asked.

"Herc and Delphi are spending the morning headhunting."

"Like, in a game?"

"It's old Earth slang for recruiting workers who already have a job with another employer," Mouser said. "You're too young for anybody to take seriously."

"Delphi is only a year older than me," Shadow protested.

"Girls mature faster than boys," Rayne said. "Sometimes I think you and Sarah are at about the same level."

"Don't get started, you two," Mouser said. "I've written down so many ideas that I had to stop because my hand was cramping up, and I plan to share them with the other teams as soon as they sign on. I just wanted to get your first impressions on a few points before I pick one and start roughing out an adventure."

"How can we have an adventure before the world-building is finished?" Shadow asked.

"We'll be doing most of it on the fly. Rayne needs to start funding work to get Flower's money into the economy, and if most of the early scenarios end up on the cutting room floor, that's the cost of accelerated development. But I don't want to be overly profligate, and that means nailing down some elements of the world and the magic system as fast as possible. The only way to do that is to dive in and start pushing the boundaries to see what makes sense."

"From my reading about twenty-first-century Earth this week I got the impression that people spent most of their time shopping or consuming stuff at home," Rayne said. "Maybe instead of a dungeon crawl, we could go on a sort of retail quest."

"Is that a pin the tail on the dragon thing?" Shadow asked, drawing a snort from Mouser.

"Retail as in direct to consumer. Shops like you see in games are usually small affairs run by a single non-player character, or maybe a family of NPCs," the treasurer explained. "By the middle of the twenty-first century, retail stores were so big that you could get lost in them, and the big corporate chains had pretty much wiped out anything like a family-owned shop or restaurant."

"That's right," Mouser said. "But I was counting on a lot of family-owned shops for employment."

"You're replacing electricity with magic," she reminded him. "That's bound to have a pretty big effect on the way the economy would have developed. Maybe you've got it right."

"I don't want to play a game about shopping and neither will anybody else," Shadow said dismissively.

"Wait until you have a girlfriend," Rayne told him.

"Truce," Mouser said, shooting Rayne an irritated look.

"Shopping and magic lessons for kids," Shadow grumbled, and then he brightened up. "Hey, how about magical shoplifting? With my stealth, I could steal a ton, and then there would be fences and police. Maybe something like that game about stealing ground transport some of the oldsters still play?"

"Of course, there will be stealing, though from what Dewey told me about Flower, I'm not sure we'd be wise to have parents teaching it to their children."

"How else are they going to learn not to get caught?"

Mouser shook his head. "That's not the point, and while I see possibilities with retail shopping, it seems overly specific for a starting point. Let me read you the ideas for broad themes I've jotted down so far, starting with—" he consulted the notebook, —"Invasion Earth. I was thinking, what if in addition to humanity having magic, alien invaders had attacked Earth before the Stryx opening."

"Magic or not, they would have kicked our butts," Shadow said.

"Dewey said that Flower is focused on the alien market and they might take it the wrong way," Rayne said. "It's pretty well established that the Vergallians were planning on taking over Earth before the Stryx beat them to the punch, and I've heard rumors that spies from other species were watching."

"It's just an idea that one of the other teams might want to run with," Mouser said. "It's not my sort of thing. I'm calling the next one Antiquer, your basic quest game where you scour Earth for artifacts. I got the idea from that Grenouthian documentary about the black market for Earth collectibles."

"Tomb raiding would be cool, but if you're talking about shopping again, count me out," Shadow said.

"You know, the aliens all love open-air markets," Rayne said. "I've heard that street fairs do very well on Earth with the tourist trade even though most of the stuff for sale is replicas."

"Feudalism is also popular with aliens, going by the number of new theme parks built around old European castles I've read about," Mouser said. "It would be easy to come up with a history where the existence of magic displaced the development of technology and the world is ruled by kings and landowners."

"Then what's the difference between that and any other swords and sorcery game?" Shadow asked.

"And Dewey did specify the twenty-first century, so the eleventh century with a thousand years of magic sounds like a stretch," Rayne said.

"Tough audience," Mouser muttered, looking back at his notes. "Revolution is always a popular theme. If we start with the twenty-first century as it was, and then introduce magic through some cataclysmic event, there's a good chance that governments would have fallen."

"That could be cool," Shadow said. "Sort of like a vampire apocalypse game, except everybody would be paranormal."

"Sounds too violent," Rayne said.

"Then you might like Isolation," Mouser said. "There's a scenario where instead of magic displacing technology, the two exist side-by-side, and there's so much destructive power in the hands of every nation that they can't go to war."

"MAD," Shadow said. "Mutually Assured Destruction. I played an old game like that where everybody has nukes and the object is to launch a successful first strike."

"Magically Assured Destruction," Rayne corrected him. "I just don't see the aliens being that interested."

"I have one with a magical version of the Internet called the Edison Web," Mouser continued. "Instead of starting an electrical lighting and power distribution company, Edison figures out how to gather and distribute the population's excess magic. When computers eventually come along, everything ends up on the same network."

"But what's the gameplay?" Shadow asked. "Who do I get to fight?"

"It sounds pretty Big Brotherish," Rayne said. "Maybe everybody is against the government? What else do you have?"

Mouser sighed and looked down again. "A post-apocalyptic Earth after an asteroid impact that triggers the rebirth of magic?"

"I'd play that," Shadow said.

"Pass," Rayne told them.

"This one I just thought of last night and I haven't sketched out much history yet. I thought it might be interesting to do a twenty-first-century Earth where the magic only interacted with technology, a sort of steampunk variant."

Shadow showed his teeth in a wolfish smile. "We could be magic hackers."

Five

"You sold us out," the producer of *Time Wars* said angrily. "Giving away all of the serious weapons from the museum means our next release will be dead on arrival." The dark bags under his eyes spoke of stress, and although he had recently celebrated his fiftieth birthday, he looked closer to sixty. He seemed to be having trouble concentrating on the meeting and kept glancing over at Delphi as if he recognized her from somewhere but couldn't quite place her.

Hercules leaned back in the conference room chair and studied the ceiling mural of a combat scene from *Heroes of Humanity*. "It's not like you ever disassembled the alien weapons and figured out how they worked. I was a beta tester on your third release, and even as a kid I knew that you were just inventing the destructive effects to match the game's physics engine."

"The whole marketing plan for *Time Wars* was built on adding rediscovered weapons technology from ancient aliens. We've spent decades branding new releases with a trailer of Doctor Destruction giving a tour of the museum. He stumbles on an ancient artifact that triggers a time warp and starts a new adventure."

"How many copies of the last *Time Wars* release did you sell?" Delphi asked.

Something in the girl's voice made the producer hesitate, but he shook it off and replied, "We don't share that information outside of the development group."

"Thirty-two thousand, give or take a few hundred. And what was the breakdown between distribution and direct sales?"

"Who's been talking to you?"

"Ninety-six percent of the sales were distribution because you and your group haven't traveled to any cons or tournaments in a decade," Delphi continued. "I bet you're lucky to net five creds on an update sold through distribution. Am I right?"

"Four and a half," the producer muttered, unhappy about being boxed in. He was staring openly at her at this point, and Hercules could almost see the gears turning in the man's head.

"So you grossed a hundred and fifty thousand creds, call it a million eBucks just to be generous since most of your customers are on Earth. And that's supposed to feed how many people until your next product comes out?"

"When I first joined the programming team, *Time Wars* was the biggest cash cow on Bits. If we could just—"

"That was almost three decades ago," Hercules cut him off. "Your audience has aged out, discovered alien games, got married, and had kids. Not one game in ten remains commercial for more than a generation."

"Sixty-two people," the producer belatedly answered Delphi's last question. "We had less than a hundred and fifty thousand creds to split sixty-two ways. If it wasn't for the tithe covering everybody's basic expenses, I would have declared the game out of production already."

Hercules nodded in sympathy "I get that losing part of the museum collection feels like a low blow, Mr. Jackson, but we have the funds to hire your whole group for at least the next six months."

"Tom. And I appreciate what you're saying. But my people signed on to do *Time Wars*, not some fantasy game."

"We're looking for different interpretations. Mouser wants at least ten full development groups working on this and you've got a great team in place. Think of it as an extended jam or a sabbatical hack-a-thon. Why not step up and try to shape a game that your people would be happy to work on? What else can you do with them?"

"We're planning a thirty-first-anniversary release, code-name *Timepiece*," Tom said.

"And is everybody happy doing that?" Delphi asked pointedly.

The producer puffed out some air and looked even more deflated than when Delphi had brought up the sales. "No. The only reason I haven't lost anybody yet is that none of the other groups are staffing up."

"Exactly," Hercules said. "All we're asking is that you agree to give it a chance. Meet with Rayne and she'll advance you enough to pay everybody for a month just to work up a storyboard prototype. Then we'll play through each other's ideas, vote on the results, and the top three designs will move forward to the next phase."

"But by participating, we're committing to throw in with whoever wins," Tom surmised.

"It's not a forced decision, though if you decide to drop out at that point, there won't be any more money for you or your team," Delphi told him. She glanced at the screen above the door that was displaying an old-fashioned clock with hands. "I'm sorry, but we only reserved the room for the morning and we have nine more meetings scheduled. The next one is in three minutes."

"Then I hope you treat the next producer with a little more respect than you've mustered for me. I've been working in the field since before you were born, and—" he stopped abruptly, and then asked in a hollow voice, "What's your mother's name?"

"Aphrodite, and, yes, you had a fling with her."

All of the remaining color drained from the man's face. "And, uh, do you know your father?"

"Your time is up," the girl repeated. She looked down and began ostentatiously reviewing notes on her smartphone.

Hercules accompanied Tom to the door, shook the producer's hand, and mumbled a quiet apology before returning to his chair. "That was pretty rough, Delphi. You shouldn't mix business with family stuff."

"Why not? Rayne did, and at least Sarah had a father for seven years before he left."

"It's not—you know the history of the hacking movement. Even before we came to Bits, there were far more men than women involved, and traditional marriages were rare. We only drifted back towards the standard family model as the demographics evened out with the children who were born here. I remember when I was working on the *Time Wars* testing team somebody told me that Tom grew up without his own parents."

"He's an orphan?" Delphi asked, the angry set of her jaw softening slightly. "Mom didn't tell me."

Hercules shook his head in the negative. "Tom had too many parents, one of those plural families with multiple wives and husbands, over two dozen of the latter, if I recall. I'm pretty sure they were one of the ideological groups where the children were considered common property, and part of the reason they left Earth was because of polygamy laws."

"Oh, I guess I've heard of that. It's creepy."

"Nobody does it anymore, at least that I'm aware of. Tom's fifteen years or so older than me, and I never hung out with the guy or anything, but he always seemed decent enough."

"He looked older," Delphi said, and something like a confused concern crept into her voice.

"I don't know how it works in other places, but on Bits, being the producer for a game means he's the one responsible for keeping those sixty-two people employed," Hercules said. "He worked his way up on *Time Wars*, it's probably the only job he's ever had, and now we're basically asking him to shut it down. And if I'm any judge of character, I'd say he never even dreamed he might have a daughter before today. It's a lot to take in all at once."

The door slid open and a woman in her early forties with platinum blonde hair in a ponytail entered. "Is this the recruitment event?" she asked with a frown. "I was expecting to see Rayne or Mouser."

"Both of them are incredibly busy right now so we're here to answer any easy questions you might have before you meet Rayne to sign on," Hercules said. "You're," he glanced down at his own smartphone screen, "Leandra..."

"Just the one name," Leandra said taking a seat. "And you?"

"Hercules, and she's Delphi. We're both in Mouser's weekly game with Rayne."

"Rayne and Hercules have been in Mouser's group since they were teenagers," Delphi added. "I joined when they lost a couple of players a few years ago."

"To Flower?" Leandra asked.

Hercules nodded. "One of them was the best paladin I ever played with, but he was into the modern stuff."

"So what can you tell me about the backers for this new game?"

"Just that their money is good and the long-range goal is a vertically integrated gameverse with everything from a board game to full interactive mode in LARPing studios."

"Is there any wiggle room on the twenty-first-century-with-magic theme?" Leandra asked, looking at Hercules over the retro eyeglasses perched on the end of her nose.

"That much is carved in stone, but how you approach it is entirely up to you."

"How many people do you currently have working?" Delphi asked.

"Over two hundred, but a hundred and eighty of them are part-time," Leandra said. "And we have more people on Earth doing customer support. That's where most of our users are, and with the Stryxnet connection there, they can get messages from other places without waiting for a visiting ship to bring a data dump. But I don't think of those workers as being part of my team because they're all employed through Bits Away."

"I keep forgetting about Bits Away because I've never worked in customer support," Hercules said. "Do you know offhand how many people they employ?"

Leandra shook her head and the glasses dropped from her nose to hang from a thin silver chain going around her neck. "At least a few thousand, but most of them are supporting the operating systems work we do for the smartphones. I was there a few years ago, my one trip away from Bits. If you're not familiar with the way we provide support, ten percent of the gross from all the work we do here goes into escrow. We don't directly manage Bits

Away because of the communications challenge, but people from here who know the technical side of our major products are always on Earth as liaisons. They have our source code library and programmers on staff to do minor patches as problems come up."

"How come I've never met anybody who worked for Bits Away?" Delphi asked.

"Because they haven't been coming back in recent years," Leandra explained. "When we first moved to Bits, it was so hard to find volunteers to go back to Earth that we had to do a lottery. Now the managers there buy homes and keep on extending their contracts. I imagine if we shut down Bits Away they would find other jobs and stay put."

Hercules made a note on his phone. "I'm not sure if the customer for the new project is going to want to go the same way for support. They're hoping to break into the alien market and I doubt Bits Away is set up to deal with that."

"You're willing to pay all of my team at their current compensation levels to spend a month coming up with a prototype, and then for another five months to push ahead with the winning designs?"

"Not their current compensation," Delphi corrected her. "Rayne insisted on a three-year average to remove any temptation for retroactive salary spiking. If you have team members without that much work history, use as much as you do have." She looked down at her phone again. "Is *Vampire Protection Services* the name of your franchise or just the latest edition?"

"The franchise, and before you ask, it's been B-list ever since the initial release, though we do have diehard fans who religiously buy the updates," Leandra said. "I don't think anybody on Bits other than our beta testers plays the game because there's not any action unless you're losing."

"So what do the vampires do?"

"Try to blend in—that's the whole point. The player takes the role of a world government agent whose job is to provide new identities and relocation services to vampires who have been exposed. It's kind of cerebral for a video game, but the people who like it can play a new release for hundreds of hours if they exhaust every possible storyline."

"Has your full-time team always been so small?" Hercules asked.

"The original was repurposed from the old *Witness Protection* game about organized crime on twentieth-century Earth," Leandra said, returning her reading glasses to her nose. "That's when I got hooked on drugstore spectacles. The development was all about scripting, music, and art. We only needed one serious coder to add some vampire-specific character abilities because it's really about storytelling and building new identities. You wouldn't believe how many forms people had to fill out back on Earth to get anything done."

"And did you have any other questions about our project?" Delphi asked, glancing up at the clock again.

"Are there going to be vampires or any kind of monsters?"

"None of that has been decided yet. I know that Mouser likes the idea of replacing electricity with magic, and where you have powerful magicians, you'd think the undead would follow. But maybe that would be more zombies than vampires."

"My game isn't completely dead yet, if you'll pardon the pun, but we are between updates, and most of my full-timers are twiddling their thumbs. How about I guarantee you the month, but we'll hold off on the longer commitment until we see what gets green-lighted?"

"That's fine by us," Hercules said. "Rayne is hoping to see everybody who wants to move ahead this afternoon. Will you be available on an hour's notice when she texts you a time?"

"Not a problem," Leandra said, rising to her feet. "Don't get up, I can show myself out."

"She was nice," Delphi said after the door slid closed, and then she reddened. "I wasn't, like, making a comparison to my probably-father."

"It's funny that I had forgotten about Bits Away," Hercules said. "With all the gamers on Bits, we test everything so extensively before shipping that any remaining bugs are minor. And without a tunnel and a Stryxnet connection, doing support for remote customers has never been possible here." He glanced at the clock display. "Who's up next?"

Delphi scrolled down her phone's screen. "Martin. I think I know him. Guy around your age with a goatee who produces that stupid game about dogs fighting."

"*Dogfighter*, and it's about aerial combat with obsolete sub-orbital aircraft," Hercules said with a laugh. "I thought I was quick to judge, but you're even worse than me."

"The name was such a turn-off that I never bothered looking into it," Delphi admitted. "Don't tell him."

Martin entered exactly on time and made his way around the table to shake hands with both members of Mouser's team. "I think I remember you from the junior hack-a-thons," he said to Delphi. "I volunteer as a coding coach."

"Yeah, you helped me once with getting my dragon to stop flying in circles," the girl said. "Hercules and I are acting as a buffer to save Rayne time later because she's swamped. Do you have any questions?"

"The package looked pretty straightforward to me," Martin said. "My team has extensive experience with translating old Earth imagery and tech into the gameverse, so in a sense, it's right up our alley. What concerns me is that we're all geared to realistic flight simulation with multi-player combat."

"Multi-player?" Hercules asked. "I thought it was a first-person shooter game."

"We included an option to play against the computer, but our real focus was on dueling and group battles. I know that we all have our niches when it comes to gaming, but didn't either of you stop by the main hall to check out our simulation of the Battle of Britain last month? We had hundreds of planes in the air at the same time."

"You know how many tournaments are taking place here. I was never an Earth history reenactor type."

"I guess I didn't see the announcements," Delphi fibbed. "There could be flying machines that work on magic in the new game. That would be up to you."

"Maybe we could make the whole thing about flying," Martin said enthusiastically. "Like, steampunk, with lighter-than-air ships based on magic and dirigibles. I have the digital blueprints for a Zeppelin somewhere and I know one of my guys is into clockwork horses."

"Where do you stand with *Dogfighter*?" Hercules asked. "Will you have to hold out some of your team to work on the next revision?"

"There isn't going to be one," Martin said. "The problem with basing a game on historical aircraft is you run out of material. After the Stryx opened Earth, the money for developing new fighter jets dried up, and most of Earth's aviation industry is utilizing Dollnick floater technology these days. I wouldn't be surprised if a few of the old nations or the city-states that replaced them still have some fighters in underground hangars, but if they do, they're probably using our game to train the pilots. Nobody sees jet aircraft in the skies."

"I hadn't thought of that. So have you dissolved the team?"

"We're spending down the money from the last release as it comes in and working on new ideas. I mean, not so new, because the leading candidate right now is to do the same thing with tank warfare, but our beta testing suggests that players just aren't into it the same way they were with flying."

"Do you have any kids?" Hercules asked.

"A boy, just turned eight," Martin said. "Is it a requirement?"

"It just struck me that we should make sure there are some parents on every development team so they can bounce the ideas off their children. We're looking for a game that can bridge generations, with whole families playing, but I don't know if it will be possible in the end."

"And since it wasn't that long ago that I was competing in the junior tournaments, I've been assigned to run focus groups of kids to look at the ideas that the teams are working on as soon as there's something to see," Delphi added.

"All right, then," Martin said. "My whole team is waiting for me at Café Storage to hear whether we made the cut, but it sounds like that was never in doubt. When will I be meeting with Rayne to sort out the money?"

"This afternoon. She'll text you an hour before the meeting."

Hercules accompanied the producer of *Dogfighter* to the door and checked the corridor to see if their next appointment was waiting. "Who's on deck?" he asked Delphi.

"Daiyu. I think I've seen that name at the top of the mixed-MMORPG leaderboard a bunch of times, but maybe it's a common name."

"Black Jade, and there's only one of her on Bits," Hercules said. "She leads the Champions of Faraway guild on *Dark Earth* and I ran with them for a couple of years. I didn't think she was old enough to be a producer. Which product does she represent?"

"*Deep Space Trader*. There's a minimum age to work as a producer?"

"No, of course not, but you need a lot of resources to produce a game, both funding and social capital. I've known teenagers who designed new games that made it to the commercial stage, but the successful ones usually find an experienced producer to help with the business side."

"But nobody cares how old you are in the gameverse," Delphi objected. "Players follow leaders with winning track records."

"In real life, most adults aren't in a hurry to make business deals with young people," Hercules told her. "They worry about your lack of experience, and to be honest, there's probably a bit of envy mixed in."

The door slid open again and a slender woman of Asian ancestry in her mid-twenties entered, her black hair coiled on her head and held in place by a large decorative pin. "Hercules?" she asked, her eyes going to the large man.

"Daiyu," he responded, dipping his head as if they were immersed in *Dark Earth* and he was acknowledging the guild's leader. "I'm surprised you recognize me."

"You look exactly like your avatar," she said, taking a seat at the table. "Who does that?"

"I'm just kind of lazy."

"He spends two hours a day in the gym and he wants everybody to know it," Delphi said. "If Bits ever runs out of food and turns to cannibalism, I have dibs on him."

"Too lean," Daiyu said. "And have we met?"

"I've seen your name on the leaderboard but that's it. I think I recognize the hairpin from your avatar."

"I've killed more dungeon bosses with my hairpin than most players have with swords," the producer of *Deep Space Trader* said. "It's part of an epic set with the combs and the ribbon."

"Cool. Do you mind if I ask how business is going?"

Daiyu grimaced. "I wouldn't be here if it was good. When *Deep* first came out, the idea was to pick up some of the humans who can't get anywhere playing *Raider/Trader.* The Verlocks released R/T over twenty-five years ago and it's really hard to break into the trading space as an independent today. We had a good initial release, but without the Stryxnet tie-in through ship controllers, we can't do the real-time market condition updates that working traders rely on. So the only thing *Deep* had left going for it was the combat mode, but it just didn't build a big enough following to keep pushing forward."

"Do you still have a development team left?" Hercules asked.

"We ran out of money for salaries a few months ago, but only two of my people found work with other teams, so I can pull them back together. My uncle raised the money for the original development and produced the first edition, but he correctly read the tea leaves and dumped the game on me rather than fighting a losing battle. Our family thought it would be a good experience, and to be honest, my mother wanted to cut down on the time I spend playing *Dark Earth*."

"Mothers," Delphi said sympathetically. "I'm nineteen and mine keeps trying to get me to go to college on Earth. I mean, who ever heard of a game music composer with a degree?"

Daiyu sighed. "I have an M.S. in Computer Science from a correspondence course. It's complete B.S. if you ask me, but it kept my family off my back for a few years. Now they're giving me a choice between going to Earth for a Ph.D. and getting married."

"Have you considered moving to a different dome?" Hercules asked.

"If you ever met my family you wouldn't have asked that. As far as they're concerned, I'm a child until I get married, and then I'll have my husband's family to deal with. It's never-ending."

"Oh. Any questions about the game we've been hired to develop?"

"I'm good with anything that will buy me another six months of work and then maybe I'll run away to a Stryx station," Daiyu said. "As long as Rayne comes across with the funds, I guarantee my team will do our best to come up with a kickass game. I'll even place a bet that our prototype makes the final three."

"Do you know if any of your team members have kids?" Delphi asked. "If not, I'll be running a focus group you can try ideas on."

The young producer of *Deep Space Trader* thought for a moment and a strange look came over her face. "They all have at least one kid. I never thought about it before, but that's probably another reason my family wanted me to take the job."

Six

"You are in a cavernous structure with a stone-hard polished floor as smooth as glass. A flat roof with exposed trusses soars above your heads, and dozens of straight passages spread out before you like an unnatural river delta ruled by geometry. Towering ledges spaced at regular intervals to either side of your path make it feel like you have entered some sort of man-made canyon. Other than the distant peeping of some baby birds waiting in nests for the return of their parents, all is silent."

"Do I detect any magic?" Hercules asked.

"Roll a perception check," the gamemaster told him.

"Thirteen."

"You reach out with your sixth sense which spreads rapidly through the structure like a bucket of water poured on the floor, thinning rapidly with distance. None of the characteristic markers you associate with magic disturb the otherwise placid surface."

"Of the puddle," Shadow griped. "Are we at a disadvantage if we move now because we're going to slip?"

"The water was metaphorical, not real," Delphi told him. "Can I cast Detect Enemies?"

"You already used it outside."

"Sorry, I forgot."

"While you stand around discussing your next move, you hear something falling to the floor in the distance, though it's impossible to determine the direction due to all of the obstructions in this closed space," Mouser continued in his role as the gamemaster. "The baby birds fall silent."

"I want to buff the party," Rayne announced. "Shield of Virtue."

"How much mana are you backing it with?"

"Five."

"The tall half-elf rubs her hands together and an eerie blue glow begins to form around the party. You all feel a surge of health and strength."

Hercules leaned forward. "I go to the end of the passage and—"

"Wait," Delphi interrupted. "What's on these artificial ledges or whatever?"

"The light is too dim this far inside the structure to make out any details," Mouser told her.

"I bring out my Orbs of Apollo."

"Three bright balls each burning with the intensity of a hundred candles appear floating above you. Where do you want them to go?"

"I'll keep one above my head, but, like, double my height, and put one each over Hercules and Rayne."

"Thanks a lot," Shadow grumbled.

"I don't think having an Orb of Apollo over your head would help with your stealth."

"That is correct," Mouser said. "Now that the passage is well lit, you see that the ledges are metal shelves, and they are stacked with stubby cylinders with cryptic markings and color coding that reminds you of alchemical preparations. There are some odd, rectangular pans on the bottom shelf, along with stacks of narrow tubes around the size of scroll casings."

"I read a scroll," Rayne said immediately

"There are no scrolls present."

"But you said—never mind."

"Can I invoke my Polyglot skill and read the cryptic markings?" Hercules asked.

"Roll for wisdom," Mouser told him.

"Sixteen, plus two for my Ring of Solomon."

"You move closer to the shelf and stare at the odd markings on a container until the words swim into focus. One Gallon, Bone White Latex."

"We're in a paint store?"

"Is this one of the big box things I read about?" Rayne asked. "How could anybody reach the higher shelves?"

"You have identified the structure as a big box home improvement store. A loud clattering sound comes through the shelves from your left, perhaps one aisle over."

"Do we have to be in here? I don't remember why we even entered. Can we leave?"

"If you all agree on leaving, I'll ask you to do an agility check," Mouser said.

"Doesn't that mean we're surrounded?" Delphi asked. "Why can't I feel anything?"

"Your passive detection ability doesn't work on the undead," Rayne reminded the teenager.

"I *hate* the undead."

"You see a figure at the end of the aisle between you and the doors through which you entered the store," Mouser said. "It is wearing a bright colored apron and moving jerkily, its head turned to the side as if the neck may be broken. I want you all to roll for initiative."

"What does any of this have to do with shopping?" Rayne asked plaintively. "I haven't been in a zombie fight for ever. We only came in the store because there was nothing else around other than empty fields. You said that the pavement of that road was so broken up that it would take all day to get anywhere."

"Seven," Hercules grunted in disappointment.

Delphi leaned over the coffee table to check her roll in the dice tray. "Eighteen."

"Sixteen," Shadow reported.

Rayne sighed and rolled for initiative. "Four."

"What are you going to do, Delphi?" Mouser asked.

"I run towards the zombie and—"

"Which one?"

"I thought the one at the front was it."

"While you were talking, two more zombies appeared at the other end of the paint aisle. They may be coming from the plumbing fixtures section. A few cans of paint fall off the shelf and roll to a stop, indicating that more zombies are trying to break through from the aisles on either side."

"We have to get out of here," Delphi said. "I run towards the one between us and the exit, and leaping in the air, I swing my staff at its head."

"Roll for an attack."

"Eight?"

"That doesn't hit," Mouser told her. "Your fear makes you too eager and you swing before you've fully emerged from the aisle. The staff impacts a display of paintbrushes and then hits the metal racking supporting the shelves. Shadow, what do you do?"

"Do I have a clear shot at the thing or is Delphi in the way?"

"Your monkish companion has slipped on a paintbrush and is lying on the floor so you have a clear view of the zombie."

Shadow hesitated for a moment, toying with his costume dagger, and then he said, "Screw it. I close within melee distance and stab it with a dagger in each hand."

"Are you invoking Double Dagger?"

"Is that one roll for the attack?"

"Yes."

"Let's do it. Fourteen?"

"That hits. Roll for damage."

"Eighteen, plus I get another ten for Double Dagger."

"The first dagger takes the zombie in the chest, perhaps it never saw you coming because of the way its head is twisted to the side. Your second thrust goes through the ear into its brain and the zombie collapses to the floor."

"So we all move to the door," Hercules said. "I don't see the point to running around in here fighting zombies when we don't even know why we came."

"It was like that with shopping in the twenty-first century," Rayne told him. "People went to stores just to look around and see what caught their fancy."

"You seem to have forgotten your initiative scores," Mouser said. "There are three other zombies close enough to attack you, but one of them rolled the same as Rayne."

"Where do you get three?" Shadow demanded. "I just killed mine, and you said that there were two coming out of plumbing."

Mouser held up his hand. "One of the zombies at the other end of the aisle appears to be confused, but the other shambles forward rapidly, its arms out and fingers extended like claws."

"Was I in a defensive stance?" Hercules asked.

"No."

"Can I get between the zombie and Rayne?"

"I'm not sure we resolved your exact positions before so I'll let you do that. What's your armor class?"

"Fifteen."

"The zombie grapples with you and tries to sink his teeth into your chest but he's unable to gnaw through the breastplate. All of a sudden, the paint rollers that Rayne mistook for scrolls come tumbling off the bottom shelf and a zombie crawls through the space to bite your leg. His teeth sink into your leather leggings, but you shake him off. What do you do next?"

"Finally," Hercules said. "I stomp on the low zombie, and with my reaction, I try to brain the other one with my mace."

"Roll for the stomp."

"Twelve, but I get plus three for the boots."

"Fifteen does it. The zombie's head caves like a ripe melon and it goes still. Roll for the mace."

"Nineteen," Hercules said with a grin.

"You better not get its brains all over me," Rayne warned him.

"The zombie is still bent over from its failed attempt to grapple and bite you so your overhand mace blow catches the back of its skull and the gore stays behind it," Mouser said obligingly. "Your turn, Rayne."

"Let's get out of here, Hercules."

"I gave up my move for the reaction, it's the main flaw in this character build," he told her.

"Can I drag him?" Rayne asked.

"Do a strength check," Mouser said.

Rayne rolled. "Eleven?"

"Eleven will get you both to the end of the aisle."

"I drag Hercules to the end of the aisle, and—is Delphi still on the floor?"

Mouser thought for a moment. "Even if she is, the aisle is wide enough to move pallets so you can get by."

"So can we just leave?" Shadow asked. "This place is giving me the creeps."

"You're still in combat with the remaining zombie that rolled the same as Rayne. It shambles down the aisle at remarkable speed for a reanimated corpse but it doesn't quite reach the end. Now you can move again."

"You're saying that we've drawn its aggression and it will follow if we don't kill it?"

"Until you get out of its aggro radius."

"I'll kill it," Delphi said with a sigh. "I grip my staff with both hands and thrust a metal-shod end directly into the zombie's forehead, thus not hitting a shelf and getting hung up."

"Roll for the attack," Mouser told her.

"Nine! This sucks."

"Nine is actually enough because the zombies aren't good at dodging. Roll for damage."

"Oh. Can I cast Iron Impact at the same time?"

"Do a wisdom check."

"Seventeen," Delphi crowed. "Does it count for both?"

Mouser shook his head. "Now roll for damage."

"Uh, fourteen."

"The iron-shod end of your staff impacts the zombie's forehead and it staggers back against a shelf which keeps it from falling. It begins to raise an arm and then slumps to the floor."

"Now can we leave?" Shadow asked.

"You move close to each other to ensure that any attackers will have to face all of you at once and you jog towards the exit. There are a number of zombies approaching, attracted by the noise, but none of them are close enough to engage. You make it through the shattered doors into the parking lot."

"The what?" Delphi asked.

"The parking lot," Mouser said. "There would be hundreds of—oops."

"What's wrong this time?" Rayne asked.

"The thumbnail history they supplied specified no cars. How were they planning for the people to get to big box stores without cars? And even if they walk or ride a horse, how are they going to bring home all of the junk they buy?"

"Why don't they have cars? They can just run on mana instead of electricity."

Mouser paged back through the rough draft of *Shopping Land* provided by one of the competing teams for an early look. "I think the problem was more with the factories. I wouldn't have any issue with a wagon maker putting a flywheel on the rear axle that can be powered with magic, but building cars is an enormous undertaking. You need raw materials from all sorts of industries that might not make sense in a magical world."

"So say the parking lot is full of wagons," Hercules said. "Maybe some of them have clockwork horses. Martin, the producer of *Dogfighter,* was enthusiastic about the idea."

"I heard that the two of you met with Tom," Rayne said, glancing at Delphi. "Did you, uh—"

"I know who he is," Delphi said. "I guess I was kind of bratty to him but it could have gone worse. I talked to mom and I'm going to have a coffee with him this evening. Wait. You knew he was my father?"

"There's a family resemblance. Did any of the zombies follow us out of the store?"

"No," Mouser said, still flipping the pages. "You're in a parking lot, but the remaining horseless wagons are abandoned, and most of those show fire damage. Some sort of magical fight has taken place here. To the west, the fields are—"

"Hold up," Hercules said, raising a hand like a traffic cop. "Why is magic being used for fighting and raising the dead? I thought it was supposed to be a replacement for electricity and maybe a substitute for money."

"He's right," Rayne said. "We should have been in there shopping, not killing monsters."

"Speaking of which, did we get any loot?" Shadow asked.

"The zombies had nothing worth taking," Mouser told him. "I shouldn't judge from what's here because they rushed to get me something, but based on the character sheets they supplied, it's hard to see *Shopping Land* developing into anything other than a standard dungeon crawl. I'm sorry the four of you went to the trouble of getting into character by coming in costume."

"I dress like a monk out of habit," Delphi said, drawing a collective groan for her pun. "Seriously, though. Herc and I have been visiting a different team every morning and we think most of them are on a good track. Forget *Shopping Land* and let's work on your game." She unzipped the detachable cowl from her robe and stuffed it in a pocket. "There. Hit us with the real twenty-first century."

"If we're not going to be fighting, I want to eat," Shadow said.

"Take a few creds from the community jar and buy two pizzas," Mouser told him. "We'll wait until you get back."

"I'll get the sodas from the fridge," Rayne said, standing up. "If my daughter could see me now I'd be in trouble."

"Are you still trying to keep Sarah away from vending machine food?" Hercules asked. "It's probably healthier than the stuff that comes in boxes full of preservatives."

"If you're ever feeling brave enough to enter mortal combat with a ten-year-old girl, try taking away her cookies."

"Costumes aside, are you up to role-playing some new character sheets I prepared as samples?" Mouser asked.

"As long as we don't have to fight zombies," Delphi said.

"There are things worse than the undead," Rayne cautioned her. "Wait until you read the sheet."

The gamemaster took up his spiral-bound notebook, turned to the back, and carefully tore out the last four sheets. He reviewed the contents of each sheet before handing it over, starting with Hercules.

"What's a boutique?" Delphi asked after reading her page.

"A high-end store that sells expensive goods, often associated with just one brand," Mouser told her. "Your character is a fashionable young lady, and working in a boutique was one of the jobs that would be attractive to you."

"I'm married to Hercules?" Rayne asked, her voice rising. "And Sarah is our child?"

"I want to work out the family angle and Shadow wouldn't be able to take being a father seriously."

"Sarah wouldn't be able to take him seriously either," the girl's mother retorted while looking over at Hercules to get his reaction. The big man was studiously committing his character sheet to memory and appeared oblivious to the conversation.

"So I start with nineteen mana every morning when I wake up," Delphi said. "What if I never go to sleep?"

"You still get nineteen mana at dawn," Mouser told her. "It's not a reward for sleeping, it's just a fact of life."

"And what happens if I had mana left from the previous day?"

"If I remember, I gave you a reserve capacity of fifty, so you don't want to go to sleep at night with more than thirty-one or you'll lose out. But mana can be stored in a talisman or other magical reservoir, and if you live somewhere with EdWeb, you can send it to a mana bank or spend it on things that aren't available locally."

"That's a school thing?"

"EdWeb is short for Edison Web," Mouser said, making a note. "Maybe I should drop the short form if it's going to be confusing."

"So you stuck with the idea of Thomas Edison inventing a magical distribution and illumination system," Rayne said. "I hope you didn't make it too technical."

"Distribution and collection. I didn't see the point of setting up a business to do lighting because any child with magic can make their own orb."

"But flipping a switch is even easier."

"Combination with meat for the guys, vegetarian for the girls," Shadow announced as he returned with two vending machine pizzas. He put one box between Rayne and Delphi and the other where Hercules and Mouser could reach it. "I love the alien technology that finishes cooking the pizzas in the boxes. It's probably the best thing we got from them."

"The alien contribution is the biodegradable heating element that turns into an insulator as soon as the pizza is cooked," Mouser told him. "It's an exothermic molecular transformation process related to Verlock heat stones, but that's all our scientists can figure out. That said, I've repaired a few vending machines, and the most complicated part is the mechanism that folds the box around the partially cooked pizza."

"All I know is they taste great."

"And here's your character sheet. It includes a basic backstory, but I'm hoping you'll all flesh those out with your own ideas."

The young man took the sheet in one hand and began reading his history out loud. "Your father brought you back to the village to live with his parents after the death of your mother when you were twelve. The next day you almost drowned when trying to make friends with the local children by jumping in the river with them even though you couldn't swim. Your life was saved by a young girl named Delphi who you've had a secret crush on ever since."

"Oh, no," Delphi said, moving away from Shadow on the couch. "For one thing, I don't know how to swim either."

"Nobody born on Bits does," Mouser reminded her. "Our reservoir is underground and there aren't any swimming pools. Also, there's nothing about the event in your history because you don't even remember pulling the boy to the river bank. It wasn't a big deal for you."

"She saved my life and she doesn't even care," Shadow complained. "Now I have to role play some loser who follows her around like a lost puppy trying to get her attention?"

"You can play the role any way you want, but you aren't going to be facing a stream of monsters, so I wanted to include some obstacle or conflict to keep the game interesting for you both."

"Let's stick with conflict," Delphi said. "If Shadow was the last man on Bits, I'd go to the Gem and ask them to clone me before I'd—my skin crawls just thinking about it."

"Fine, a conflict, but there aren't any Gem on twenty-first-century Earth," Mouser said. He eyed the thin-film thermometer on the nearer pizza box that indicated it was almost cooked. "The four of you—five when Sarah joins us—are living peacefully in a small village that serves as the commercial center for the farms within walking distance. Hercules is an artificer who builds and repairs farm equipment. Rayne is the village healer and herbalist. Delphi bicycles to River Junction, a large town where she's the salesgirl in a boutique. Shadow works part-time for Mercury Courier Service, better known as MCS, while taking a correspondence course in technical magic."

"What's technical magic?" Hercules asked.

"In a world where everybody has magic, referring to some people as wizards or mages would be redundant. But there should be a difference between casual users and those who practice magic in their profession, so I came up with the idea of technical magic."

"But my profession is delivering packages," Shadow pointed out. "Why would I need specialized magic?"

"You took the MCS job because your grandparents were worried about you spending all of your time in the attic fooling around on the EdWeb. You wanted to be a magical hacker, and I've given you larger balances in mana accounts than everyone else in the village put together."

"Does he store mana in a talisman as well?" Rayne asked.

"He thinks that's too old-fashioned, but his reserve capacity is over two hundred thanks to constantly practicing magic. Now, tell each other more about your histories, and feel free to improvise while the pizza is cooling."

"So I work in a boutique where I sell fashions in return for mana, I get paid in mana, and the store buys goods with mana," Delphi surmised. "Do we have a mana register and people carry out a transaction by casting a spell or something? Is it like a video game where a prompt pops up asking if they're willing to pay five mana for whatever it is?"

"That would be just like programmable Stryx creds," Shadow said. "The register must be connected to the EdWeb. If it was started a few hundred years ago, everybody would be hooked up by now, plus it's the only way the Rules Committee has of tracking everything so they can collect the tithe."

"It's not Bits with our tithe, it's twenty-first-century Earth. All of the national governments were oligarchies, or kleptocracies, something like that."

"I thought it was mainly city-states with a governor-general."

"That came after the Stryx opened Earth and most of the national governments collapsed," Delphi told him. "Don't you remember anything from History Module 3?"

"I passed the test, but it's not like I ever used it for anything again. Nobody talks about that stuff."

"Watch some Grenouthian documentaries," Hercules suggested. "Our library has them all available for streaming and they're a bargain compared to dramas."

"They're not pirated?" Shadow asked in disbelief. "What kind of hackers are we?"

"It's smarter not to mess with the Grenouthians."

"What's the government?" Rayne asked, directing her question at Mouser.

"Sinister. In the background. It's closer to an oligarchy than anything else because of the concentration of mana, but I'm still trying to work out the implications."

"Concentration of mana?"

"It's a problem that's inherent in the system as soon as you tie everything together," Mouser explained. "Most of the major industries are monopolies or duopolies. At best, each niche is dominated by large concerns, with all of the small players added together barely reaching a double-digit percentage of market share. I wouldn't say that the economy is entirely stagnant, but the centrality of the EdWeb makes doing business on a large scale any other way impossible."

"So there are still cottage industries?" Hercules asked.

"You should know, you're running one," Rayne reminded him. "I suppose it's the same for me as a healer."

"Other than the magic, or should I say, due to magic, medicine is probably the biggest departure between our game and twenty-first-century Earth," Mouser said. "By the time the Stryx opened the planet, the medical industry accounted for over a quarter of the economic activity in the so-called advanced countries with aging populations. Magical healing eliminates the hospital-industrial complex. It's not in competition, it's a direct replacement."

"So what's happening to all of the excess mana that's getting soaked up via the EdWeb? Does it all go into mana savings accounts? Do depositors get a return on their investment, or is it just an option to building a talisman collection at home?"

Mouser grimaced. "Any way I look at it, the people who end up controlling large pools of mana, even if they have to borrow it, end up with such an advantage in any business that they can drive the competition bankrupt."

"I don't see where having access to extra mana changes much on the small scale," Delphi said. "Take this boutique where I work. According to my sheet, the store is so small that I usually work alone."

"Your boutique is owned by a chain," Mouser told her. "Look, there are exceptions to every rule. Maybe there's room in the fashion industry for a few small, independent players. But businesses that count on profits to pay their bills can't compete with large players who are willing to operate at a loss year after year because they have access to endless supplies of mana from investors."

"Investors?"

"Investors, savers, it amounts to the same thing in this case. The fact is that the population generates more mana than it needs to survive, and Edison's magical network works to concentrate that magic in the hands of the most sophisticated players."

"Nobody is going to want to play in that world," Hercules said. "Isn't it better to rethink the rules now than to lose time heading down the wrong path?"

"But I had in mind a sort of social revolution where the players take back their mana and relearn how to function independently," Mouser said. "With magic, anything should be possible."

"Doesn't sound very promising to me either," Rayne said. "You're getting lost in the economic weeds when you should concentrate on creating a challenging game. Let's say Herc and I moved to the village because we don't approve of the mana harvesting that goes on in the bigger towns and cities. That's enough to set up a scenario where there are two sides. It's the underdogs against the establishment, and you don't have to go into every last detail of how it got to be that way."

Mouser sat back in his chair, took a bite out of a too-hot slice of pizza, and thought for a moment. "Okay, I guess that could work."

Seven

"How old were you when you came to Bits?" Sarah asked her grandmother.

"Thirtyish," June replied, moving one step closer to the counter in Bits Bakery. "Young and dumb."

"Thirtyish is old."

"Ninety is old, thirty is young. You're still a baby."

"But I babysat for Thor yesterday," the girl protested. "Nobody would hire a baby to watch a baby."

"Sometimes I wish I'd never taught you logic," June said. The pair shuffled a step closer to the counter as a middle-aged man with a large loaf of bread under each arm brushed past in the opposite direction. "Good. They're doing the standard one-kilo loaves today."

"I like the crust. They should make bread that's all crust."

"I remember back on Earth they tried that with muffins. Some people only liked the tops and—you've never had a muffin, have you?"

"Are they like cupcakes, except more bready?" Sarah asked.

"And they puff up over the tin so you can nibble around the edges. Muffins often have little pieces of fruit or nuts in them."

"So what did they do with all of the bottoms?"

June looked puzzled for a moment before figuring out what her granddaughter was getting at. "You mean the bottoms of the muffins? I didn't work in a bakery so I'd only be guessing, but they might have just baked tops on cookie trays and pretended."

"Do you miss Earth?" the girl asked. "Thor's grandparents moved back on the last ship that stopped here. That's why I got asked to babysit."

"I knew Thor's grandparents when we first came to Bits but our friendship didn't survive my serving as the Rules Committee treasurer," June said. "It's a lonely job in some ways. Everybody wanted to be my friend until I turned down their request for development funding."

"Like all the people who have been coming around to see mom the last couple of weeks?"

"Now that she has the biggest budget to hit Bits in decades your mother is the most popular person on the planet," June confirmed as they moved forward again. "It's funny when I think about it, but our original group of settlers left Earth because we weren't happy with the changes being introduced with all of the alien imports. Four decades later, many of us are moving back precisely because of those changes."

"I don't understand," the ten-year-old said.

"Almost all of our members were programmers and hackers whose livelihood was under threat from alien technology, but Earth was also a depressing place to live at that time. Half of the population had already left to work on alien labor contracts, and the infrastructure was crumbling because government funding had dried up and their debts were still in place. It took a lot of inflation and defaults to clean that mess up, and eventually, the whole world adopted the eBuck as a monetary—am I talking over your head?" she cut herself off when she saw her granddaughter's look of impatience.

"You always do that, but I don't mind. It's just that I thought you were going to tell a joke."

Again, June had to think for a few seconds to make the connection. "Because I said it's funny. I was thinking about Thor's grandparents moving back to Earth, but the reason they and so many of the older folk on Bits have been returning home is because of the very thing we feared. It turns out that the alien businesses opening up back on Earth in the last decade have revived the economy. And retirees from labor contracts all over the tunnel network returning home means that there's plenty of money for the kinds of services that old people like to have."

Sarah shook her head. "I still don't see why it's funny."

"Next," the young man behind the counter called, and June realized that they'd reached the front of the queue while she was talking.

"Two, please," June said, handing over her ration card.

"One per family."

"Didn't I give you my daughter's card with mine?" June checked her belt pouch and saw that Rayne's card was still there. "Here."

The baker's helper immediately recognized the treasurer's photograph. "You're related to Rayne?"

"My daughter. Will it get us a better loaf?"

"They're all about the same, but if there was a difference, I'd give you the best one," he said, returning the ration cards. "Hey, I'm going to make up some molasses cookies for our team while the oven is still hot and I could give you a dozen of those."

"Yes, please," Sarah piped up immediately, and then looked up at her grandmother. "Do I like molasses?"

"You like everything in cookies," June said. "And what will they cost us?"

"Line's a little long for twenty questions," somebody called out irritably from a few steps behind them.

"Just a word with Rayne when I stop by to deliver them later," the baker's assistant said, putting two loaves of bread on the counter, one of which June passed to Sarah. "My real job is writing dialogue, but my team hasn't had enough work lately so we're picking up hours wherever we can."

June leaned over the counter and whispered, "Gamma Dome, Sixth Ring, 736."

"Did we get the cookies?" Sarah asked as they exited the bakery.

"They're coming special delivery. I just hope your mother's home when he gets there."

"She said she would be working in her room all afternoon so I have to catch up with my lessons in case she tests me. Can you help?"

"How far behind are you?" June asked.

"Just three days. We can do it this morning, easy."

"It's a good thing you kids have so many projects to keep you busy or you'd be driving all of the adults nuts. I've heard that on Earth the public schools are making a comeback, though the curriculums have changed radically, and most children still homeschool with teacher bots."

"What's a curriculum?"

"A fancy word for the subjects they teach," June explained. "Back before the Stryx opened Earth, all of the lessons that you do yourself on the computer used to be done in classrooms with dozens of other children. After the governments collapsed and most of the economy shifted to work-from-home, teacher bots and family replaced school for all but the wealthy."

"But Dad says that all of the kids on Flower go to classes and that there are also schools at most of the human communities where they stop," Sarah said as she stepped onto the moving sidewalk that looped between the circle of residential domes.

"I don't know anything about life aboard Flower, but I've met people who worked on alien worlds, and they have regular schools for children as part of the contract terms. The tunnel network has strict laws for advanced civilizations employing workers from backward species, and the basic benefits package, including education and retirement, are one of the reasons the majority of the population left Earth."

"Why didn't I have any of this in my history course? It's just been a lot about old games and computer languages so far."

"Because you just turned ten," June said with a smile. "I probably shouldn't always talk to you as if you were an adult, but it's what I did with your mother, and she turned out fine. The history of games is very important for a young girl growing up on a planet where the only occupants are hackers and game designers who left Earth to preserve their lifestyle."

"And the Hortens rented us the planet because they didn't want it anymore?" Sarah asked.

"Is that what the children tell each other? The Hortens didn't finish the terraforming work because there was a glut of habitable planets on the tunnel network at the time and completing the work didn't make business sense. To get a Stryx tunnel connection, a world needs to reach around a hundred times the population we have here. Our planetary lease probably covers the financing cost for the Horten developer who put the job on hold. The opportunity just fell in our laps when one of the founders of Bits, Nir Barad, made it to the final round in a Horten tournament before being beaten by the developer's grandson."

"The Horten asked his grandfather to give us the planet because he felt bad about winning?"

June shook her head even though she was standing on the moving sidewalk behind Sarah. "This was almost forty years ago when humans and aliens didn't have many relationships outside of contract work arrangements. The Horten, his name is Porl, was impressed by Nir's playing style, and the two of them got to know each other. When Nir explained his fears about the hacking culture on Earth disappearing, Porl thought of his grandfather's ongoing terraforming project and the rest is history. Our history."

"So all of the domes and stuff were already built when we got here?" Sarah asked.

"Long before. There were around three hundred thousand Hortens living on Bits at one time to work on the terraforming plan. Everything around us—" June swept an arm to take in the glass-encased moving sidewalk and the circle of connected domes visible on the planet's surface, "—was mothballed and available for immediate occupancy. The developer even helped arrange for an ancient jump-capable transport that could make the trip to bring us here as part of the deal."

"The ship landed on Earth and picked you up? Why didn't you take the space elevator?"

"It wasn't finished yet, either of them. When I was your age, leaving Earth meant a trip on an alien spaceship, whether it was up to orbit to change to a bigger alien spaceship, or a large transport capable of going the whole way. Most transports only have to travel far enough to enter the Stryx tunnel and then they're in hyperspace until they come out close to any other planet on the tunnel network. Bits is off by itself so only jump-capable ships come here."

"Do I get credit for my lessons if I remember what you tell me?" Sarah asked.

"No, but when it's time to learn these things you'll already know them," June said. She stepped off the moving sidewalk behind her granddaughter, who jumped with both feet together. "Now that we have fresh bread, what do you want for lunch?"

"Cookies."

"Maybe I'll just surprise you."

"Aren't you playing any games today?"

"I'm starting to cut back," June said. "The first few years after I got your mother to take over the treasurer's job I signed up for every tournament and beta testing invitational that showed up on the calendar. I must have played at least six hours a day for a thousand days straight."

"The big board in the cafeteria shows people who have played over ten thousand days straight," Sarah pointed out.

"The Rules Committee work kept me too busy for that, and I was never as hardcore a gamer as your grandfather."

"Do you miss him?"

"I do miss him, Pumpkin, but we grew apart. His family had a small vineyard and winery, and when his older brother died unexpectedly, your grandfather was the only one who could keep the business going. Your mother and I didn't want to return to Earth at that time so he went alone."

"Why wasn't there anybody else?"

"So many questions," June said, swiping her hand over the access plate to open the apartment door. "All of your mother's cousins left Earth to work for aliens, and ironically, at least one of them is making wine on a Frunge world. Your grandfather keeps in touch with them, and they plan on returning to Earth to take over the winery when they retire."

"That's good then," Sarah said, going into the kitchen and putting the loaf of bread on the counter. Then she brought up three days worth of overdue lessons on the home entertainment system and worked her way through everything before lunch without needing to ask her grandmother a single question.

"Do I smell French toast with cinnamon?" Rayne asked when she arrived home.

"Best use of powdered milk and powdered eggs I've ever come up with," June replied from the kitchen.

"Does that mean they had fresh bread today?"

"We got two loaves, I brought your ration card. It wasn't that many years ago that we kept bread in the freezer to stretch its life, but now we let it go stale to make French Toast. I used up all of the old loaf for this."

Rayne went over to the living area where Sarah was playing a game on her smartphone. "I finished all of my lessons," the ten-year-old said without looking up. "You can check them."

"I will," her mother said. "Not because I don't trust you, but I want to keep up with what you're learning."

"But you know it already."

"I don't remember everything I learned when I was your age."

"Then why do I have to learn it?" Sarah asked, putting aside her smartphone to watch as her mother reviewed the lessons.

"Here, I have something for you," Rayne said, taking a folded sheet of paper out of her purse. "It's a character sheet that Mouser made up. He's hoping you'll role play on our team for the presentation."

Sarah studied the sheet with an intensity that belied her age. "Hercules is my father now?"

"It's just role-playing. I haven't married him in real life."

"And I can do magic?"

"Just a little," Rayne said. "I think most of your gameplay will be magic lessons."

"The French Toast won't be any good if you let it get cold," June called from the kitchen. "And I have a surprise I've been saving up."

"A surprise?" Sarah shot off the couch still clutching the character sheet and raced into the kitchen. "What is it?"

"Ta-da!" her grandmother said, brandishing a grey plastic jug. "It's real maple syrup from Vermont, exported by Drazen Foods. I've been keeping it in my room."

"How much did that cost you?" Rayne asked. "I saw that there was a case with the last big shipment but I would have sworn it was ten creds a jug."

"The price isn't important. Sit, both of you."

The syrup was worth every cred of the price, and Sarah offered to slice up one of the new loaves of bread to let it go stale so they could have French Toast all week.

"It's a treat," June said. "If we eat it every day, it won't be special anymore."

The door chimed, and Sarah jumped up and ran to answer. "It's Hercules," she shouted back to the kitchen.

"I forgot to tell you," Rayne said to her mother. "Mouser wants Sarah on our role-playing team for the demo but she won't be interacting much with Shadow and Delphi. I thought it would be best if we get some practice time without them. Would you be able to stand in as gamemaster?"

"Of course," June said. "I like Hercules, maybe more than you do, and I miss being a gamemaster."

"Good. I got Mouser to copy all of his notes onto my phone when we were in the meeting this morning. Some of those artistic directors can go on forever about trivia."

Rayne excused herself to send a few texts from her bedroom to free up her early afternoon from appointments. Her mother joined Hercules and Sarah in the living room. The man and the girl played a racing game on the entertainment system while June took ten minutes to skim Mouser's notes on the concept of his game before she began.

"A father and daughter are sitting in the kitchen area of their one-room cottage enjoying the heat still radiating from the stove after burning a load of wood to prepare breakfast."

"If the wood is all burned, why is the stove still hot?" Sarah asked.

"Because the mass of the iron holds the heat that didn't escape up the chimney, my daughter," Hercules told her. "You weren't born yet when I brought that stove home from my blacksmith shop, but I can tell you that it weighs more than I do."

The girl stared at the large man whose frame carried far more muscle than fat. "But you're so big and it's so small."

"That's because it's made out of iron, and metal is heavier than flesh."

"Even aluminum?"

Hercules shot a look at June, and the gamemaster made a rolling motion with her hand, telling the role player to skip past the metallurgy lesson and get on to the magic.

"Well, iron is heavier than flesh," he continued. "If you're finished with your breakfast, we'll start your lessons."

"What subject?" Sarah asked suspiciously.

"You open a crudely bound book titled 'Third Year Homeschooling Guide' and flip a few pages," June said. "Your mother has already checked off Math, Reading, Composition, and Nature for this week. The remaining choices are History and Magic."

"Magic! Magic!"

"Do you have your talisman?" Hercules asked.

Sarah stood and looked around for something that would serve as a talisman. Then she patted herself down as if she was unfamiliar with the dress she was wearing and needed to check for secret pockets.

"Didn't you ask me for a leather cord to make your talisman into a necklace so you wouldn't keep losing it?"

Sarah's eyes went comically wide, and she reached in the neck of her dress and pulled out an invisible bauble. "Here it is."

"Bring the talisman and sit down."

"Where are you going?" she asked her father as he rose from the couch.

"To get the magical teaching supplies," he said, glancing towards June again. The gamemaster nodded and pointed to a brown plastic box to which somebody had added two parallel bands of black electrical tape meant to invoke the general idea of a wooden chest. Hercules brought it back to the table and made a show of hiding the contents from Sarah as he lifted the lid and peeked inside. Then he brought out a half-dozen carved animals, including an elephant and a squirrel, not to scale. "Choose the one that speaks to your soul."

Sarah picked up each one of the carved animals in turn, holding them up to the light. "Is that a lantern?"

"What?" June asked, breaking any remaining suspension-of-disbelief remaining in her role as an omniscient narrator.

"Father said I should hold the carvings up to the light," the ten-year-old explained. "Mom said there wouldn't be electricity, so is it a lantern, or like a magical orb?"

"It's a magical orb that your parents maintain," the gamemaster said after a few seconds of consideration, and she scribbled a note with her fingertip on the smartphone. "Please continue and try not to talk directly to me."

"So which animal speaks to you, my daughter," Hercules said, trying to reestablish the role he was playing.

"This one," Sarah said, pushing forward a carved owl.

"Good, you keep it. I'll take the bear and put the others away. Have you gotten far enough in your history lessons to know why we use talismans and tokens for storing magic?"

Sarah shook her head in the negative. "Don't I need to get magic somewhere before I can store it?"

"The reason we begin magic lessons in the third year of schooling is because that's when most children are old enough to generate excess mana," Hercules said. "All living creatures arise with a new supply of mana every morning. Your capacity will increase as you grow and study, but not even the most powerful among us have an infinite amount of mana on tap. That's why learning early how to store mana is so important. It will stimulate your soul to create more, while also building a reservoir that you can use to pay for other things you need."

"But I don't *feel* like I have any magic," the girl said. "How can I store something that I don't know I have?"

"Your mother and I may have made a mistake not bringing out your magic earlier as some in our village choose to do, but it's a tradition in our families to wait. We believe that the later a child starts to actively work with magic, the stronger they'll ultimately become."

"Then why now? Why not wait until I'm eleven, or twelve?"

"Because there's also an upper limit where if you wait too long, your magic won't be as strong," Hercules improvised, and added, "Your mother will explain it to you when the, uh, time comes."

Sarah clutched the owl in her fist and furrowed her brows as if she was concentrating with all of her might. "No. I don't *feel* anything."

"Watch me." Hercules placed his bear token on the palm of his left hand and then rested the tip of his right index finger on its head.

"The bear begins to glow with a blue light," June intoned.

Now it was Sarah's turn to look over at the gamemaster. Her grandmother nodded encouragingly, so the girl turned back to Hercules with an expression that plainly expressed her incredulity before saying, "Yes. I see the blue glow."

"Excellent," Hercules said. "Open your fist so you can see your owl."

Sarah did as her father instructed, and then touched the little carving with the forefinger of her free hand. "Nothing happened."

"I saw a little green spark. Didn't you feel it?"

The girl removed her finger, tried again, and shook her head. "Maybe I'm empty."

"As your father, I can see your aura and you're definitely ready for this. I want you to think about a waterfall of light that starts in your chest and pours down your arm until it comes out the tip of your finger and enters the owl."

"If you say so," Sarah said, adding a theatrical sigh. She closed her eyes in concentration.

"A rush of green mana infuses the owl token," June told her.

"Did it? Or are we just playing make-believe?"

"Let's take five," Hercules said, getting up from the table. "I need to check my messages."

"Sorry," Sarah said. "It's just weird role-playing without any costumes. I keep forgetting."

"It's my first time in years and you're doing just fine," her grandmother said. "It's okay to ask questions, but part of the fun in games is staying in character."

"So if my eyes were open, I wouldn't have seen any green magic coming from my finger?"

"You might have. It depends on how your imagination works. What I can promise is that if you give it a chance, you'll believe that you're in the kitchen of your parent's cottage in Old Hearth Village."

"My real dad left us and is living on Flower."

"I know that, Sarah. But your mother is still a young woman and she may find you a new father one day. Think of the game as practice."

"The two of you are more than enough for me," Rayne said as she joined them. "What happened to Hercules?"

"I'm coming, I'm coming," the large man said as he emerged from the bathroom. "Listen, I had an idea. How about people who are related to each other can share mana directly through touch?"

"Do you mean related genetically, or would a married couple be able to share?" June asked.

"I hadn't thought that far. Maybe shared genes. I was thinking we could keep topping off Sarah so she could practice storing magic. Maybe she just doesn't have much because of her age."

"That's kind of technical for this stage, isn't it?" Rayne asked. "I thought the idea was to explore as many different core elements as possible to get an idea of how they'll play out."

"I'll see the glow this time and I won't ask you any questions," Sarah promised.

"The door of the cottage flies open and a woman with a load of wood in a canvas sling enters," the gamemaster said. "She walks directly to the large copper pan next to the stove that serves as the firewood holder and dumps the split wood and kindling. Then she hangs the log carrier from its peg by the handles and joins her family at the kitchen table."

"Just in time," Hercules greeted his wife. "I've started our daughter's first lesson in mana storage and she's looking very promising."

"Did you discuss the lesson plan with her first?"

"The what?"

Rayne reached past him to retrieve the imaginary book and flipped it open to the first magic lesson. "All living things generate mana—"

"I told her that."

"—but only humans have the ability to store their surplus magical energy or transfer it to others. Thomas Edison was the first to develop a central system for the storage and distribution of mana, but this soon led to abuses and the concentration of magical reserves in the hands of a new class of elites. The birth of the modern homeschooling movement was in large part driven by the common people pushing back against the public school system harvesting magic from students in return for providing an education."

"The teachers take the children's magic?" Sarah asked.

"Not the teachers, the schools," Rayne said. "They use the magic to pay the teachers, build new schools, do all of the things we do with creds on Bits."

"No real-world references," Hercules reminded her. "We're supposed to be able to do this without them."

"I want to learn how to do spells and make things happen, like in my Youngest Witch books," Sarah said. "Esmerelda could clean her room with magic, and she had a wand."

Eight

"Whatever are you doing, Junior?"

"You agreed to stop calling me that, Mom, and I'm trying to get my stupid hair to stay down."

"I work with a dozen young women who would kill for a natural wave like you have, *Shadow*," his mother said, moistening her fingers with a bit of saliva. "Do you want me to fix it?"

"I'm eighteen now and I've been telling you for at least the last twelve years that I don't appreciate being groomed with your spit," Shadow said as he backed away. "You explain it to her, Dad."

"Don't tease the boy, Mandy, or he'll end up with a complex about women touching him," Shadow's father said from the couch. Then there was a loud crash, followed by the sound of a trumpet playing taps over the wreckage of a motorcycle. He held the game controller up over his head for his wife's turn. "I died, Babe. You're up."

"I never realized how close the apple falls to the tree until this moment," Mandy said, going over and taking the controller from her husband. She hit the 'Player 2' button and did a wheelie out of the starting gate as soon as the lights turned green. "Two men in my life and they both have head problems. One won't wear a helmet during speed trials, the other has more bad hair days than his sister."

"You can use my clippers and give yourself a buzz cut," Frank Senior offered his son. "That's what I did when I was your age and I never had to think about my hair again."

"I don't want people asking if I plan to join the mercenaries," Shadow said, leaning to the left as his mother swerved to avoid a fan who ran out on the race course. "How can you two still play this game? I can see the individual pixels from here. It must have been obsolete a century ago."

"Games like this are half the reason we came to Bits. And if you don't want to cut it, at least do a ponytail. You look like the drummer in a hair band."

"Only old guys like Mouser have ponytails. And what's a hair band?"

"Your father is showing off what he learned from the Grenouthian documentary about twentieth-century Earth music that we watched last night," Mandy explained as the motorcycle she was controlling hit a ramp and jumped an improbable number of school buses before landing with barely a swerve. "It's all in the wrist."

"Hair bands," Frank Senior continued. "Late twentieth-century musical style, a cross between glam rock and heavy metal. From the archival footage, it looks like the band members had to be wearing wigs, but maybe they put chemicals in their hair to make it all puffy like that."

"Perms," his wife said as the bike hydroplaned through a poorly drained tunnel. "Women these days are more likely to go the imitation-Frunge route and put their hair up on a trellis."

"The helicopter is going to come after you at any moment."

"We're on level one, it won't catch me. I still can't believe you died."

"I'm going out," Shadow said, knowing that his parents would become more and more immersed in the simple video game as the levels progressed until the point that they spoke only in monosyllables. "If Lisa comes home, tell her I went to The Cave."

"Good luck, and if a girl touches her own hair while you're talking, it means that she likes you," his mother called after him.

Shadow glanced in the mirror again and grimaced at the deep wave in his hair. At least the acne that had plagued him for years after puberty had disappeared, and while he sometimes thought his lips were too full for a man, his sister assured him that it was better than being thin-lipped. Before he left the apartment he took the smartphone out of his pocket and slipped it into the holder of the new bracer he was wearing on his forearm. Stepping out into the corridor, he almost ran into an athletic girl with long blonde hair piled up in a messy bun on her head.

"Hey, Lisa. Just back from the dojo?"

"It was so great," she said, showing off perfect teeth in a wide smile. "The new martial arts instructor I told you about started on Drazen style this evening. Even without a tentacle, you can learn enough of the basics to spar." She grabbed her younger brother by the bicep and squeezed, hard. "At least you're finally lifting and have put on a little muscle in the last couple of months. I still haven't gotten over the fact that you're half a head taller than me. It seems like just yesterday you weren't up to my shoulder."

"The folks are playing *Speed Demons* again," Shadow told her, pulling his arm free. "You know how they get by the third or fourth level."

"I'm just going to grab a shower and change. Where are you headed?"

"The Cave. It used to be all kids, but a new place with retro pinball machines opened nearby, so now it's shifted to our age. They have plenty of board games for after if you haven't eaten yet."

"You know I haven't," Lisa said, stepping around her brother. "I'll see you there in a half hour."

Shadow continued down the corridor until it intercepted a moving walkway which he stepped onto with the fluidity of somebody who had grown up in the domes. It took ten minutes to reach the corridor that connected to his destination, and he spent the whole time catching up with message traffic for Mouser's group.

"Hey, Shadow," a short young man with jet black hair and matching eyes greeted him as he entered the café. "I hear you hit the jackpot."

"What are you talking about?"

"Mouser's group. I always thought you were nuts for role-playing games with that old dude, but now you guys hold the fate of Bits in your hands."

"We don't even know whether or not Mouser's game is going to make the final cut," Shadow protested. "Everybody who participates is going to have a vote."

"Come on," Botan said. "Everybody knows that the Rules Committee treasurer is the only one authorized to spread the money around and Mouser is the committee chair. Are you telling me they'll agree to fund somebody else's game?"

"Yeah, they aren't normal. Mouser is like, I don't know, he looks at this new game franchise as the last chance to do something big with his life. And Rayne, well, she likes games, but I doubt she would be on Bits if she hadn't been born here."

"What are you drinking?"

"Root beer. Do you want to play a quick round of *ExpressGo*? The table's open."

"How quick?" Botan asked.

"My sister will be here in maybe twenty minutes."

"That's not enough time, and making your sister wait scares me."

"She could break us both in half," Shadow agreed cheerfully. "You have your cards?"

The smaller teen took two decks of game cards out of his pockets and handed them over. "You pick which one you want to play. I'll be back in a minute and we'll do a speed round."

The ice in Shadow's glass hadn't melted before the game came to the end.

"Do you want to swap decks and try again?" Botan asked his friend.

"It won't make a difference, you always win the strategy games that depend on magical affinities," Shadow said. "I can't keep all of the colors and point systems straight, at least not when we play fast."

"That's because you're used to role-playing with a gamemaster. How's work going?"

"They're finally letting me do some serious coding for the app, but it's just part-time. I still think we should both quit and work on our own app. You could do the graphics and I'll do all the coding."

"Anybody can build an app, the trick is making money from it," Botan said. "My parents would kick me out of the apartment if I quit my job."

"You work for your father."

"Exactly. And this is the first evening off I've had in two weeks. We're buried with extra work from the teams competing to be selected for the new game."

Shadow swirled the ice in his glass and looked around to see if his sister had arrived yet. "I wonder if Hercules and Delphi made it clear to the teams that they'll be competing on concepts and playability. Mouser won't give bonus points for having the best art."

"Everybody judges on appearances even if they say they don't," Botan told him. "I guarantee you that at least two out of the three teams selected to continue will have the best-looking artwork."

"Why not three out of three?"

"Because one of the teams will be Mouser's, and he's not spending anything." The smaller teen raised a hand to forestall Shadow's protest. "I know, you told me that he doesn't play that way, but this is the opportunity of a lifetime for him. And everybody says he is the best gamemaster on Bits, so I bet the other teams concentrate on the videogame or the massively multiplayer approach."

"But how much of an MMORPG can they hope to demonstrate with only a month to pull it together?"

"Not much, unless it's just a new skin on an old game, which makes the artwork even more important. Hey, there's that girl you're always talking about."

Shadow looked in the direction that Botan had just indicated with his chin. "Delphi? You're nuts. When have I ever had anything good to say about her?"

"You don't, dude. That's what makes it so obvious that you like her. How long have you been doing Mouser's game together?"

"Just three years," Shadow said, trying to make it sound like no big deal even though it was always the highlight of his week. "He lost a couple of long-time regulars to Flower and wanted to get some teenagers in the group so he wouldn't end up with a game that only old people would play. My parents know Mouser from way back. Lisa didn't want to do it so I got stuck."

"How come she's not coming over?" Botan asked.

"Because we don't like each other. I told you it's all in your head."

A pair of strong hands grasped Shadow's shoulders from behind and their owner stooped so her head was right next to her brother's. "Aren't you going to invite your girlfriend to sit with us?"

"Knew it," Botan crowed triumphantly,

"Quit it," Shadow said, reddening as he tried to knock his sister's hands away. "What are you going to order?"

"Already did," Lisa said, letting go of her brother's shoulders and taking a third chair at the round table. "Seriously, you should ask Deli over. With four of us, we could play Drazen checkers."

"I see where this is headed," her brother said in a long-suffering tone. "It's going to be Drazen everything with you now, just like it was Frunge everything when you were studying their martial arts style."

"I'm willing to learn," Botan said, and then corrected himself, "Checkers, not martial arts."

"Hey, Deli," Lisa shouted, waving her arms to get the girl's attention.

Delphi nodded and pointed at the barista.

"You know her?" Botan asked.

"She was in a bunch of my coding classes before she got too far ahead of us," Lisa said. "Deli is a few years younger than me but she's really smart. I wasn't surprised when she started composing music, and she's been selling ringtones since she was like twelve."

"On Bits?"

"Nobody pays for ringtones on Bits because none of us make voice calls—she sells them on Earth through the smartphone store." She turned to her brother. "Do you remember the text alert tone I used to have that drove our parents nuts?"

"Duh-duh-*duh*-duh-duh-duh?" Shadow asked. "It drove me nuts too."

"That was one of hers. She did this whole collection of text tones to annoy your friends and family and they were the hot thing for a while. I'll bet she still has a royalty account full of eBucks. It's not like there's anything around here to spend it on."

"Delphi does have the most expensive dice I've ever seen," Shadow said grudgingly. "They're all handmade, and the D20 looks like—"

"Are you talking about my dice behind my back?" Delphi asked as she set a tray down on the table. "The soup and sandwich are yours, Lisa. They asked me to bring it over."

"You have to love The Cave," Lisa said, taking possession of her late dinner. "They're trying so hard to be a throwback to the early days of Bits that they end up exaggerating all of the communal stuff. Can you go see if they have a Drazen checkers board in the game pile, Shadow?"

"Don't you need four for that?" Delphi asked.

"What? You've got somewhere else to be?"

"I'm meeting my dad if he can get away, though it's probably fifty/fifty tonight. They've got one more week to prepare for the selection, and even though Tom is officially the producer for his team, he does a little bit of everything."

"I didn't know you had a dad," Lisa said.

"I just found out a few weeks ago and I'm still kind of struggling with it. The weirdest part is finding out I have a younger sister."

"Really? That's so cool. How old is she."

"Six," Lisa said. "I don't know if I should ask to meet her or offer to babysit. I'm just glad that Tom's wife isn't anybody my mother knows. She's like fifteen years younger than he is."

"I'll see if they have a board," Shadow said. "We can play until your dad gets here. Botan's probably going to win in any case."

"Sounds like he owns you," Delphi said, and then took a tiny sip from her espresso. "Have we ever met?" she asked the other boy after Shadow headed off to hunt for Drazen checkers.

"Maybe in passing at a tournament," Botan said, offering a little wave in place of a handshake. "I work for—pirate on deck!"

Both of the girls turned in the direction Botan was staring and saw a Gem wearing a hodgepodge of uniform scraps with a holstered weapon on her hip. Although she was proportioned about the same as a human, there was something in the planes of her face that screamed 'alien.' The tattooing across her cheeks and around the eyes declared her allegiance to the Free Republic.

"What do you think she's doing here?" Delphi whispered. "I thought that the clones all kept to their dome and didn't mix with us outside of market days and tournaments."

"She doesn't look like one of the Old Empire Gem to me," Lisa said. "They all have that defeated look that makes me want to tell them to stop playing Cloner and just get on with their lives. Maybe she came over from Base Sixteen."

"Hexadecimal?" Botan asked, and then flinched when he saw the way the two girls were looking at him. "Oh, you meant the pirate base on the next world out. But I heard that they all decided to boycott Bits because we wouldn't change the rules for that stupid game with—"

"—the asteroid deflection system," Lisa completed his sentence. "I think that's just the story that the Rules Committee put out to explain the fact that pirates haven't been coming around much recently because we never have any money to buy anything. Interplanetary trips just to say 'Hi' are a huge time waster, not to mention the fuel."

"Only two inhabited worlds in the star system and we can't be bothered to make social calls," Delphi mused. "I don't know how the tunnel network does it."

"The tunnel network treaty prohibits the members from fighting with each other so they end up competing in business as a proxy," Botan said. "My dad has been making me study up on the business climate because—" He cut himself off mid-sentence and looked embarrassed.

"Is your family thinking of moving to Flower?"

The young man looked around to make sure nobody else was nearby before replying in a low voice. "My parents and grandparents think that the writing is on the wall for Bits. It's gotten to the point where my Mom hasn't bothered replacing one of the elements on the stovetop because she doesn't think we'll still be here in a year."

"What about the new game?" Delphi protested. "If it goes full franchise and catches on with the aliens it could directly employ thousands, and that means thousands more jobs for contractors and subcontractors. And you know how success feeds success. In a few years, Bits could be back to what it was when our parents were our age."

"It's not just about bringing in work," Botan said. "For my grandparents, it's not even about money. They all read the library's subscription to the Galactic Free Press, even though it's old news by the time a ship stops here with a data dump of back issues. My grandmothers both read the latest first, but my grandfathers are a full year behind, reading a new issue every day. You wouldn't believe the fights they have when my grandmothers start talking about something that my grandfathers haven't read yet."

"Okay, but what does that have to do with leaving Bits?"

"It's the stories about Earth, mainly. The world is getting its act together, and with the population barely more than a third of what it was a century ago, you can get free land in most places in return for paying taxes. My grandparents want to return to Japan before they die, and a lot of their friends feel the same way, wherever they came from. Moving here to preserve twenty-first-century computing was all well and good when they were young but nobody wants to be buried on a leased planet."

"I never really thought about it that way, maybe because my parents were kids when they came here," Lisa said slowly. "I guess if the whole first generation pulls up stakes, the population here will fall so much that the place will just feel empty."

Shadow returned from the games pile and put a large box on the table. "No Drazen checkers but I got *Spy Versus Assassin*. That's pretty cool with four people and—we don't have to play anything," he concluded, noticing the depressed look on his sister's face.

"Huh? Oh, SVA is fine by me. We were just talking about the future of Bits and it got pessimistic. Let me just finish my sandwich and we can get started."

Delphi looked around the café again to see if her father had slipped in unnoticed. "Is that clone coming over here? I think she just smiled at me, but it's hard to tell with all the facial tattoos."

"Did you do something to her?" Shadow asked. He decided to play it safe and remained standing, acknowledging the approaching Gem with what he hoped would be recognized as a welcoming head bob. "Can we help you?"

"I'm new on Bits," the clone said in English, her pronunciation and accent surprisingly good for an alien. "I was looking for a place that served hot chocolate, which proved to be surprisingly difficult to find." She held up her large mug as if presenting evidence to back her words, and Botan immediately noticed that she wore a ring on each of her four fingers with stones that corresponded with the cyan, magenta, yellow, and black of a printer's plates. "You may have heard that it's difficult for members of my species to eat alone, and I was wondering…"

"Please, sit," Shadow said, giving up his chair. "I'll just drag one over from the other table there."

"Is that acceptable to you all? Now that I look at you more closely I believe I've identified two matched pairs. I wouldn't want to intrude on your mating rituals."

"We're brother and sister and they're our friends," Lisa told the Gem. "Do you know Keemchat Dee?"

The clone's eyes widened, but if she had any other physical reaction, it was lost in her movement to sit. "I'm surprised a Human would even be familiar with the Keemchat Dee. Have you studied our martial arts?"

"My dojo does an ongoing workshop on alien styles, just six months each, so it's barely an introduction. But we had a real Gem instructor a couple of years ago when we did Keemchat Dee and I loved the sparring."

"Humans and Gem have similar builds so it translates well," the clone said. "I had the opportunity on a Stryx station to study Jujitsu and Kendo with a Human sensei."

"My mother's father has a bamboo sword and armor, but my grandmother won't let him practice since he broke an arm sparring," Botan volunteered.

"That saddens me to hear," the Gem said politely, and then took a sip from her hot chocolate. "Delicious. I really can't understand why Humans don't take chocolate with all of their meals. If not for our nutritional requirements, my sisters and I would eat nothing else."

"It is addictive," Lisa agreed. "So what brings you to Bits?"

"I was in the neighborhood and heard about a colony of Earth expatriates who attempted to create a digital utopia. When I found out it was the same Bits that produced Cloner, I had to stop in. I'm a games journalist," the Gem continued, producing four thin business chits and passing them around, "and I contribute to Gem Today."

The young people sat bolt upright when the clone mentioned being a journalist because they all understood the value of free publicity in a crowded galactic market. "Is there a particular game that you're interested in?" Delphi asked. "I know at least a dozen producers who I could introduce you to and we have friends on the Rules Committee."

"Then it seems I've stumbled on the right table. Although I've just arrived, I'm beginning to think of doing a full feature on Bits. Such a willingness to break away from your civilization and pursue a utopia dedicated to the hacking and gaming lifestyle may strike a chord with my revolutionary sisters. As an around-the-clock broadcaster, Gem Today is always in need of quality long-run content."

Delphi and Shadow exchanged a look, and then the girl continued with, "You've arrived at the perfect time. We've been commissioned to create a whole new gaming franchise for chocolate chips and our top development teams are competing for the winning concept."

"Chocolate chips?" the Gem inquired.

Delphi shook her head in frustration when she realized that the magical non-disclosure agreement had kicked in. "Some of the information is confidential, but I can introduce you to Mouser, who is in charge of the creative side of the development."

"That's very kind of you," the clone said. "I'll ask for an introduction after I've settled in. And any background you can give me about growing up on Bits would be very useful in helping me shape a narrative for the story. I can even imagine a multi-episode documentary-style approach if I can find a thread of, if I may coin a phrase, Human interest?"

Delphi and Shadow again exchanged looks, the excitement of potentially appearing on a network watched by tens of billions of Gem written on their faces. Botan had swiped to life the smartphone strapped to the back of his forearm and was flipping through photos of his family, looking for one of his grandfather giving a Kendo demonstration.

Lisa seemed to be bothered by something and asked the clone, "Do you mind a personal question?"

"Not at all," the Gem responded. "You've been so open with me it's the least I can do in return."

"Did you originally come to this system to do a story on the pirates?"

"What makes you ask?"

"Your facial tattoos. I can't imagine ever doing something like that just to advance my career."

The Gem looked puzzled for a moment, and then she smiled in the manner of her species and snorted a short laugh. "You mean these?" She pointed at her face with the fingers folded tight, almost as if she were about to strike herself with the fist, and then she reached over with the other hand and tapped her rings in rapid succession. The tattoos came to life and began to flow off her face, separating into four different color streams that ran over the knuckles and into the respective rings.

"How?"

"Nanobot ink. Nanotech and cloning are the only sciences where we lead, or can at least compete with, the other tunnel network species. The nanobot tattoos are so unnoticeable that I forgot I had them on."

Nine

"I haven't been down here in years," Hercules said as they stepped off the escalator at the bottom of the spiral. "I think it's to the right."

"Left," Delphi corrected him. "My practice studio is down on the right. The space is cheap because nobody likes being near the geothermal heat exchangers. I don't know why when they don't make any noise."

"They make plenty of sounds that are neutralized by active interference. Mouser tells me that the Hortens have developed some interesting acoustic technology, though nothing like the Dollnicks."

"What did you think of the proof-of-concept Leandra's team is working up?"

Hercules shrugged. "It looked like they replaced the bloodsuckers in *Vampire Protection Services* with aliens, updated it to the twenty-first century, and force-fit a magic system. But it's not a surprise that people who have been working on a game for years want to reuse the algorithms if they possibly can, and the artwork was first-rate."

"Shadow's friend Botan works in his family's art studio and he said that all of the teams are scrambling to hire contract artists for the push."

"Part of the goal was to spread Flower's money around, so I guess we're succeeding on that account," Hercules said. He stopped in front of a door with the silhouette of a black rat stenciled on the alloy. "Paper Rat. This is the place."

Delphi waved her hand over the scanner and the door slid open without a sound. They entered a cavernous room that might have once served as a warehouse but was now blocked off by what looked like a solid wall of office partitions. She cupped her hands around her mouth and shouted, "Hello?"

"Come right in," a muffled voice called back a few seconds later. "The opening is on the left."

Hercules led the way to the near wall on their left but it didn't become apparent that there was a break in the partitions until they were within a few steps.

"That blue fabric they used for the partitions blends in so well that it's hard to see where they start and end," Hercules commented as they entered. "I think I would go nuts working in cubicles all—where is everybody?"

"I think there's another opening there," Delphi said, pointing two partition sections ahead on the left. "I can see a shadow."

"Yeah, but..." the big man hesitated for a moment. "Are you okay with me picking you up?"

"In the air?"

"To see over the partitions. I think we're in a maze."

The girl nodded in understanding. "That would fit in with the paper rat theme. Sure. My mom made me take six years of gymnastics for the sake of the exercise so I can probably balance on your shoulders if you don't mind my climbing up."

Hercules put his hands together to form a stirrup and crouched to make it easier for the girl to get her foot in. She kept her hands on his shoulders as he straightened to raise her feet as high as his abdomen, and then she got her other foot up on his shoulder.

"Try not to move," she said, climbing up onto his shoulders. She balanced for a few seconds before jumping off behind him.

"Are you alright?" Hercules asked as he spun around.

"I guess it's not the same as riding a bicycle so I got down before I lost my balance," she said with a grin. "It's a maze, all right, but only if we enter the next opening. This way."

Delphi led the way past the first opening and continued another thirty steps before a second missing partition let them into an open-floor-plan office where at least a hundred people were at work on a knee-high maze made of clear plastic partitions.

"A maze inside a maze," Hercules said. "Does it play?"

"Welcome to Paper Rat," a white-haired woman who might have been a youthful-looking sixty greeted them. "You met with our producer Daryl a couple of weeks ago but he pulled an all-nighter and I sent him home to sleep. I'm Sash, the director."

"Hercules, and she's Delphi. I'm sorry we're getting to your team so late in the process, but Daryl put us off the last two weeks, and now there's just one week left until the selection."

"Daryl is a perfectionist. He used to be our chief of quality control but he slowed everything down so much that we all voted to promote him to his level of incompetence. *Find The Cheese* was so hot back then that the producer didn't matter."

"He did seem a little less business-oriented than the other producers we met with," Hercules said. "So, do you want to tell us what you're working on?"

"I'll give you three guesses," Sash said.

"A maze, a maze, and a maze," Delphi responded without hesitation.

"Three hundred percent correct. Our game takes place on an Earth where information flows freely but physical travel is restricted by magical barriers that are erected and maintained by communities at every level of organization."

"Do you mean governments?"

"Not necessarily," the woman said. "The thing about magic is that it makes controlling people who don't want to be controlled a challenge. You can deal with it by creating dystopian military dictatorships or the like, but we went with a system where magical barriers maintained from within by a sufficient population are inviolable. That led Earth to fracture into tens of thousands of land-locked islands that each march to their own drummer. Every type of government you can imagine is represented many times over, but there are also extended families, groups who have embraced a particular lifestyle, even artists and musicians creating utopian societies."

"I can see how the magical barriers make that theoretically possible, but how do people live without the distribution of food and goods?" Hercules asked. "Is there a functioning economy, or is every community an isle unto itself?"

"That's where the maze comes in," Sash said, leading them to the edge of where the game designers were all hard at work mapping, adding or subtracting partitions from the maze, and even pouring water into it in one case. "We've created a class of characters called Maze Runners. These are the players who travel between the virtual islands and profit from trading."

"So it's a trading game," Delphi said. "You should talk with Daiyu. Is magic used for anything other than the barriers?"

"It could be, but we're trying to keep it simple for the demo run. We've adopted the Internet from the twenty-first century so everybody has instant access to information, but there's no same-day delivery of plastic cha-chas from across the world."

"How about *A Mazing Earth* for the title?" Hercules suggested.

"It's already on the shortlist," Sash said. "We're also working on a variant where instead of running the maze as traders, the players are basically on a scavenger hunt for Earth artifacts. My artistic director—" she looked around and pointed at a thin woman who was down on her knees painting what looked like a farm scene at the periphery of the maze, "—is part of a hobby group that studies alien museum catalogs for signs that they may have visited Earth in the past and acquired originals that are never mentioned in our history."

"Is that something that really happened?" Delphi asked.

The director managed a sly smile. "If you have a few days to kill, ask her. It's hard to prove either way in the absence of physical evidence."

"But thanks to that Grenouthian documentary about the aliens collecting famous works from Earth, the game could get a lot of free publicity. It would have a natural audience with art students around the tunnel network, and I'll bet there are plenty of those."

"Our board game strategist—that's Heinrich over there—says that famous artworks are the perfect fit for card decks, and we already have the imagery in the library.

But without knowing who the customer is I'm not convinced that going with a pure quest game would be the right move. Trading is the most popular inter-species activity on the tunnel network, and sometimes it's better to have a small slice of a big pie than the whole of a cake that nobody wants to eat."

"Is there any combat?" Hercules asked, studying the maze. "If those magical barriers are keeping out anybody the community doesn't want in, it doesn't seem like there would be much call for traditional role-playing character types."

"But you're forgetting about the maze," Sash said. "In order to maintain trade, there are serpentine paths that are open to small groups with the right magical credentials. Just because the majority of the population in each area is willing to act together to maintain the barriers doesn't mean that they're all good people or that they want to pay the prices that Maze Runners demand for their goods."

"So it's more like an old-school caravan system with armed guards than the long-haul truckers of the twenty-first century."

"We're still developing the ideas through limited gameplay. Our eight volunteers for today are in make-up getting ready. If you stick around another hour, you can watch them do a trial run."

"Your beta testers go through make-up just for development?" Delphi asked. "That's pretty hardcore."

"It works better than having them wear signs that read, 'I'm a four-armed Dollnick' or 'Blue-furred Grenouthian.' We're trying to concentrate on gameplay for aliens in hopes that will set us apart."

"Our schedule doesn't give us the luxury to stand around waiting, but if we come back in say—" Hercules caught Delphi's eye, "—two hours?" The girl gave a little nod.

"Oh, we'll be at it until well past supper the way things have been going lately," Sash told them. "I just hope that whichever teams get the go-ahead to continue aren't so burned out from the competition that the work just stalls."

"That's why we plan to offer work to everybody who participated," Hercules said. "If you're chosen to proceed, you can plan on your team tripling."

"And what happens when we get to the end of the road and your mystery client chooses one game for the franchise launch. Do the other two get thrown on the trash heap?"

"I'm not privy to the contract details, but my understanding is that we're all essentially working as employees, so the work belongs to the client. But you could always repurpose around it, so instead of twenty-first-century Earth with magic, it could be set in medieval times or something like that."

"I suppose we'll cross that drawbridge when we come to it," Sash said. "May I inquire how the other teams are getting along? We've been doing regular posts on the board that Mouser set up to keep everybody informed of our general progress. I've seen the other teams reporting on elements they're developing that might be reusable by the winners, but it doesn't give you a feel for whether anybody is falling behind schedule or running into dead ends."

"Nobody has dropped out yet if that's what you mean," Delphi told her. "Most of them are making more use of outside contractors than you are, but Paper Rat had the second largest team to start with, and we only invited you to participate because we, uh..."

"You saw that our first major release in three years was dead on arrival. It turned out that the Hortens had developed a nearly identical game a few hundred thousand years ago and one of the reviewers who received our prerelease happened to be a game historian and wrote a scathing review." Sash sighed and ran a hand over her white hair. "The saddest part is that she sent us a copy of the game that still runs on a standard Horten holo-console and it had everything ours did and more."

"It's tough to come up with original ideas on the tunnel network when the youngest of the member species have been cruising the stars for over a half-million years," Delphi said sympathetically. "It comes up in music all of the time. All you can do as a creator is try your best and not worry about the fact that somebody else has probably discovered the same rhythm or chord progressions a billion times in a billion galaxies. It's just bad luck if you run into a critic who remembers it."

The trip back up the long spiral escalator took another three minutes, and then Hercules and Delphi caught the moving sidewalk to the main dome. They passed through the largest gaming hall on Bits with its piles of obsolete computer junk at the back and entered the sadly reduced Museum of Alien Weaponry. Just to the right of the entrance, where one might have expected to find a gift shop, was the door labeled *Time Wars*. Inside, they were confronted by an empty reception desk.

"Think they took the money and ran?" Hercules asked Delphi playfully.

"They're probably doing an all-hands-on-board test," she told him. "We can go through. Dad—Tom added me to the security system so I could visit any time."

"Have you been, uh..."

"Yeah, you were right. He's a nice guy and he works too hard. I was up really late the other night trying to finish an instrumental I'm hoping that Mouser will use for the intro and I stopped by just to prove to myself that he's not here around the clock. It was like two in the morning and he was all alone working on scheduling."

"Hope he doesn't collapse before they reach the finish line," Hercules said as he followed her down the hall. "Did you get a sense of how it's going?"

"We didn't talk about that," Delphi said. "They'll be in here."

She swiped open another door and the sound of street traffic was almost overwhelming. A sketchy hologram of an urban setting was flickering like the projectors were pushed beyond their limits, and dozens of real people were standing motionless as if glued in place. A second look showed names chalked on the floor that served the function of an actor's marks on the stage. The girl tapped Hercules on the shoulder and held a finger to her lips.

"Second position," a voice called out. The staff members moved to new marks and then froze again. Thirty seconds went by and they moved to a third position, then a fourth. "All right, that's it for now," the director announced. "Tom, our guests are here."

Delphi's father, who was dressed in what might have been the peak of twenty-first-century business fashion, broke free of the crowd who were now joking and congratulating each other. "One more shoot and we should have enough," he greeted Hercules and his daughter. "I never thought I'd end up as a scaffolding actor for holographic anime but we decided that's the best way to demonstrate how the game might work in a LARPing studio."

"Your team is the first we've seen that's gone to such lengths," Hercules said. "I'm surprised you could afford the time."

Tom lowered his voice and glanced at his team members, who were still congregated at the center of the floor and either congratulating or critiquing each other's stop-action acting skills. "See how energized they are? I've been pushing them hard for three weeks and they needed a break. The fact that it might help with our demo is just icing on the cake."

"Why was it necessary to hold your poses so long?" Delphi asked. "I would have thought it would be easier to capture live motion."

"We don't have the equipment on hand," Tom said. "Come with me." He led them around the milling employees to the back of the room and pointed at the wall. "Do you see all of the sensor strips? We taped them around three walls of the room, and if you look up, they're on the ceiling as well. Everything is wired back into a Dollnick thermal imaging controller."

"Infrared? You mean after all of that work the holographic anime is just going to show you as colored blobs?"

"Is every silver dot in this tape an independent sensor, or does the whole strip count as one?" Hercules added to the girl's question.

"Now you're starting to see," Tom said with a grin. "That's the beauty of the Dollnick technology. If you only had a few dozen thermal sensors the resolution would barely be enough to keep track of where people were standing in the room. But there's an individual sensor roughly every five millimeters in the tape, which means thousands in each strip. I think we ended up with over a hundred parallel strips on the walls plus a few hundred more on the ceiling. When you feed all of that data back into the imaging controller, it even does a decent job rendering passive heat sinks, like clothing."

"But why would the Dollnicks have developed such a technology when there are so many better ways to capture three-dimensional images?"

"Thermal imaging can be surprisingly useful for troubleshooting mechanical systems. I borrowed the controller from the repair dome on the other side of the tarmac. The last terraforming crew left some interesting stuff behind."

"And all of the tape with the embedded sensors?" Delphi asked.

"You know how it is with the aliens and multi-purpose technology," Tom said. "If you hook up a different pair of leads the sensors emit infrared light. There must be hundreds of kilometers of the tape on giant rolls in the warehouse attached to the repair dome. I think the engineering crews must have used it to mark large areas of the planet's surface that they wanted to sculpt from a space-based platform. I suspect that the Hortens are glad to employ Dollnick technology when it comes to terraforming."

"From the little bit we saw, it looked like you were acting out a street scene," Hercules said. "Was it strictly background, or will you all be recording dialogue as non-player characters?"

"Strictly background," Tom confirmed. "Our casting director wants a big barbarian type as the..." He trailed off, looking Hercules up and down as if he were seeing him for the first time. "Esty! How about this one?"

A striking woman in her mid-thirties broke away from the group still congregated in the middle of the room and her dark eyes lit up when she saw who Tom was openly pointing at.

"I was thinking of calling, but I knew you were involved with Mouser's team and I didn't want you to think I was trying to buy your vote," Esty said to Hercules. "HunkWatch has you in the top ten physiques on Bits."

"HunkWatch?" Hercules asked.

"The app," Delphi told him, swiping the smartphone strapped to the back of her forearm to life. She tapped a couple of times, swiped, and held her arm out for him to see. "You're currently number four."

"How did they get a picture of me in the weight room? It looks like I was posing in front of—is the mirror two-way glass?"

"Be a good sport and don't let on that you know," Esty said. "So, will you do it?"

"Do what?"

"We need high-resolution imaging of a big man with your muscle definition. I've got a standard holo-recording booth set up in the other room and it will take less than a half hour."

"You want me in your demo?"

"It's a full NPC role, and if the game goes ahead, we'll need you to record lines," Esty told him. "You aren't going to keep that body forever, you know. This is your chance at immortality."

Hercules hesitated. "Like you said, it could be seen as a quid pro quo for supporting your game."

"Everybody already believes the contest is rigged so it won't make a difference. I can alter your face if you're worried."

"Go ahead, Herc," Delphi said. "We have plenty of time to kill before we can go back to Paper Rat."

"Bring them in the recording studio," Esty told Tom. "I have to tell my holo-booth operator that it's time to go back to work."

By the time Hercules had changed into a pair of boxing trunks and nothing else, Tom had been called away to deal with the latest emergency, and Delphi was left standing with Esty. The casting director brought her into the control room, where they watched as Hercules began going through the standard calibration routine dictated by the operator.

"He really is a hunk," Esty said conversationally. "I had the biggest crush on him back when we were in the same drama group."

"Herc wanted to be an actor?"

The casting director shook her head. "He only joined because of a girl he liked, but she only had eyes for Gorgeous George."

Delphi gaped. "Are you talking about Rayne? Hercules was carrying a torch for her?"

"Given that he's never managed to stay in a long-term relationship, I suspect he still is," Esty said. "Sometimes I think that the aliens have it right with all of the professional matchmakers, compatibility testing, and family involvement in courting. It seems that we humans waste a tremendous amount of time and energy making ourselves unhappy about people we can't have. At least Hercules never strung the girls along the way some guys do."

"And how about Rayne? Did she know?"

"I think he proposed to her when they were kids. Women can be just as cruel as men that way. If some guy you just don't feel that way about ever reveals his heart to you, do him a favor and cut him out of your life."

"That seems pretty extreme," Delphi said. "I mean, don't you think women and men can be friends?"

"Sure, if one of them isn't carrying a torch for the other," Esty said. "That's just torture. I never exactly told Hercules how I felt, but he figured it out and let me know he was a one-woman man. It hurt, but I stopped mooning over him, and within a few years I was happily married with two kids."

"It's hard to think of somebody his age being in love."

"His age?" The casting director laughed. "If you haven't found somebody in another five years and Hercules is still single, I'll bet you start thinking that he's just the right age to settle down."

"No way," Delphi said, making a face. "He's like an uncle or something." She glanced at the monitor showing the progress in the holographic capture booth and giggled. "A really built uncle."

"So, how are the other teams coming along?" Esty asked conversationally. "I heard you mention Paper Rat. It was tragic what went down with their big release, but it can happen to anybody."

"They were working hard, but I don't know how it's going because they asked us to come back later for a demo. And you know how tough it is to understand how a game plays without actually playing it. I probably know more about what you guys are doing than any other team and I still can't quite put it all together in my mind."

"Think of it as *Time Wars,* except it's stuck on one time and place, twenty-first-century Earth, and there aren't any wars."

"Thanks. That's really helpful."

Esty laughed again. "I guess that does sound rather vague, but it's the same basic idea of a chase game, except instead of alien weapons, you have all the archaic human technology to work out, plus the magic."

"I never really spent any time playing *Time Wars* so that could be the problem," Delphi said.

"In *Time Wars,* the space-time continuum is breaking down and you chase the bad guys through the galaxy using all of the period weapons we base—used to base—on the museum displays. In this game, the bad guys are aliens passing as humans, and you're an intelligence agent from one of the tunnel network species trying to track them down before Earth finds out that UFOs are real."

"You explain it better than my dad does. I thought it was about stealing cars and hacking computers."

"There's a lot of that because of the chases. You, I mean as an intelligence agent who isn't supposed to be on Earth to start with, can't bring any gear that would affect the course of human history if you lost it or got killed. So you're stuck working with the weapons and computing systems of the period."

"No cheating at all?" Delphi asked.

"Well, that's where it gets interesting," Esty said with a grin. "Technology that twenty-first-century humans would never be able to figure out is acceptable as long as nobody sees you using it. Think about bringing a smartphone back to the Stone Age. A caveman would probably try to punch a hole through it and put it on a thong as a necklace."

Ten

"Are you sure about this?" Rayne asked Mouser. "It's not that I was dying to role-play a village healer in front of everybody on Bits but I don't see how it helps your credibility to have me up there. They already believe that the fix is in for your game because that's what they would all do in the same circumstances, and most of them know by now that I'm in your regular group. Besides, you're already using Sarah."

"Stop worrying about—" The rest of his words were drowned out by the ship proximity alarm and he threw the boot he was about to pull on at the silencer button.

"Pretty impressive," Rayne said when the alarm went silent. "You can't even see the button from where you're sitting."

"It's screwed to the workbench so it never moves," Mouser explained. He rose to his feet and limped over to retrieve the boot. Almost as an afterthought, he keyed the microphone to active and barked the standard Bits greeting. "What?"

"The Little Princess, requesting permission to land," a voice crackled out of the ancient radio cabinet along with an unusual volume of whistles and pops.

Mouser took his finger off the microphone key and turned to Rayne. "Sounds like Dollnicks. There haven't been any visiting Bits in at least a decade. Did you know about it?"

"Are you asking if anything came up at the last three Rules Committee meetings that you skipped, Mister Chairman?" Rayne asked sarcastically. "No, but see if you can get fifty creds out of them."

"There's a fifty cred landing fee for unscheduled visitors to cover ground control expenses," Mouser said into the microphone. "You can put down anywhere, but we're having a major event this weekend so there won't be anybody to greet you."

"We're already parked," a familiar voice said. "Despite my reassurances, the captain insisted on shielding until touchdown because of the old rumors you have ancient alien weapons you don't know how to operate. I'll be with you in a minute."

"That was Dewey," Rayne said to Mouser. "How did he know we were staging the contest today?"

"We did say after four weeks, and it's not hard to guess we would do it on the weekend." Mouser returned to his easy chair and pulled on the second boot. "Alex," he called to the voice-activated controller. "Show the ship on the tarmac."

A large flatscreen display that was most often used for playing old-fashioned video games came to life. Every pixel was bright white except for a message in an unknown language that appeared as a vertical banner.

"Did your monitor just fail?" Rayne asked. "I thought it was manufactured on Earth. Is that Korean?"

"Look at the dust floating around," Mouser said in a hushed voice. "That's live video. Alex. Zoom out." The vertical text shrank, but the picture was otherwise unchanged. "Alex. Zoom out again." This time a slice of the old maintenance dome across the tarmac appeared at the right of the screen, proving that the camera had been showing the hull of a glossy white spaceship whose prow was still well above the frame the lens was able to capture. "It's bigger than a Gem cruiser."

"I should hope so," a new voice announced from the doorway, and they turned to see Dewey accompanied by a towering four-armed alien who spoke English that sounded a little like it was coming from a parrot. "The Gem are hardly known for their space engineering prowess, while we Dollnicks wrote the book on atmosphere-capable capital ships."

"Mouser, Rayne," Dewey addressed the surprised Rules Committee members. "I'd like to introduce my good friend, Lume. He's been with Flower since she started on her current mission and is one of her closest confidants."

"You didn't mention anything about returning to judge the proof-of-concept stage," Mouser said accusingly. "Did you plan this all along and keep us in the dark?"

"Rest assured that your artificial friend knew nothing about this until three days ago," Lume said. "Flower is currently stopping at the only major sovereign human community on a Horten open world, just a few star systems—" he peered at the ceiling and then pointed off to the left, "—that way, and one of our naval ships happened to be concluding a treaty visit when she arrived. Somebody owed somebody a favor, and to make a long story short, we have a fourteen-hour window to visit before we have to return to catch Flower."

"I thought that Flower was on the outs with the Dollnick establishment," Mouser said.

"Old news," Dewey told him. "Any remaining animosity was smoothed over by the Container Prince in return for

Flower's help with the sale of his first terraforming job. How much time do we have?"

"We were just getting ready to leave for the contest," Rayne said. "The schedule has eleven teams making half-hour presentations with a fifteen-minute break between each for questions and setup. It's all going to be streamed live on our network if you don't want to be seen."

"Is there a reason we should remain in hiding?" Lume asked.

"No? Then let's get going before all of the Danish is eaten."

"Magical nondisclosure," Mouser explained to the Dollnick while double checking that his five-subject notebook was packed in the rollaway.

"That's odd," Dewey said. "The NDA should have deactivated when I told you that Lume is a trusted agent."

Rayne looked back and forth between Dewey and Mouser and then laughed. "Sometimes a pastry is just a pastry. If they aren't worried about people guessing that Flower is our customer, I really do want to get going before the Danish is gone."

"I shall identify myself as a manager of a family investment office," Lume said. "If the people here believe that Flower is still a pariah to Dollnicks, that can only work in favor of my cover story. Can we help with any of those bags?"

"This is the only one I'm bringing," Mouser said. "Some of the teams will be presenting artwork, holograms, even physical models of specific locations in their games, but I'm used to setting the scene with words. And the two of you should accompany us onto the stage so I can introduce you as special guests from our client."

"An old-fashioned man on an old-fashioned planet," Dewey said. "I always thought that you were one of the few people not born here who didn't seem out of place."

"The Bitters who came here from Earth are that different from the generation born here?" Lume asked as he followed the others into the corridor. "I had the impression that adaptability to new locations was one of humanity's greatest virtues."

"The difference here is that there's a belief system involved," the artificial person explained to his alien companion. "The first generation that came to Bits made a conscious commitment to move away from the tunnel network so they could continue working with obsolete computer systems, even if the processors are mainly simulations. Humans who accepted contract work on alien worlds are primarily economic or political refugees. These people are closer to being religious refugees who came so they could practice their beliefs."

"I've never heard it put that way, Dewey," Rayne said over her shoulder. "Did you hear that from one of the Traitors?"

"It's my own analysis, and I used the religion analogy in a paper I wrote for a peer-reviewed academic journal where it's still making the rounds. The main point is that I see those who voluntarily left Earth as converts of a sort, people who underwent a conversion experience. Those born here, including yourself, Rayne, have never known another life so it all comes naturally to you. Someone like Mouser, on the other hand, lives with first-hand knowledge of the artificial constraints he's put on the technology he's using."

"Constraint equals creativity," Mouser muttered the Bits mantra.

"And I believe if you all remain another generation you'll see a growing gap between the way the first generation of those born here deal with technology and what their children are willing to accept," Dewey continued. "If I had to bet, I would put my money on the second generation accepting alien technology wherever it solves problems that currently go unanswered."

"That's the feeling I get from my daughter," Rayne admitted. "You won't believe how she's shot up in the last few years, Dewey."

"Your daughter has become a drug addict? That's terrible. I know a doctor I'm sure can help if you let me take her back to Flower."

"I mean how she's grown. But don't be offended when she doesn't recognize you. Sarah only knows you as a wheeled robot with a shelving attachment."

The little group made their way into the dome's main gaming hall where row after row of old monitors, keyboards, and game controllers of various types were arrayed on long tables. The seats were all taken and every head turned when Mouser's group entered the room. People began saving games and turning off monitors, pushing the screens down into the parked position so they didn't obstruct the view of the small stage at the front.

Hercules, Delphi, and Shadow were waiting on the stage, and Sarah hopped down and ran to greet her mother. "You came! I thought you said you weren't going to play."

"I came to see you," Rayne said, and shot a look at Mouser. "But I suppose it doesn't make a difference so I may as well participate."

"Are those video cameras?" Lume asked Dewey, gesturing at the boxy objects with long lenses set up on tripods around the edges of the stage. "They look like antiques."

"I'll take you through the computer museum if we have time," the artificial person replied. "They have paper punch cards and magnetic tape."

Mouser stood the rollaway next to a folding chair with a microphone hanging from a long cord dangling in front of it. He gestured for Dewey and Lume to come to stand with him.

"Dewey!" Sarah exclaimed. "You came back to see me play an Earth girl with magic."

"How did you know it was him?" Rayne asked her daughter.

"It's Dewey," the ten-year-old repeated, sounding puzzled. "Can't you tell?"

"But he's in a new—never mind."

Mouser lifted the dangling microphone and said, "Testing. One. Two."

"All good," somebody yelled from the back row of tables.

"Before we begin the competition, I'd like to introduce you all to Lume, who works in the family investment office of our backer, and Dewey, who all of you know as the first and only sentient artificial intelligence created on Bits."

"And the first and only to leave," an old voice pointed out unnecessarily.

"I only found out a few minutes ago that our special guests could be here today to participate in the evaluation of our ideas," Mouser continued. "We'll be getting the game I've been developing out of the way first, and I know that many, if not all of you, believe that the fix is in and it will make the final selection. But I never set out to create a full game that can be expanded into a franchise. My interest was to explore the economics of a magic system grafted onto twenty-first-century Earth, and I hope that some of the elements may be adapted by the winners."

After a half-hour role-playing session, in which Sarah somehow managed to accumulate the most mana of the players and then expended it all on a spell to turn her bedroom pink, Mouser called an end to the demonstration and asked if there were any questions.

"So why do all the city people upload their mana on the EdisonNet instead of using it to do something?" a man in the front row asked.

"They believe when they need to use magic in the future it will be available with interest," Mouser explained. "Part of my point is that the ability to wield magic is akin to being a self-employed businessman. Not everybody is cut out for it."

"But what if they all want their mana at once and the, uh, mana bank has loaned it to somebody who used it up?"

"The mana banks all run on the fractional reserve system, but they're backed by the Central Bank of Mana, which—"

"Isn't that why the Stryx had to open Earth in the first place?" somebody else interrupted. "Because our monetary policy got so out of hand that the social contract broke down and the world was teetering on the edge of the apocalypse?"

"Well, yes, but the whole point of alternative history games is to examine how the future might be different if you change one major event, like the outcome of a war, or magic replacing money."

Lume turned to his left and whistled something softly in the artificial person's ear, causing the latter to rise and address Mouser. "Did you consider roles for any of the other tunnel network species in your game, or would they always be playing Humans?"

"I thought they might enjoy the change," Mouser said. "The thing that fascinates me is the concentration of mana. I believe that over time the rent anyone would have to pay to borrow mana would tend towards zero, and—"

"But did you develop a goal to achieve through playing, or is the game only about mana accumulation and rules for a magic economy?"

"Humans were obsessed with the accumulation of mana, I mean, money, before the Stryx opened Earth. So it's authentic to the period. I guess you could say that it's mainly rules, but with a good gamemaster and serious role players, the play could develop in all sorts of interesting directions."

"Is there any combat?" Lume asked directly.

"Not per se, though there's nothing to prevent players from trying to use their magic on each other, or anything else, for that matter," Mouser said.

"Watch out or the little girl will turn you pink," a woman called out from the side.

After a few more questions about the setting of the game, Mouser took his leave from Dewey and Lume and abandoned the stage to five members of the *Vampire Protection Services* team led by Leandra.

"We had a last-minute technical problem with our holographic recording, so with myself acting as gamemaster and these four brave volunteers, we're going to try to give you a flavor of our game by role-playing," Leandra began. "I apologize that we're doing this unrehearsed, and I'll have to ask you to make a superhuman effort to suspend your disbelief, especially as my volunteers will all be playing aliens passing as humans."

"Interesting," Lume whistled softly in Dewey's ear. "And I can't help wondering about their technical failure."

"Could I ask one question before you begin?" the artificial person addressed Leandra.

"Of course," the producer replied when she realized he was waiting for an answer.

"Is the technical failure something you could address if your time slot is moved to the end of the day?"

"I'm afraid not. My team was unfamiliar with the Horten holo-recording equipment, and when we attempted to prepare the permanent rendering for projection last night, somehow we performed a permanent memory wipe instead."

"It was my fault," a young woman on the team with puffy eyes spoke up. "The interface was all color coded and I found out last night that I'm red-green colorblind."

The audience let out a sympathetic moan, though there might have been a bit of relief blended in from the competing teams.

"It was too late for us to plan anything with costuming or makeup, so I hope you can suspend your disbelief and accept that our two female team members are high-caste Vergallian, Manny here is a Verlock with an active holographic disguise letting him pass as an overweight man—"

"Thank you for that," Manny interjected.

"—and Peter is a Frunge male wearing a knit hat over his hair vines, along with gloves, and a facemask over his nose and the whole lower part of his face printed with 'I'm allergic to everything.'"

"Why the facemask?" Lume inquired softly of Dewey.

"Because anybody on Earth would immediately recognize a Frunge as alien," the artificial person replied.

"Really? Other than the hair vines, you two-armed types all look the same to me."

"You're on a shuttle that has just landed on Earth," Leandra addressed her four team members. "The tour operator passes out emergency recall beacons disguised as smartphones. A native wearing some sort of uniform is standing next to what appears to be a ground conveyance that travels on rubber tires. He opens a door of the passenger compartment at your approach and the four of you slide in, sitting one pair across from the other in the surprisingly spacious interior. The native takes his place in the front of the vehicle and says, "Help yourself to drinks."

"Does he speak Vergallian, or do I speak Humanese?" the older of the two young women asked.

"You all have translation implants and took a crash course in Humanese during the trip to Earth, so you know how to say a few hundred words. Your smartphone beacons also serve as external translation devices with a delay."

"Won't that give away that we're aliens?"

"The natives had developed simple translation technology using smartphones and cloud computing by this point. What do you want to do?"

"Have a drink," Manny said. "What's in the minibar?"

"Hold on a second," the girl with the puffy eyes said. "We should find out where we're going before you start drinking."

The older Vergallian leaned forward and rapped on an imaginary sheet of glass. "Conductor? When will we get there?"

"Assuming there hasn't been an accident in the tunnel, we'll be in downtown Boston in ten minutes," Leandra replied in a sort of brogue, and then reverted to her normal speaking voice. "The driver glances in the rearview mirror as he replies and you notice that he doesn't look back to the road. A strange vibration comes from the right side of the vehicle as the tires begin running over a strip of evenly spaced ruts that appear to have been intentionally scalloped out of the road's surface."

"Driver!" Manny barked. "Watch the road."

"The limousine swerves back into the travel lane just before making contact with a concrete barrier."

"What happened?" the girl who had erased the holographic production asked.

"You and I are upper caste Vergallians, which means we're the most beautiful females the Humans have ever seen in their lives," the other woman reminded her. "We'll have to put on our sunglasses and raise our hoods when we get there."

"But it's almost dark out."

"That just makes it more likely we'll be accosted."

"Do we have any native money?" the Frunge asked.

"The tour agency supplied you each with two hundred creds in the local currency known as dollars," Leandra reported. "But be aware that much of the economy has switched to using smartphones for cashless payments, and you don't have any of the necessary accounts established to participate."

"Why do we have to go through a tunnel?" the Verlock asked.

"The spaceship that brought you was disguised as a private jet plane of the type that was commonly used by wealthy individuals in the twenty-first century," Leandra explained. "Since the airport is located on the other side of Boston's inner harbor, a water crossing is necessary. The limousine emerges from the tunnel and the driver expertly navigates from the highway onto the city streets." She shifted back to the brogue, and asked, "Are you sure you want to get off at the Common?"

"That will be fine," the older Vergallian said, pulling a pair of oversized sunglasses out of her purse. She put them on, pulled up her hood, and muttered, "I feel like a vampire."

"You look like a vampire," the Verlock grumbled. "I look like your livestock."

"Are we supposed to stay together as a group or are we going to go our own ways?" the Frunge asked.

"He didn't read the quest package," the younger Vergallian said in frustration.

"I believe it robs games of their spontaneity if you overprepare."

"Like knowing the rules and the objective?"

"It's not like I'm the leader. Who is, by the way?"

"I'm the leader," the Verlock declared. "And the objective is to investigate reports of Human magic use. Earth isn't yet aware of the existence of aliens and we're prohibited from interfering."

"The four of you exit the limo near a small newsstand on the sidewalk running around the perimeter of the Boston Common," Leandra continued. "Passersby stare at the poorly disguised Vergallians, trying to guess whether they're famous movie stars or merely rich. What do you do?"

"Can I sense any magic?" the Verlock asked.

"You drop your mental shields and your senses are overwhelmed by the pressure of raw magic coming from every direction, but it feels undisciplined—uncontrolled."

"Do I have any cool spy technology that detects magic?" the Frunge asked.

"Check your kit."

When the time ran out and the clumsy role-playing scenario stumbled to a conclusion, the audience applauded from relief. The remaining nine demonstrations were all highly polished by comparison, and then Mouser returned to the stage to read the results of the secret ballot conducted over the Rules Committee app that was available on the smartphone of every Bits citizen. Before announcing the winners, he leaned over and quietly asked Dewey a question. After receiving the answer, he took up the microphone again.

"Several of the competing teams have asked us what happens to the work they've done during the last month if their game isn't selected for further development," Mouser said. "Dewey? If you would explain?"

"My associate and I have a Dollnick warship waiting for us on the tarmac so we won't be able to stay for the meeting tomorrow, but I have a message from the family investment office that we represent," Dewey said. "Think big. We're looking for a franchise that includes all of the elements you've demonstrated here today. We've done a great deal of market research for this project, especially with non-human tunnel network species to whom many of you have had limited exposure. Even the least polished of the presentations we saw here today has something to offer on that score."

"We know an alien when we see four arms," somebody called out.

"Wonderful. Now sell him something." Dewey waited for a few long seconds while the silence drew out, and then nodded. "That's what I thought. The reason we chose Bits to create a game set on twenty-first-century Earth should be obvious to you since, for all intents and purposes, you have recreated the early part of that century here in these domes. But one thing we learned here today is that you are creating back stories and instructions for using technology that make sense to yourselves, people who are already fluent in the period. We need you to keep that in mind when you're building the universe, writing dialogue for non-player characters, and creating guidebooks. Don't write for yourselves—write for tunnel network members who only know that Earth is the place that exports all of the contract workers."

"Are you saying that you want us to shoehorn all of the game scenarios presented here today into a single game?" Mouser asked. "I can't see much common ground between at least half of them."

"We're looking for a fully articulated gameverse," Dewey said. "A properly constructed twenty-first-century Earth that can contain any of these prototypes can contain all of them. The players can simply enter through different doors as they do in the period games marketed by other species." Then he returned to his seat and let Mouser handle all of the shouted questions.

"Uh oh," Lume whistled in the artificial person's ear. "There goes trouble.

"Who?"

"The Gem sitting near the back on the left. I didn't notice her earlier or I would have done something."

"I don't think I've ever seen her before, but you know how hard it is to tell with clones," Dewey said. "If that little scar over her eye ridge is real I'll recognize her next time."

"You have better eyes than me," Lume said in surprise.

"I splurged on the optics upgrade when I bought this body."

"Dollnicks have evolved the natural ability to focus at a distance, but my point is, she's a spy."

"From the Old Gem Empire?" Dewey asked. "Bits has always had a number of those coming through, and I understand there are a few thousand former military now living in a dome here."

"New Gem Empire, I met her at a conference sponsored by EarthCent," Lume said. "Flower was hoping to keep the project quiet for at least a few more months."

"I wouldn't worry about it. There are no secrets more fleeting than gaming secrets, and the Gem are in no position to compete with anybody at game production. In fact, Old Empire hangers-on purchasing Cloner helped keep Bits in business for decades."

"That's Old Empire, she's New Empire, and they've made real progress." The Dollnick glanced out at the audience again and pointed subtly towards the museum entrance with his upper left hand partially shielded by the upper right. "There, we made eye contact. I'm going to go talk to her."

"I'll come with you," Dewey said. "I have an idea."

Eleven

"Why do I have to be the executive producer?" Rayne demanded. "You have far more experience than I do and you're much better with people."

"You're the one Dewey said Flower wanted, and you're also the only person authorized to distribute funds from the programmable cred she supplied to finance the whole shooting match," Mouser said. "I doubt anybody else on Bits other than your mother even knows how to use the Stryx register."

"I never understood how it and the mini-registers can work when we don't have a tunnel network connection."

"Stryx creds are their own thing. Supposedly it has something to do with quantum coupling, but I wouldn't be surprised if that's just what they tell technologically backward species like ourselves because we can't prove otherwise."

"That doesn't give me a great deal of confidence in Stryx leadership," Rayne said.

"I don't buy your idea that they're pulling the strings on our project," Mouser said. "I have to believe the Stryx would have better sense than to have appointed me creative director for *A Mazing Earth*. I think Dewey is following vague instructions from Flower and that's as far up as it goes."

"Do you really think the three prototypes that were voted through can be merged with the useful elements from the other teams into one coherent game?"

Mouser shrugged. "I've never seen it done before, but if I had to pick a phase in a game's development to start making major changes, a month in is probably about right. My suggestion is that you name three associate producers and let them do all of the work."

"What do you think about Tom, Diayu, and Leandra?" Rayne suggested.

"Tom and Diayu's teams won, so that makes sense, but why Leandra?"

"It couldn't have been easy to get up there in front of everybody on Bits for half an hour and attempt to show what we would have been seeing if their holographic presentation hadn't been wiped. It demonstrated she can improvise under pressure."

"I still can't believe everybody voted my game into the top three," Mouser said. "It wasn't on the merits. I think it must mean that they were so convinced the vote was rigged they decided to play along."

"People are funny like that," Rayne said. "We have a subconscious desire to be on the winning side. I've been reading more of Earth's earlier history as background for the twenty-first century. They used to have opinion polling for elections that turned out to influence the outcomes by changing different voting bloc's motivation to vote."

"Thanks for reminding me why we left." Mouser checked his notes before continuing. "By the end of the month you'll have thousands of people on the payroll so you're going to need all of the management help you can get. My advice is to stick with finance, pick somebody as co-producer to supervise the overall production, and keep the top people from all of the teams in management positions."

"I think Delphi's dad would make the best co-producer," Rayne said. "He's old enough to command everybody's respect, but not too old to work the hours the job is going to demand without killing himself. I'll tell him to find slots for all of the other producers and directors."

"Now you're delegating," Mouser said with a smile. "You can even tell him to find his own replacement for the associate producer slot you gave him two minutes ago. Are you coming to my first creative meeting? I booked the dome's main conference room so there will be plenty of seats at the table. Development leads, directors, and producers."

Rayne shook her head as she rose from the old couch. "You just told me not to spread myself too thin. I've never had this much money to manage before so I'm going to talk to my financial mentor."

"Your mother?"

"Keeps it in the family."

Mouser puttered around his workshop for a few minutes after Rayne left, basically killing time before the meeting so he wouldn't end up answering the same questions for people who arrived early and then again for those who showed up on time. He checked the windup pocket watch he'd built from a replica kit and was surprised by how much time he had left.

"Alex. Is it only a quarter of?"

"Yes, and you have a first-time visitor," the smart speaker informed him.

"Open the door," Mouser instructed, curious to see who on Bits hadn't already been authorized entry to his workshop when he was there. At first, he couldn't put his finger on what was off about the clone, but he soon realized it was her clothes. Instead of wearing the jumpsuit that was standard issue with all of the Old Empire Gem, she was dressed in what might be current tunnel network fashion, and of a higher quality than anything available in the stores on Bits. "Can I help you, Miss..."

"Belle," the Gem introduced herself, coming forward to offer a handshake.

"I'm Mouser."

"You look surprised," the clone said, putting him on guard, as the few local Gem he had met over the years kept to themselves and weren't known for being able to read human expressions. "Am I the first of my sisters from the New Empire that you've met?"

"In person, yes. One of your ships stopped last month to bring an old friend for a lightning visit but none of your sisters came inside the dome."

"You're talking about Dewey," Belle said, taking the place on the couch that Rayne had recently given up. "Do you have a few minutes to talk?"

"I have to be at a meeting soon, but I could give you ten minutes," Mouser said. "May I ask if your name is, uh..."

"My real name, as opposed to a label I've chosen for convenience when meeting with Humans? You may have heard that Gem identify each other through what you might term telepathy, though that's not entirely accurate when talking about clones. As we've begun reestablishing the lost bloodlines of our species, we've found it desirable to take names so that the newly cloned males can address us individually."

"And you chose Belle?"

"It's a long story and we have limited time, but I promise to give you the details later if you remain interested,"

Belle said. "I met with Dewey and Lume after your competition yesterday. They explained Flower's plan to me, or at least, as much as they felt that I needed to know. The New Empire is sympathetic to EarthCent for the same historic reasons that played into my choice of a name, and I'm here to offer whatever help I can for the next five months."

"I don't want to sound paranoid, but do you have any proof of what you're saying?"

The Gem reached in her fashionable purse that was branded with three embroidered feathers and removed a smartphone that looked a generation newer than anything available on Bits. "I picked this up during a recent visit to Earth," she told him as she passed it over. "Just tap the video icon."

Mouser started the video, which proved to be a wide-angle selfie with Dewey in the center, Lume crowding in on his right, and Belle on the artificial person's left. The Dollnick's right arms weren't in the frame, so one of them must have been holding the phone out in front of the trio.

"I'm sorry we had to run off after the competition, but you understand that the ship's captain was doing somebody quite a favor in stopping here," Dewey began. "Belle is an old acquaintance of Lume's who arrived on Bits a week ago, so she already knows as much about the game in development as we do. Flower authorized me to take representatives of other tunnel network species into our confidence as necessary, and as a freelance gaming journalist for Gem Today, Belle is in a position to do us some good. I hope you'll cooperate and allow her to document the development of the game. We have to get going, but expect to see me back with Flower in five months."

Mouser continued looking at the phone for a few seconds after the video stopped to let the artificial person's words sink in. "You're a gaming journalist?"

"Among other things," Belle said, holding out her hand for the phone. "If there are any other people who should see the video, just point me to them."

"I think Rayne would be it." Mouser sat back in his chair and tried to get a read on the clone's alien features. "Did you really come all the way to Bits on a whim and stumble into our biggest development project ever, or is there something more to this that I'm missing?"

"It's possible that word is out in certain circles that the situation on Bits is rapidly evolving."

"Do you mean that Flower has started a whisper campaign without telling us?"

Belle took a moment before responding. "Interestingly enough, I hadn't thought of that possibility, but it does make sense. Flower has been pushing into anime production for several years now and would certainly have built up a list of entertainment industry contacts with access to the rumor mill."

"How else could word get out?" Mouser asked. "Dewey has been here twice in the last month, and you slipped in on a pirate ship, but that's it for traffic. If the rumor didn't originate with Flower herself, where could it have come from?"

"I'm sure you've heard of industrial espionage. I happen to know that Bits once produced a game of that name."

"Maybe twenty years ago. It was too complicated to play and people lost interest."

"Certain people, or should I say, certain sentients, found *Industrial Espionage* to be fascinating, if vastly oversimplified."

Mouser stared at the clone, trying to decide if there was anything to be gained by asking her outright if she was a spy herself. His thoughts were interrupted by the door opening to admit Hercules and Delphi.

"Belle," the girl greeted the clone. "I thought you were going to ask me for an introduction to Mouser when you had time to meet him."

"I ran into a mutual acquaintance at the competition yesterday who tasked me with delivering a message to Mouser," Belle said. "I've been stopping by The Cave every night in hopes of running into you and your friends again, but you aren't regular customers."

"Shadow and I were preparing with Mouser's team every night for the competition," Delphi explained. "This is Hercules, by the way."

"Pleased to meet you," the big man said, offering the clone a handshake and wincing comically at the strength of her grip. "Do you want to get going to the meeting, Mouser, or are we shooting to arrive fashionably late?"

"Early is on time," Belle said.

"You'll be coming with us?"

"May I?" the clone asked, turning to Mouser. "It would be very useful for documenting the development of the game."

"Does she know about the pumpkin pie?" Delphi asked.

"Dewey has approved her as our embedded journalist for the project and she's aware of Flower's involvement," Mouser told the pair. "I suppose we better get going. Will Shadow be meeting us there?"

"He picked up another part-time gig, I don't know if it's on his old game or something new."

"If he'd rather be coding than working with us to coordinate the production I'll ask around and find him something full-time."

None of the producers or story directors waiting in the conference room appeared surprised by the Gem's presence, and it didn't escape Mouser's notice that most of them seemed to recognize her. There were five empty seats on the arc of the rounded end of the giant U-shaped conference table, and the place cards confirmed that whoever prepared the room had done so in expectation of Rayne and Shadow attending. Delphi nodded at her father as she passed, and Tom returned a smile, though he looked like his thoughts were elsewhere.

"Does anybody have anything they need to say before I begin?" Mouser asked once they were all seated.

"This will just take a minute," Tom said, rising to his feet. "Rayne texted me around a half hour ago and we had a brief meeting. She's been appointed executive producer for the combined game and she asked me to take on the job of co-producer in charge of production."

"So what does she do for top billing?" one of the younger directors asked.

"She hands out the money," the freshly minted co-producer said. "I've already asked Leandra, Daiyu, and Martin to serve as associate producers and they've all accepted," he continued, pointing with his whole hand at each of them as he spoke their names. "I'll be asking all of the former producers here to take on management roles as soon as I get the chance to talk to you alone." He glanced around the table to see if there were any questions, and added, "That's all I had to say."

"Thank you," Mouser said. "I'll just take a moment to introduce Belle, our embedded games journalist from Gem Today. She'll be documenting the development of our project from this point forward with the authorization of our financial backer."

"She already came in to see us last week," Leandra spoke up. "I guess I just assumed it was okay to talk with her."

"Same here," somebody else said.

"Brought us chocolate," a third voice added.

"So before we begin, I'd like to remind you all that entertainment is the biggest business category on the tunnel network," Mouser said. "I've learned that word has already leaked about our project to build a new vertically integrated gaming franchise, so it would be best not to discuss the particulars with people who aren't on your development team."

"But that goes against the whole hacker ethos," an older man said. "We've always discussed technical issues with members of other development teams even when we're competing in the same market."

"May I say something?" Belle asked Mouser. He nodded, and she turned to address the whole table. "Have any of you ever played *Insertion Orbit*?"

"Of course," the man who had just objected replied. "*Insertion Orbit* was the first game developed on Earth that had a full astrophysics engine capable of working out gravity slingshot maneuvers. It's widely known that several space agencies in the pre-Opening era used it to confirm their computations of trajectories for probes sent to Jupiter's moons. But it wasn't particularly successful as a game, and I haven't seen it since I was a kid back on Earth."

"Around five years ago, a Horten tourist visiting Earth stumbled across a copy in a retro gaming boutique and was taken by the artwork on the retail package. He also had the foresight to purchase a system capable of reading the disc, and three months later, Morp Educational Games came out with *Deep Space Probe,* a fun way for children to learn about the history of primitive space vehicles."

"But the aliens, I mean, tunnel network species, must have developed thousands of superior products in the millions of years some of them have had interstellar travel," Hercules protested.

"Yes, but those are old and this was new," the clone explained. "It's already sold over a hundred million copies, making it the second-most popular cross-species title for children on the tunnel network in the last decade."

"What's the most popular?" somebody asked.

"*Coloring with Aisha*. It's a Grenouthian release based on *Let's Make Friends*."

"What about intellectual property law, or is *Insertion Orbit* out of copyright?" Tom asked.

"I don't think anything produced on Earth in the last two centuries will ever go out of copyright," Belle said with a laugh. "It seems that extending the protection period over and over again is the only thing your remaining governments can agree on. But *Deep Space Probe* isn't a copy of *Insertion Orbit*. It's simply inspired by it and covers the same ground in a similar fashion. I doubt the Horten programmers who created *Deep Space Probe* had any exposure to the Earth game beyond a functional description. But it never would have existed without Morp's vacation purchase, and a whole new business centered around game prospecting tours to Earth has sprung up."

"So there's no point in taking unnecessary chances if some of that competition starts coming this way," Mouser said, and then paused a moment to make clear he was moving on to the next subject. "Now, I'm not a big fan of meetings, especially with this many people, and I'll try to keep it short so we can all get back to work. I've been chosen by our client to be the creative director for *A Mazing Earth*, which means I'll be riding herd on the rule books everyone comes up with for the gamemasters."

"Are you going to coordinate all of that online, or will there be regular meetings?" Tom asked.

"I've set up a dedicated message board for sharing rules and backstories, but I think meeting with story directors in my workshop once a week would help keep us from getting too far out of sync with each other. Our client wants me to maintain overall artistic control, which is ridiculous. The project is too large and I'm too old, but at least I can provide one-stop blaming if it all goes sideways. I don't have the energy to run around checking on everybody so I'll be relying heavily on Hercules and Delphi to be my go-betweens. If you have any questions or concerns, please don't hesitate to contact them any time of the day or night."

"Thanks a lot," Delphi muttered under her breath, though her blush gave away that she was pleased to be entrusted with so much responsibility, especially in front of her recently discovered father.

"So let me get this straight," a woman wearing a *Starship Bloopers* T-shirt said. "Dewey and his four-armed friend sat through our prototype demonstrations, decided that all of the ideas had some value and should be integrated with the three winners, and you're the one who is supposed to blend it all together at the end?"

Mouser shook his head. "The reason all of you story directors were invited today is that we need to divvy up the usable pieces from the runners-up among the three games that were voted most likely to succeed. And I hope you can tell from Dewey's choice of *A Mazing Earth* as the title that despite my team being voted into the top three, the mazes of magical barriers proposed by the Paper Rat team will be a foundational element. It's the responsibility of all of us to make sure that the overall storyline and feel of the three branches converge back to a coherent starting point, or at least, don't become incompatible with each other."

"So we're sticking with the three-doors concept?" Tom asked.

"It's what Dewey said the client wants," Mouser replied, though he didn't look very convinced of the wisdom of this approach. "He said it's a common technique with game franchises published by the advanced species. One door always leads to a family-friendly option, a second door drops you in a maximum action scenario, and the third door leads to the most challenging path from an intellectual perspective."

"That could be your version of twenty-first-century Earth where magic replaces money," Daiyu said. "It might not be a bad idea to lump all of the wonkier stuff together behind one door and maybe the other species will find it interesting."

"I don't get it," one of the younger directors spoke up. "You're saying that players will be able to choose from three distinct games and the only thing they'll have in common is the setting?"

Leandra mumbled something under her breath, and Tom asked, "What was that?"

"I said that I've been playing *Plus One* for years," Leandra said, and when nobody reacted, she went on to explain, "It's a Vergallian game where you're a disinherited princess and you have to take over an unaffiliated planet and bring it into the Empire of a Hundred Worlds."

"Where did you even get something like that?" Daiyu asked.

"I bought a pirated copy years ago, from, you know."

"Pirates," somebody said unnecessarily.

"It's not like I could tell anybody that I'm addicted to an alien game when we're not even supposed to—anyway," Leandra cut short her excuses, "it starts with three doors, and you can go the builder route, the warrior route, or try to pull a Rasputin."

"I'll guess the builder route is the family-friendly option, like a farm game," Delphi said, "and the warrior route must be the action option, but what's a Rasputin?"

"The power behind the throne. It's the most intellectually challenging of the three options and I never made it past the first level without getting executed," Leandra said. "But the reason I brought it up is that the three options are all in dialogue with each other."

"There's a chat where you can talk to friends who started through the other doors?"

"Not a dialogue between the players, a dialogue between the storylines. It's hard to explain, but the history of the planet you're trying to take over is the same behind all of the doors until you show up. Once you choose a door and start playing, it affects the history and starting point should you choose a different door the next time."

"You're saying the three options aren't truly isolated," Tom said.

"And it's not just one-way," Leandra said, speaking slowly as she tried to find words to describe the concept. "It's almost as if the other options are pushing back, like the builder storyline doesn't want the warrior storyline to include destroying a city or cutting down an orchard. I can't really describe it other than to say that I don't have a clue how the game devs pulled it off without A.I."

"Storylines in dialogue with each other is an excellent analogy," Belle spoke up unexpectedly. "Vergallian game developers have a special word for it that doesn't have a direct correspondent in Humanese, but it's something akin to an echo. It mainly affects the non-player characters whose knowledge of their world is altered by what occurs behind the other two doors. The Grenouthians and Verlocks both do something very similar in their trading games, though they focus on the availability of goods and market pricing."

"I suppose we could do something relatively crude in terms of keeping the history in sync so that somebody who starts *A Mazing Earth* through the family-friendly door and moves on to one of the others sees echoes of their previous gameplay," Tom said. "It's going to mean more work for the two of you," he added, lifting his chin to indicate his daughter and Hercules.

"I think I understand what you're getting at, but if she's willing I'll talk it over with Belle," Delphi said.

"Of course," the Gem said. "That's what I'm here for."

"I thought you were here to get a story for Gem Today," Mouser said.

"In my line of work, it pays to make oneself useful to as many people as possible," the clone replied. "And as a journalist, I don't see any conflict of interest in sharing my knowledge—you could even say that it's my calling."

Twelve

Shadow studied the split screen of the debugger where all of the variables and data for the current thread were displayed in real-time. He glanced to his left at the monitor where the results of the process were shown and double-tapped the space bar on his keyboard, advancing the execution of the main thread by ten lines. The fire spell cast by the player's avatar bloomed out from her open palm. He looked back at the debugger screen, clicked his tongue, and double-tapped the space bar again while watching the results.

"Gotcha!" he cried as the fireball dissipated rather than zooming towards its target. Turning back to the debugger once again, he stepped backward through the main thread one line at a time and identified the object call where the parameters for the fireball suddenly zeroed out. "Nothing like old code where the hackers didn't believe in comments," he said happily.

"Did you find it?" a middle-aged woman asked, standing to look over the low partition that separated their cubicles. "According to the error report from Bits Away, that fireball glitch only comes up a few times a month, and never for the same player. They've been receiving in-game complaints about it for years. This was the first time a player bothered providing them with the complete debug log. I guess the fireball failing got her killed."

"It would have to be rare for them to put it in your queue since we'll only fix it in the next release," Shadow said. "There's a typo in the expansion multiplier where instead of using the clock elapsed time the programmer just used the clock."

"You lost me," his boss said. "I know the fireball has a random factor to keep it interesting, but…"

"There's a random factor too, but this is a fiddly adjustment that one of the artists must have insisted on. It's a reciprocal that at most should have made a difference of five percent in the expansion speed."

"And using the wrong clock..."

"Unlike the elapsed time, the real clock goes to zero every day at midnight. The variable only uses integer seconds, but there are still eighty-six thousand or so of those a day. That must be how the bug got through beta testing here without ever being caught. It's almost surprising it comes up as often as it does."

"I'll bet a lot of Earthers play late at night," his boss said. "Good job, Shadow. You can head home early if there's nothing else on the list. I thought those bugs would keep you busy for a month and you got through them in a week."

"I'm the best," the eighteen-year-old said, slipping his smartphone back into the bracer on his forearm.

"No, I'm the best for hiring you. And next time you see Mouser, thank him for referring you my way."

"How do you know him?"

"He didn't tell you?" The woman's laugh floated over the cubicle partition as she sat back down. "My little brother is married to his daughter. Bits wouldn't function without nepotism."

Rather than stopping home, Shadow headed directly for the dome's gym to beat the Friday after-work rush. He put in a solid hour in the weight room before hitting the shower. Then he sniffed at his sweats, decided they were good for another week in the locker, and began changing back into his street clothes. Hercules arrived and started changing into his own sweats.

"Hey, Herc," Shadow called across the locker room. "Does Mouser still want us all day tomorrow?"

"Unless he changed his mind in the last ten minutes."

"I was just checking. You're working with Delphi all the time now, right? What happened to her last weekend?"

"If you hadn't been late you would have known," Hercules said, unable to resist the urge to tweak the younger man over his chronic tardiness.

"Come on."

"Her little half-sister had a birthday and Delphi thought it would be fun to make herself a present. It was the first time they met."

"That's pretty cool. Did she jump out of a box or something?"

"I'm not going to spoil that story in case she wants to tell you herself." Hercules tied the drawstring of his sweatpants and pulled on the light workout jersey he'd taken to wearing in the weight room since finding out that the mirror was one-way glass with a camera behind it.

"Is she still composing, or is coordinating between all of the games taking up every second of her time?"

"Why don't you invite her for a coffee and ask her yourself? I don't know much about her schedule when we're not working other than she's started spending a lot of time at The Cave. It usually shows up as her location when she texts me about anything in the evening."

"Thanks," Shadow said, feeling like a dog that had been thrown a bone. "I'll see you in the morning."

"On time," Hercules tossed over his shoulder as he headed into the weight room.

Shadow took a long detour on the way home, going by The Cave, but he didn't order anything when he saw that Delphi wasn't there. When he arrived at the family's apartment, his sister was performing a kata in the living room with their parents for an audience.

"Come and sit down, Junior," his mother called. "Lisa is showing us the scaffolding she's doing for character selections."

"She's helping the devs build the avatars for all of the alien females," his father added.

"Not the humans?" Shadow asked, going to stand by the couch.

"Humans are the trivial case," his sister said. "I can do a human in my sleep but I really have to work at getting the alien moves right for the motion capture booth. I don't know if I could have managed them all so close together without Belle's help. It turns out that she knows more about alien martial arts than my sensei."

"Doesn't that make her your new sensei?"

"Maybe, I hadn't thought about it. Now, you'll have to imagine I'm twice as bulky for this Grenouthian style, but the name translates to Pushing Paws." Lisa went through a series of choreographed kicks and paw strikes that the aliens who resembled giant rabbits had been practicing for millions of years. Shadow couldn't help joining their parents in applause when she finished.

"You look pretty pumped up for just having gotten home from a new coding job," Lisa observed, throwing in a solid punch to her younger brother's bicep for good measure. "Did you get fired already?"

"More like promoted, or at least, I'm sure they're going to keep me. My boss let me leave early today after I finished cleaning up a big bug list she thought was going to take me a month."

"I still can't get used to the idea of hackers working regular hours," his father said. "It's so Earth."

"We should take the kids out for dinner to celebrate," his mother said.

"And we would if we didn't already have plans."

"Oh, right. Sorry. Another time."

"How about I treat you since I've caught on at work and all," Shadow said to his sister. "I was thinking of eating at The Cave."

"Because you're suddenly a big vegan fan?" Lisa asked, eyeing him skeptically. "Well, I won't look a gift brother in the mouth. Let me grab a shower and send a few texts. I can't believe how busy I've gotten with all of this avatar scaffolding work."

As soon as Lisa disappeared into the bathroom, Shadow's mother asked him, "Did you understand what she was talking about?"

"You know how she butchers sayings. It's the Trojan horse thing."

"What?"

"You're the one who butchers sayings in this family," his father said. "Trojan horses are bad gifts you shouldn't accept. Not looking a gift horse in the mouth is because a horse's teeth can tell you a lot about its age and health. The point is that you shouldn't be critical of gifts."

"Now you're both confusing me," Shadow's mother said. "I'm talking about this scaffolding work. She's never explained it to me and I waited too long to ask."

"Oh," Shadow said, embarrassed to find that he'd been referencing Trojan horses inappropriately his whole life. "It's what they call it when you have a live actor provide the underlying framework for an avatar to save time for video game artists. Lisa either puts on a motion capture suit or gets in one of those holographic booths so they can build a vector model of how she moves. Botan tells me that anime artists work with putting skins on scaffolding all the time. That's what he wants to get into if his family leaves Bits some day."

"Lisa is becoming an actress?" Shadow's mother asked. "Why didn't she tell us, Frank?"

"She's been talking about her scaffolding work for months," Shadow's father replied. "I remember when she came home and explained it. You were playing *Kangaroo* on the console and you kept on saying, 'Yes, I understand.'"

"I'm not responsible for what I say when I'm in the zone. House rules."

Shadow decided to change into his lucky shirt, the one he had been wearing when he won an under-eighteens tournament a year earlier. While he was in his bedroom, he spotted the small bottle of cologne that his sister had given him for his most recent birthday and vacillated over dabbing a little on before chickening out. Then he texted Botan his plans and got caught up in playing an old stacking game on his phone.

"Let's go," his sister said, breaking him out of his Tetris coma. "I'm hungry."

"Where did the folks go, anyway?" he asked, following his sister out of the apartment.

"It's that adult-game beta testing group they signed up for," Lisa said.

"You mean a rated-X game? They didn't say anything to me about it."

"That's because you're the family prude. I must be the only big sister I know who never caught her little brother looking at porn."

"Have you forgotten threatening to beat me up if you ever found me looking at pictures of naked women on my phone?" Shadow demanded, giving his sister a friendly shove. "I was like ten. I think you traumatized me for life."

By the time they reached The Cave, both siblings were in high spirits, and Lisa asked, "Did you tell your artist friend that we were heading out?"

"Botan? I texted him. Why?"

"He's cute. And smart. That's two out of three."

"His birthday is a week after mine," Shadow told her.

"Good. I wasn't sure he was legal," Lisa said with a grin. "That's three out of three."

"You don't think it's weird, a girl being interested in a younger guy?"

"Not if he's mature and she isn't."

"Sometimes it's painful how honest you are with yourself," Shadow said through his own laughter. "What do you want to eat?"

"Let's check the blackboard," she said. "I want to see if they have any fake meat."

"What's the point of being vegan if you eat fake meat all the time? Why not just eat your vegetables and grains straight?"

"I'm not vegan for aesthetic reasons," his sister said. "I just think it's healthier and better for Karma not to eat things that are ambulatory. The upper caste Vergallians are vegans. I read about their diets when I was studying their martial arts."

"Have you been watching Vergallian dramas again?" Shadow asked suspiciously. "I thought you swore off them when you were sixteen. You know how addicted you got."

"I'll have a beet burger with sweet potato fries and a side of fried tofu," Lisa told the counterman. "Water for now, we'll be back for drinks later."

Shadow grudgingly duplicated his sister's order, paid with his phone, and the two of them found a good table. They'd barely sat down when Botan joined them.

"You guys hear the latest?" the artist asked.

"You mean the X-rated game," Shadow said, trying to sound nonchalant.

His friend looked at him funny and Lisa laughed. "No," Botan said. "I mean about the Horten ship that set down on the tarmac around an hour ago. Supposedly it's one of the planetary survey models, but what would one of those be doing here?"

"I'll text Mouser." Shadow tapped away on his smartphone and then waited impatiently for a response. "He said nobody has come in the dome yet. The ship is just sitting there."

"Maybe they got tired of Zero G and Bits is an off-the-tunnel-network spot where they can take a break without getting caught by their bosses," Lisa suggested.

"Do you think survey ship crews have bosses?" Botan asked. "I thought it was one of those independent jobs."

"Everybody has bosses," Shadow said. "Mine told me I'm a genius so tonight is my treat. Have you eaten?"

"No, but I already ordered and paid. You can get the drinks."

Lisa quizzed Botan about his family during the meal, trying to tease out whether they were still planning on leaving Bits. It turned out that they had so much subcontracting work processing twenty-first century images from cloud backups brought from Earth that his parents had gone quiet on the issue. But Botan's grandparents, all four of whom were in their seventies and in good health, were studying old satellite maps of Japan in preparation to choose land in the prefecture where they had grown up.

Shadow almost jumped up from his seat when he saw Delphi come in. She didn't notice him and headed over to a table where her father was sitting with a woman in her late thirties and a young girl.

"That must be her half-sister," Lisa said, following her brother's eyes. "I didn't know who they were, but I saw they were already eating when we got here, so Deli is just stopping to be polite. I bet she uses us as an excuse not to go home with them."

"Maybe they invited her for dessert," Shadow said. "After all, she didn't know we were going to be here either."

"You didn't ask her to come? When I saw you'd changed into your lucky shirt I figured you finally got up the courage to ask her out."

"The point of the lucky shirt was to get her to show up," Shadow explained, He reddened when he realized both how stupid that was and how obvious he was being about his interest.

"She's pointing to us, dude," Botan said after sneaking a look in the family's direction. "I'll bet your sister is right."

"This is starting to remind me of the social group my parents made me go to when I was watching too many Vergallian dramas," Lisa said. "Humans are so screwed-up. When an upper-caste Vergallian woman wants a man she just doses him with pheromones."

"What percentage of their population is upper caste?" Botan asked.

"It's basically the royals, retainers, and the occasional recessive genes showing up in the general population. I don't think they publicize statistics like that but it's got to be less than one in a thousand. Maybe less than one in ten thousand."

"How do they maintain control?" Shadow asked. "I always thought it was one in ten or something."

"The queens are really good at their jobs—it's what they were bred for," Lisa explained. "There are a dozen other caste levels before you get to the mass population. You know that the Vergallians aren't all originally from the same species, right? The empire has been absorbing compatible humanoids for millions of years. They probably do a bit of genetic engineering on the sly to make interbreeding possible, but some of the other aliens believe it's the classic case of panspermia. The Vergallians think that humanity is a patent infringement on their basic build."

"And now there's like a trillion of them," Botan said. "Hey, here comes Delphi."

Shadow stood up and immediately felt foolish when he remembered that nobody did that sort of thing outside of dramas. "I was just about to go order drinks," he improvised when the girl arrived. "Can I get you something? I'm celebrating a work thing."

"Cool," Delphi said. "I'll have an orange juice."

"A pot of Sencha," Botan told Shadow. "It's too early for alcohol."

"That's green tea, right?" Lisa asked, and received a nod from the young artist. "I'll try it."

"You guys are a thrill a minute," Shadow said, and attempting an old Earth accent, added, "I'll be back."

"Did you hear about the Hortens?" Botan asked Delphi. "Shadow checked with Mouser and he said that the ship is just sitting on the tarmac."

"Tom told me that he already texted all of the managers on the project to remind them about industrial espionage," Delphi replied. "It seems weird, aliens spying on each other's game development, but I guess commercial espionage is practically a sport on the tunnel network."

"But we're not on the tunnel network, and our whole civilization depends on this project working out."

"Civilization?" Lisa asked with a laugh. "There are barely a hundred and fifty thousand of us left living on Bits and we don't even raise our own food, beyond salad stuff."

"I don't think quantity is the defining factor," Botan said seriously. "A civilization is about people living together with a social order and a system of communications."

"Don't you think it takes a little more than that?" Delphi asked. "I always thought of Bits as a colony."

"Of what? Of which civilization on Earth?"

"Was there more than one when our parents left to come here?"

"That's an interesting question," Belle said, and they all looked up to see the Gem journalist standing at the table. "May I?" The clone took Shadow's chair and continued talking. "I studied up on Earth before my visit, and while the planet wasn't exactly homogeneous prior to the Stryx opening, your Internet and the ubiquity of smartphones had made it much more so than any time in your past."

"I would have guessed that there were only enough people for one civilization if you go back far enough," Lisa said.

"Perhaps at the beginnings of humanity, but if you make urbanization a requirement of civilization, it's doubtful your people had any significant urban centers before they had already spread over much of the globe. If you ever get there yourselves, I can recommend a tour I took of ancient sites that supposedly gave evidence of alien contact at the dawn of civilization."

"Did you..."

"The Gem?" Belle chuckled and shook her head. "Even if we had discovered Earth, we were too busy fighting each other to become the sole inheritor of our species to be interested in playing sky gods to primitive peoples."

"But is there any real evidence that aliens came to Earth before the Stryx opening?" Botan asked.

"There certainly is, though I didn't see any of it on the tour."

"Then why did you recommend it?" Delphi asked.

"It was well organized, highly entertaining, and one of the civilizations in question developed a drink based on chocolate," Belle said. "That's more than enough reason to visit a planet, in my humble opinion."

Shadow returned with a tray and distributed the drinks, including a hot chocolate for the Gem. "Belle and I met at the counter," he explained even though nobody asked. "I'll return the tray and be right back."

"How is the documentary coming?" Lisa asked the clone. "I was psyched when you came in with the cameraman the other day when I was doing motion capture but you left before they gave me a break."

"You presented a highly compelling visual," Belle said. "If the cameraman Mouser found for me had you framed and focused properly, I'm sure I'll be able to give you thirty seconds of fame. My sisters are fascinated with the entertainment industry."

Shadow returned, pulled up another chair, and finally took a sip from his coffee. He wished he had thought of asking for a shot of Dutch courage in it, but he was still shy about ordering alcohol, especially if he was the only one drinking. "How's the game looking?" he asked the clone.

"Delphi would know more about it than me," Belle replied. "She and Hercules visit different working groups every morning. I keep running into them on my rounds."

"Not really," Delphi said. "I mean, I could tell you who's ahead of schedule and who's behind, or how the magical barriers in the maze mess up the ability of undercover alien agents to chase alien rogues, but as to the overall thing?" She shook her head. "Mouser and Rayne seem to think it's all on track, and my—Tom says that everything is going surprisingly well, though I doubt he sleeps more than five hours a night."

"Managing large projects is an art of its own. It's different with us, of course, as the vast majority of our population remains based on a single individual's genes. But the first generation to start coming of age after our revolution is proving to be far more independent-minded than those who came before. Some of my sisters are beginning to study best practices in management in preparation for the new bloodlines that are joining the workforce."

"You're studying Earth's best practices in management?" Lisa asked in disbelief.

"Perhaps not as much as those of the other tunnel network members, but if we learned one thing from our long winter as a clone species, it's the importance of keeping an open mind."

"But seriously,' Shadow said to Belle. "You're a gaming journalist, right? Are we building a game that you would play, or is this all some sort of employment project foisted on us by popcorn?"

"What's in that coffee?" his sister asked suspiciously. "You can't be drunk already."

"I could eat popcorn," Botan added.

"It's a non-disclosure agreement we signed, Botan, and that's all either of us can say about it other than cheesecake," Delphi told them. "We get that being here is your job, Belle, but what do you think of the project as a game?"

The Gem took a sip from her hot chocolate and nodded. "I think the basic concept will be attractive to the other tunnel network species, though I really can't say for your people. Twenty-first-century Earth is a fascinating period because it combines the peak of your technological culture with the worst of your economic systems. I took a tour of the Wall Street Preserve run by the Grenouthians. The guide claimed that every serious economist at the time understood that monetary policy was on an unsustainable course, yet they all hid their faces."

"Do you mean they averted their eyes?"

"My reading makes me believe that hiding one's face or turning away is a stronger expression of willfully ignoring an existential threat," Belle said. "But let's not get bogged down in Humanese semantics. The game's setting is excellent, everybody loves a new magic system, and the three doors approach is familiar to most species and should work well. The main problem I'm seeing, again in terms of tunnel network uptake, is that the culture you're creating beggars belief."

"But how can we introduce magic without asking the players to suspend their disbelief?" Shadow asked.

"Not the magic, the culture. Coming from a species that subsisted for thousands of years on a manufactured nutrition drink that had the texture of sand, it's difficult for me to cast aspersions, but at least it didn't damage our health. Humanity was a poorly governed species on the brink of economic collapse intentionally making food choices that were deleterious to your health. It's almost as if half of your population had a death wish."

"I don't quite get what you're talking about."

"At least on Bits, you import frozen vegetables. Soda and chips are so expensive, relatively speaking, that they're more of a treat than a staple," Belle said. "Tell me. What did you have for lunch today?"

"Vending machine pizza," Shadow replied.

"And yesterday?"

"Vending machine pizza."

"And Wednesday?" the clone prompted.

"All right, so I eat vending machine pizza for lunch at work every day. I like vending machine pizza."

"And you don't see anything wrong with that," Belle stated, rather than asking.

"Of course not. It's got bread, cheese, and tomato sauce. Those are the three main food groups right there."

"That's what I meant about beggaring belief. Any member of an advanced species who doesn't have previous exposure to Earth culture would find such a diet unbelievable. And there are lots of other things, from the number of traffic deaths you found acceptable, to your approach to education, and practically everything about your health care system."

"We're supposed to make it as faithful to the period as we can," Delphi said.

"You're faithfully reconstructing these things in the game because your parents remember them and you still cling to some of those practices on Bits," Belle said thoughtfully. "But the vast majority of your people who work on long-term contracts for the other tunnel network species end up emulating the socio-economic systems and lifestyles of their employers to the greatest extent they can manage. I'm not sure their children will find this version of Earth any more believable than the average tunnel network member."

"You're saying that to make the game more realistic, we have to make adjustments to our past?"

"It's a game, not a history lesson," the clone reminded them. "Magical barriers, undercover aliens, shopping quests—all of those are fine. But if all of the non-player characters get out of bed every day and act as self-destructively as the people in your twenty-first century, nobody is going to believe that it's real."

Thirteen

"Why can't I go with you?" Sarah asked her grandmother. "You always bring home the wrong kind of cookies."

"Our Seniors Club monthly meeting for seniors is strictly for the sixty-five and up crowd," June told her. "Even if they let you in you'd be bored out of your mind."

"I'd play games on your smartphone, in silent mode."

"That's exactly why we have the meetings in the auditorium of Dome Six. When the doors are closed it's a Faraday cage. It's the only location in the domes without any cellular reception."

The ten-year-old appeared to be shocked. "What if something happened?"

"I imagine we'd open the doors," June said. "And it's not that I pick out the wrong cookies for you, it's that people my age have sophisticated tastes. We like dry, crunchy cookies that aren't too sweet."

Sarah made a face. "The only good thing about those cookies that come in big round tins is the tin. You can bring me one of those if they leave them out. They're good for storing things."

"Yes, Your Highness." As June dropped an elaborate curtsy, her granddaughter darted forward and planted a kiss on the old woman's cheek.

"Anything you bring me is fine. Just promise you won't retire to Earth."

"The meetings are really just an excuse to get together and complain about our children. What makes you think they're going to push for a return to Earth all of a sudden?"

"Kids hear things," Sarah said mysteriously. "I need you here to help me take care of mom."

"There is that." June hid a smile as she slipped out of the apartment and began walking toward the nearest moving sidewalk. Along the way, she fell in with Agnes, a woman in her early eighties who had been on the Rules Committee for a stretch of years while June was the treasurer.

"Did you hear the latest?" Agnes asked immediately.

"About Earth?"

"About the Horten surveyors. There are two of them in environmental suits going through the domes and measuring every room. And their ship deployed a huge swarm of drones that are flying all over Bits doing a low-altitude optical scan."

"Do you mean there are Hortens going into our living quarters and snooping around? Who gave them permission?"

"They're leaving our apartments alone, but they're checking every larger space and logging the equipment as well," Agnes explained. "The chat rooms are going crazy with rumors that we're being evicted."

"My daughter made the annual lease payment just a few months ago," June assured her. "What do the Hortens say when people ask them?"

"Not much, and since they're encased in environmental suits, we can't tell if they're lying from their skin color changing."

"Is that why they're wearing them?"

"Who knows," Agnes replied. "If they've never been around humans before they're probably worried about germs. The Hortens are the worst hypochondriacs on the tunnel network."

They reached the moving sidewalk and Agnes grimaced. "Could you give me a hand, June? Whoever designed these things didn't have elderly women with low bone density in mind."

"It won't be too long before I'm the one asking for help," June said, supporting the older woman as they stepped onto the moving sidewalk together. "Have you heard from Celia lately?"

"The Horten survey ship brought an electronic mail dump so its last assignment must have been on the tunnel network. It sounds like I'm going to be a great-grandmother."

"Congratulations," June said. "I knew about the mail because Sarah received a long video from her father last night. The great-grandchild will be your first, right?"

"Yes, thank you," Agnes said. "And Celia invited me to come and stay with them again. There's no shortage of cabin space on Flower and she even said something about special accommodations for older people, though I find that hard to believe."

"My ex-son-in-law makes living on board Flower sound like paradise, though we take it with a grain of salt because he obviously wants us to move there with Sarah."

"Wouldn't that just create the same problems he and Rayne had here?"

"There's at least a thousand times as much living space on board Flower as we have here in the domes, and nearly ten times the population. They have self-sustaining agriculture, factory decks, everything you can imagine," June added. "Sometimes I think that the original Rules Committee made a mistake not taking Porl up on his grandfather's offer to pay us to continue the terraforming work here as time allowed. Bits isn't that far from being a habitable planet and the Hortens would have provided the expertise."

"But that would have interfered with the goal of preserving the hacking culture, which was the whole point of our leaving Earth," Agnes reminded her, and then frowned. "I wonder if that's why the surveyors are here now."

"To prepare a major reboot of the terraforming work? Wouldn't that be a positive?"

"Not if they plan on bringing somebody else in to do the job. Why else would they be going around measuring the rooms in the domes and checking the status of all of the equipment?"

June sighed. "I hadn't thought of that."

"I only told you about the Hortens a couple of minutes ago, you haven't had time to digest it. A group of us were discussing the possible implications in the *Gladiators of Rome* for the last hour."

"I still can't understand how you play that game with your arthritis. My fingers hurt just thinking about the controller, and with my reaction time, I'd be lucky to live through a bout with an angry squirrel."

"Didn't I tell you that my arthritis is improving?" Agnes asked, her face lighting up. "A shipment of pills from a new pharmaceutical company arrived on the last transport and they've worked for everybody who's tried them so far, provided you do the exercises in the instructions." Then her head turned to the left and she asked, "Wasn't that the auditorium corridor?"

"Wait for the new skid plate just around the bend," June said. "It moves with the sidewalk as you step off and dissipates your momentum over its length."

"I thought the Rules Committee decided we couldn't afford any of those."

"Mouser told Rayne to do a little creative skimming with the game funds and spread the money around. If the customer asks, she'll explain that spending a little to cut down on broken hips keeps family members working who would otherwise be pressed into eldercare. The skid plate can only be used by one person at a time so I'm going to walk forward ten steps to put enough space between us. I'll go first so you can see how it works."

June took the skid plate like a pro, thankful that Rayne had dragged her out a few days earlier to show it off. Agnes stepped off a few seconds later, a broad smile on her face. "Tell your daughter we need these in every dome, two per location would be even better. I can't tell you how nervous I've been stepping off sidewalks in recent years. Getting on is easier for some reason, and you know how much the young folks hate it when we use the emergency override app to stop a whole section."

"Mouser told Rayne that it would be just as easy to make skid plates for getting on, though I think they'd need a different name," June said, leading the way back to the corridor they had passed. "Nobody ever said that old age was going to be a picnic."

The meeting was just getting underway when they arrived and an improbable hologram was projected over the stage. It showed dozens of senior citizens sitting on blankets or folding chairs on a broad lawn and enjoying a string quartet. The caption read, "Join us for a picnic at Flower's Paradise. We'll be stopping at Bits in sixty-two days."

"All right," said a tall silver-haired man standing in front of the hologram. The old-fashioned microphone on a stand picked up his voice and sent it into the public address system, but many in the audience who had hearing difficulties were using their smartphones to access the public address channel and play it through their earbuds at a higher volume. "Most of you already know me, but for those attending their first Seniors Club meeting, I'm Ralph, and I have the geriatric seat on the Rules Committee."

"What's with the propaganda hologram?" somebody in the audience demanded loudly. "I got the same spam in my account from that ship of traitors this morning and I deleted it without reading. I hope you all did the same."

"Please, let's not turn this into a shouting contest. If you want to come up here and talk after I say my piece you're welcome to do so. Our only rule of order for club meetings is that whoever stands up is allowed five minutes if they aren't booed off by popular acclaim."

"Boo, Boo," hooted the man who had objected to the hologram, but only a handful of others joined him, and they were easily drowned out by the cries of, "Let him speak."

"Thank you," Ralph said. "The Horten ship that arrived yesterday brought a mail dump that included a rather impressive presentation from an independent living facility on Flower whose name should be obvious from the hologram. It didn't make any mention of an additional mailing campaign, so if any of you received spam, I can only imagine that an overzealous marketer purchased a mailing list from one of our expatriates on Flower and employed it in a clumsy manner."

"It wasn't spam, it was fascinating," a woman sitting near the front called out. "If it's not included in your five minutes, I'd like to go after you."

"Very well. So before I tell you about the offer from Flower's Paradise, let's get all of the shouting out of the way. The letter began by referring to a rumor that humans will be evicted from Bits."

This did bring about several minutes of angry back-and-forths between people who cherished different rumors. A dozen or more people got up and stalked out of the auditorium before a measure of calm was restored.

"I didn't start the eviction rumor, and neither did Jack, the president of Flower's Paradise who contacted me," Ralph continued. "My daughter has been hearing whispers about it at work for months, and my grandson brought it home from playgroup."

"We've all heard it," a new voice called out, and this time there was a chorus of agreement.

"I'm not expressing any opinion as to whether or not I think there's truth behind the rumor, though the arrival of a Horten surveyor ship does seem a bit ominous. But we all know people who have left to retire on Earth, and we all have friends, or perhaps family, who are talking about doing so in the future. I present the material from Flower's Paradise in that context. For anybody thinking about retiring away from Bits, Flower provides an interesting option without any long-term commitment. Now, how does this thing work?"

Ralph tapped at the smartphone mounted on the back of his forearm, and after a long thirty seconds that included him raising his arm in front of his eyes so he could see what he was doing, the hologram came to life with the sound of chamber music. A tall man in his seventies and a petite woman in her early eighties rose from their lawn chairs and the hologram zoomed in on them.

'I'm Jack, the president of Flower's Paradise, and this is my wife Nancy, who coordinates our lecture series and advises on the continuing education program."

"We met in Flower's Paradise," Nancy said, glancing fondly up at her husband.

"Flower has set aside an entire deck at her heart-healthy eighty-percent of Earth-weight radius for independent living," Jack continued. "As a top-of-the-line Dollnick colony ship, she has space for at least five million humans on board, but she's currently operating at less than twenty-five percent of capacity. Before showing you the standard presentation we've created for retirees looking at their options, I want to stress that with Flower, everything is a la carte. If you want to move to our deck and set up your own cooperative and restrict the membership to retirees from Bits, you're free to do so, and I'll offer whatever help I can."

"Just be prepared for mandatory exercise and volunteering," Nancy added. "The rest is up to you."

The hologram blinked and was replaced by a waltz, complete with a full orchestra playing for the dancers, all of whom were in their golden years. Members of the Seniors Club sat in stunned silence as the presentation went on to highlight the cafeteria, room service, dining on the other decks, and morning stretches with everybody standing in the corridors just outside their cabin doors.

The next segment focused on the field trips cooperative members took to planets where Flower stopped, and nobody objected as the projection time stretched well beyond the five-minute limit. When it finally reached the continuing education segment, spotlighting free lectures on the independent living deck and courses in everything from crafting to documentary filmmaking, somebody cried, "It can't be true. It's all made up."

Ralph left the hologram frozen on the final scene showing a woman in her late sixties manipulating a pair of floating immersive cameras while interviewing an alien. "I've been up here way past my time limit, so I'll just add that I have a nephew living on Flower, and he says that the whole setup is so unlike anything on Earth that we won't believe it unless we visit. My understanding is that Flower will be stopping here when the development for *A Mazing Earth* is scheduled to wrap up so it's likely the funding group behind the game lives on board. I plan on taking advantage of the opportunity to visit Flower in orbit and we might want to prepare a signup list so that those of us who are interested can travel together."

As Ralph stepped down from the stage, the woman who had volunteered to talk about the marketing material she'd received came forward, but an angry-looking man brushed past her, growling, "I was first."

"It's Howard Long," Agnes whispered to June. "We should have known he was going to be a problem back when he tried to make everybody address each other by their family names."

"Sometimes I think he's still living in the twentieth-first century," June said. "Dealing with all of his objections and calls for audits was the least pleasant part of the job when I was the treasurer."

Howard Long didn't feel the need to introduce himself. He launched directly into a rant about how everything was lies, from the alleged Horten survey vessel to the existence of a Dollnick colony ship named Flower. Rather than booing him off the stage, club members began whispering and pointing, and then the whole audience burst out laughing.

"Do you think you'll trick me into looking behind myself?" Howard raged. "I may be old, but my father didn't raise any fools, and—" he broke off when a hand tapped him on the shoulder.

"Excuse me," an alien encased in an environmental suit addressed him via an external translation pendant that introduced a delay. "We just need to shoot the stage and then you can get back to your lecture. It sounds highly informative."

A second alien carrying a sort of tripod with a fancy bit of surveying equipment set it down just a few steps from where Howard was standing and the first alien tapped a few symbols on a wrist controller. The center extension of the tripod shot up over their heads, and the device began to spin, shooting what might have been laser beams in every direction.

"Watch your eyes!" somebody in the audience shouted, but whatever the surveyors were doing, it was already over. The one who hadn't spoken folded the tripod, checked some readings on a small screen, and nodded to his companion.

"Thank you for your cooperation," the first alien said, and then turned to exit into the wings.

"Wait," a woman cried from the audience. "Could you answer a few questions for us?"

The alien paused, glanced at his wrist controller again as if checking the time, and then faced the crowd. "It works both ways," he said. "I'll trade you answers one for one."

"Are we really getting evicted?" the same woman asked.

"Eviction is a legal process for tenants who violate the terms of a lease. Nonrenewal within the terms of a lease is a different issue. Now my question. Every office we measured this morning was full of employees busily working on what we're told is a vertically integrated game franchise. Who is paying for all of it?"

"An anonymous group of investors," the woman responded.

"That's not an answer so I'll ask a different question," the alien said. "Have any survey teams or realty firms been here assessing your domes? They might have come disguised as diplomats or something else."

"The last alien ship to visit Bits was a Dollnick military vessel, but Dewey and a friend were the only ones to enter the domes," somebody in the front row volunteered.

"What's a Dewey?"

"An artificial intelligence who was created here and moved to Flower. He and, what was the Dollnick's name?" the man asked his wife.

"Lume," she muttered.

"Dewey and Lume," the man in the front row continued. "They were here from Flower to check progress on the new game franchise, not to inspect the domes."

"Ah. My mistake." The alien turned to leave once again.

"But we have more questions," cried the woman who had originally stopped him, but this time she didn't receive a reply.

"What do you think that was all about?" June asked Agnes. "I don't see the connection between real estate and game development."

"You know the Hortens are gaming fanatics," the former Rules Committee member said. "Maybe the owner of the planet would get bad publicity if he kicked us out while we're developing a new game."

Howard Long, who had been thrown off his rant by the appearance of the aliens, didn't have the energy to get himself worked up again when left in full possession of the stage. He had to satisfy himself with grumbling loudly as he climbed down the stairs and was replaced by the woman who had read the marketing mail. She was wearing a colorful wig and was dressed like an anime character.

"I've never spoken at one of these meetings so please forgive me if I lack the charisma of Mister Long," she began.

"Your name?" somebody called out.

"I'm Pam, which rhymes with spam, but the electronic brochure I received couldn't have been more welcome. It was from Flower Entertainment, and it described a permanent living area for cosplayers on the deck where they hold cons for every genre you can imagine. In the last year they've done comics, anime, games, science fiction, fantasy—everything I've been missing about Earth since moving to Bits."

"We have cons," somebody objected from the audience.

"We have the same con over and over again, with the same little cliques of people who end up fighting over the same trivia that I've been listening to for decades. I want to go to a con with cosplayers I don't recognize and voice actors from all over the tunnel network. According to the demographic breakdown in the brochure, the anime cons draw more aliens than humans."

"Is there going to be a con in progress when Flower stops here?"

Pam shook her head. "There aren't enough people on Bits to justify it, and nobody else would travel here to attend because we're not on the tunnel network. They always have a big con when Flower makes her semi-annual stops at Union Station, but otherwise they schedule them to coincide with visits to heavily populated worlds or orbitals."

"But we can visit the con deck?" another voice inquired.

"That's what the cover letter for the brochure said. Free transportation, both ways, and free food if you show up in costume."

After Pam ceded the stage, eight more members of the retirement club got up to talk about what they had heard from friends or family who had moved back to Earth or joined Flower. For some, the availability of cheap land in their home countries combined with Dollnick floaters being manufactured by humans under license was a convincing argument to think about returning to Earth. For others, the facilities available on Flower no more than a few minutes in a lift tube away were a compelling argument to give the independent living deck a look.

"We're coming up on our time limit for the evening," Ralph said when he retook the stage. "At the risk of gilding the lily, I should point out that in the letter I received from Jack, he told me that Flower would offer free transportation to Earth for anybody who boards at Bits and lives on board until she gets there."

"Does that include room and board?" somebody called out.

"Don't be greedy. It's transportation for you and a reasonable amount of baggage. Food and lodging will be covered by the tithe, providing the Rules Committee agrees." Ralph paused and squinted towards the back of the auditorium. "It looks like our volunteers have arrived with the hot drinks, so enjoy the cookies, socialize, and please be patient if you text me this evening and I don't get back right away."

"That was interesting," Agnes said to June as they took advantage of their seats at the rear of the auditorium to be among the first to reach the snack tables. "Oh, dear. Is it wrong for a woman my age to crave a chocolate chip oatmeal cookie with raisins?"

"Where are they?" June demanded. "I'll grab a couple for my granddaughter."

"I was complaining about their absence from the selection, not about my lack of willpower. It looks like the usual cookies from tins. Why doesn't Bits Bakery make any good cookies?"

"I'm happy to get the bread," June said, pouring herself a coffee despite the hour. "And the workers there do bake cookies and pastry, but only for themselves. Don't you remember what it was like when all of our bread came frozen from Earth?"

"I try not to dwell on the past."

The two women returned to their seats with the nosh and the club president turned into their row on his way to the refreshments.

"Hello, Ralph," Agnes said.

"Agnes, June," the Rules Committee member greeted them. "I wondered if I could have a moment of your time."

"Which one of us?" June asked.

"Both of you," Ralph replied. "I'm hoping that between the years Agnes served on the Rules Committee as a regular member and your thirty years as the treasurer you'll be able to steer me in the right direction for accessing money from the tithe."

"It's not like guaranteed pension income," June explained. "The tithe supports people living here on Bits. Our members who retired to Earth or moved to Flower left with their personal savings and we no longer support them. I doubt Rayne could make ends meet for those of us remaining on Bits if we were paying for retirees who left."

"But I thought that the software royalties, whether from games or the operating systems, were divvied up among the individuals who did the work."

"They are, after deductions for Bits Away support and the tithe," June explained. "For most people who haven't been working recently, it comes to a couple hundred creds a month at best. But those who stay on Bits have their basic expenses all covered by the tithe."

"We had a discussion about this in my time when a group of developers from one of the high-earning games decided to leave Bits," Agnes told him. "They asked for a lump sum to make up for the fact that they would no longer be receiving benefits from the tithe, while the tithe would still be getting the first cut of the royalties their prior efforts were still bringing in."

"Did you pay it?" Ralph asked.

"Of course not."

"But if our lease isn't renewed and we have to leave the planet, it will be a different circumstance," June pointed out. "I prepared a liquidation plan years ago, just as an intellectual exercise. I'll have to dig it out and see if it makes sense."

Fourteen

"How much of this equipment is yours?" the alien asked, his stylus poised over the tab he had just used to take pictures of the workshop.

"Take your mask off and I'll tell you," Mouser replied irritably. "If I had known why you were here, I would have denied you permission to land."

"You couldn't have stopped us. And not cooperating with a duly appointed representative of the planet's owner is a direct violation of the lease terms."

"Show me."

The alien used his stylus to rapidly navigate a number of screens on his tab and displayed the resulting page to Mouser. "Paragraph 962, subsection 004, part G."

"I don't remember any of this," Mouser said. "I was at the signing and it was a single piece of parchment."

"It's a planetary lease, not a spaceship rental," the alien said, and the exasperation came through in the translation. "The parchment was just a presentation piece. Are you going to cooperate or not?"

"This equipment was all purchased or built by your humble servant. What are you really doing here?"

"We're surveying the physical plant with an eye to re-starting the terraforming process, not that it's any of your business."

"I'm the chairman of the Rules Committee and that makes everything that happens on Bits my business," Mouser said, cracking open a can of ginger ale and putting his feet up on the table. "Want one?"

"Are you insane?" the alien demanded. "Do you think I want to poison myself with carbon dioxide and sugar substitutes?"

"Suit yourself. If you don't mind, I have work to do."

"Anything I can help with?"

"What?" Mouser stared at the interloper in disbelief. "You come in here to measure my workshop like you've already got a new tenant lined up and now you want to help? Don't let the door hit you on the way out."

"I'm serious. I've been all through the domes in the last week and I can offer an outsider's view of this game franchise you're developing."

"We're all set for criticism, thank you," Mouser replied, hoping that the alien's translation implant would pick up the sarcasm.

"You don't trust me, do you?"

"You've given me no reason to trust you. Take off the mask."

"I'm all finished here, I was saving your workshop for last," the alien said, placing his tab in a large belt pouch and sealing the magnetic strip. "But I like you Humans, so I'll give you one on the house. Don't trust that clone who hangs around watching everybody work."

"Belle? She's a journalist for Gem Today and she came highly recommended."

"By Lume?" the alien inquired and successfully read Mouser's expression. "I thought as much."

"Wait. What are you really doing here?" Mouser demanded, but the alien didn't even glance back as he headed out the door. "Alex. Ping Hercules and Delphi for me and ask them to come by. And bring up that survey ship on the screen."

"Hercules is on the way, Delphi will be a couple of minutes," the smart speaker replied after a brief delay.

"Capture an image of that ship at our highest resolution. Fit it to the frame."

The image on the large display expanded, and then the Horten who had just left the workshop seemed to freeze on the ramp as the high-resolution scan was in progress. When the image returned to life a few seconds later, the hatch which served as the entry ramp was rising into place.

"Can you get a reverse image from the camera on the maintenance dome? Capture any registration numbers on the ship."

The image shifted to pure black.

"Swap back. The camera isn't working."

A moment later, the Horten ship lifted off without raising a cloud of dust. Mouser shook his head and said to himself, "I get the feeling we've been had."

Hercules entered the workshop, glanced at the video of the tarmac, and asked, "What's up? I was on my way here when your virtual assistant texted me."

"Did any of the teams you visited this week mention those Hortens coming by?"

"It was the first thing most of them brought up. In a couple of cases, the Hortens asked the people to leave the office so they could use a high-intensity laser measuring rig. Somebody on Maxine's team couldn't find her tab afterward but they didn't want to accuse the aliens of stealing it without proof."

"How about questions?" Mouser asked. "Did they try talking to our people about the game?"

"A few developers mentioned that, but in a positive way," Hercules said. "Like an artist working on the magical barriers scenario caught a Horten looking over her shoulder, but he praised her work and compared it to a classic game she'd never heard of. Apparently he offered some useful suggestions."

"Meaning he drew her out about details."

Hercules shrugged. "If they were doing industrial espionage on the side there's not enough time left for anybody to act on it before our release date. Besides, they were sent by the owner of the planet. We couldn't ban them from surveying the domes."

"Rayne checked their credentials but they could have been forgeries," Mouser said. "Without a Stryxnet connection there was no way to find out."

"We could send the landlord a message on the next ship that stops here."

"And by the time we hear back the same way, months will have passed and the point will be moot. Hello, Delphi."

"Why the text?" the girl asked, stopping by the refrigerator to grab a soda. "We were all meeting here for a lunch session in any case."

"I forgot, and I guess on some level, I was trying to get an answer before the Horten ship lifted off." Mouser shook his head and snorted. "Now that I think about it, I was just being foolish. Even if we caught them red-handed, it's not like we could have done anything other than ask them to leave."

"Is this about the missing tab? Maxine texted me that it showed up this morning, but they had to reinstall from scratch because the software was corrupted."

"Mouser thinks that the surveyors may have had a side gig spying on our game development," Hercules told the girl.

"Oh, Belle warned us about that," Delphi said. "I thought she was just being paranoid for the sake of her documentary. She said that any aliens who showed up on Bits before the release shouldn't be trusted."

Mouser shrugged. "As I said, we aren't in a position to do anything about aliens coming around and snooping other than keeping our mouths shut. But if they were monitoring our network traffic while they were here we may have a problem."

"It's all encrypted."

"I'm not sure that the Hortens would find our encryption that challenging."

"Really, it doesn't matter," Delphi said with a grin as she settled onto the couch. "Belle has been spreading the word about being careful for months. I'll bet for every person who was sweet-talked into leaking some details there's another who had a blast making stuff up. Now that I think of it, maybe we should have a plan in place to provide disinformation the next time we're in a position like this."

"That could work," Hercules said. "The best defense is a good offense."

"Spoken like a true barbarian."

The door slid open and Shadow entered carrying two boxes of vending machine pizza. "I got a promotion this week so it's on me," he said proudly.

"Title promotion or a raise?" Delphi asked.

"Both. I'm the lead troubleshooter now and my slice of the royalties got bumped by forty percent."

"You're making more than me!"

"Is he?" Mouser asked. "I never really thought about what I'm paying you and Hercules to be my eyes and ears."

"Rayne is giving us what we earned on our last jobs," Delphi said. "It's okay, though, at least for me. I still make more from my ring and text tones."

"And I'm doing well with the side work I picked up scaffolding for the game," Hercules said. "It looks like I'm going to do a bit of acting as well." He looked almost embarrassed by this admission.

"It's about time you got paid something for all the iron you've pumped in the gym," Shadow said. "Muscles may not count for much in hacking but they rule in video games."

"Pizza!" a young voice piped up as Rayne and Sarah entered. "I thought I smelled it in the corridor."

"Mouser's corridor always smells like pizza," Rayne said as her daughter made a beeline for the coffee table where Shadow had deposited the boxes. "Who do I owe?"

"Shadow got a promotion and a raise," Delphi told her. "Wait for it to cool, Sarah."

"I just want to see the thermometer work," the girl said. She added accusingly, "We never get pizza at home."

"So, did everybody get a chance to work through the new scenario I wrote up?" Mouser asked.

"I liked it," Sarah said earnestly. "Everything except for the dice. Why can't my spells just work every time?"

"Because that would make you overpowered and then the game would be boring," her mother told her.

"Not for me. I promise."

"Without a random element, it would be more like co-operative storytelling than a game," Mouser explained.

"I *like* storytelling," Sarah informed him. "Creative writing is my favorite group."

"I like storytelling too. But if there isn't something for everybody you'll be left talking to yourself."

"I get the magical barriers and everything, but I don't quite see how my character is supposed to fit in," Shadow said. "Sarah, Herc, and Rayne are playing a family of traders, and Delphi is their guide between all of these little islands of humanity, but I seem to be something between a real player and an NPC."

"You're an artificial person," Mouser explained. "An alien artificial intelligence passing as human. Didn't I include that?"

"Shadow only skims when he's reading anything other than code," Delphi said. "What I don't understand is how my character can play a guide when it's my first time in the game. Don't I need to know where we're going?"

"You have a strong affinity for pathfinding. You'll need to roll every time you make a choice, but your basic level is so high that at worst you'll pick a less direct path."

"It's ready!" Sarah cried, opening the box in front of her. "Yuck, it's got meat."

"The other one is vegetarian," Shadow told her. He sat on his heels and slid a couple of slices from the open box onto one of the plates Rayne had brought over and then moved back to perch on the edge of a crate of visors. "I'm ready."

"Welcome to *A Mazing Earth,*" Mouser said, motioning at the same time for Hercules to hand him a plate with a slice of the combination pizza. "After choosing the left-hand portal into the twenty-first century, you find yourselves in possession of a horseless wagon powered by a flywheel charged by magic. Sarah and Hercules, the two of you are in the back of the wagon working on a crafting project. Rayne and Delphi, you're—"

"What's the project I'm working on?" Sarah interrupted.

"You choose."

"A doll."

"You're crafting a doll. Rayne and Delphi are sitting on the front bench of the wagon and Rayne is steering it with the tiller. Shadow is jogging alongside, which is about the top speed for the wagon while loaded. You see a river ahead of you and—"

"What kind of wagon is it?" Delphi asked. "Like one of those Wild West things that floated?"

"The wagon is designed for both land and water travel, but you have to manually engage the propeller with a lever in the back," Mouser said. He looked regretfully at the slice of pizza cooling on his plate and continued. "The river marks the boundary between the somewhat industrialized area you have just traveled through and an academic enclave that draws scholars from as far away as the Atlantic seaboard. There are no other people in sight on either side of the river, though both sides are farmland planted with young winter wheat. What do you do?"

"Are we on this road for a purpose, or is it just that we've seen what there is to see in the industrialized area that we're leaving?" Rayne asked. "I mean, it sounds like you have us going to the academic enclave for a reason and it would be good to know upfront."

Mouser shook his head while chewing and held up a finger for a pause. "You can turn and go back if you want. It's just a starting point."

"But we're traders, right? Are we already loaded with trade goods?"

"I look behind me in the wagon," Delphi said.

"You cast your eyes over the recently purchased load of heavy cutlery and hope that the wagon won't sink when it enters the river," Mouser told her. "Hercules notices you looking back and gives the hand sign for stopping."

"Why didn't I have to roll for perception or something?"

"You helped pack the wagon. You know what's in it."

"So I've been traveling with my clients for more than a day?"

"You've been working together for months," Mouser said, holding his slice in one hand and keeping his notebook flat with the other. "It's common for guides to attach themselves to traders, even to the extent of paying for part of the trade goods."

"Do you want to take a break and eat?" Delphi asked.

"No time. But I think Hercules called a stop to have a little conversation with you."

"I disengage the flywheel thingy and stop the wagon," Rayne said.

Hercules stood. "I climb out the back, help Sarah down—"

"I don't want to get out," the girl said. "I'm working on my doll."

"I pass my daughter a threaded needle and suggest that she sew the eyes on her doll while we're stopped. I'll inspect the canvas top of the wagon as I walk to the front."

"Nothing is out of order," Mouser said. "It's a standard trader's wagon in good repair."

"I'll stop and jog back a few steps to join the others," Shadow said, and then in the new voice he'd been practicing, asked, "Why are we stopping."

"I called the halt," Hercules said. "I need to be outside of a barrier isle to employ my Trader's Sense skill on a new domain, right?"

"Right," Mouser replied. "And it's a cantrip."

"What's a cantrip?" Sarah piped up.

"Technically, you're still in the back of the wagon and you can't hear this conversation," the gamemaster told her.

"I climbed over all the stuff after Hercules left and I brought my doll with me."

"I'll allow that. A cantrip is a spell that you've used so much that you don't have to prepare to cast it and it doesn't take up a slot."

"You mean, I can have as many cantrips as I want and just do magic all of the time?" Sarah asked.

"You have to earn them," her mother said. "Children usually don't have cantrips unless it's for something they do every day, like cleaning their room."

"Roll for insight," Mouser told Hercules, stretching for another slice of pizza.

"I thought insight was to check for lying," Delphi said.

"Trader's Sense is a second sight thing, so he's basically checking to see if somebody has ensorcelled an area to mislead him."

"Eleven?" Hercules reported tentatively, looking up from the dice and adding his modifier.

"Eleven," Mouser repeated, a sort of half-smile on his face. "You sense many trading opportunities in the academic enclave, but there's a slight fuzziness about the feeling, as if that's not the whole story."

"There better not be zombies," Delphi said.

"More importantly, is there a magical barrier in the river?" Rayne asked. "Are we going to be drifting downstream in our heavily laden horseless wagon trying to find an opening?"

"Let me check something." Delphi flipped through a few screens of text on her smartphone before looking up again. "I have to meditate for twenty minutes to see barriers so you guys may as well break for a meal or something."

"How long do we have to rest to top off our mana?" Rayne asked.

"It's not D&D," Delphi reminded her. "You get your daily recharge every morning at dawn, plus whatever is left in your reserve capacity."

"She's right," Mouser said. "Resting only affects your fatigue level. As you've all been riding in a wagon on a good road, you haven't been expending much energy."

"How about me?" Shadow asked.

"As an artificial person, you don't have a fatigue level. Your fuel cell is good for weeks without a charge, and you can generate energy with your microturbine by drinking sufficiently strong alcohol."

"That works for me."

"You don't get drunk," Mouser added.

"So let's say Delphi has been meditating for twenty minutes," Hercules said. "What does she see?"

"It's only been three minutes," Sarah pointed out.

"Do you really want to sit here for another seventeen minutes doing nothing?" her mother asked.

"I don't want to cheat," the girl said and looked at the gamemaster.

"It's not cheating," Mouser assured her. He set down a crust and turned to Delphi. "You open your eyes and a maze of glowing barriers is superimposed over the landscape. You see an opening right where the road ends in the river but it leads to a dead end. Downstream appears to be a continuous barrier, but to the north you see a crossing that leads into a small maze with an obvious exit."

"We need to leave the road and follow the river upstream," Delphi said. "I know where we can cross, though there's a bit of trickery on the other side."

"I'd rather run a maze on land than in the water," Hercules said. "Let's get started so we don't get stuck doing this in the dark."

"If we can't walk through the barriers, does that mean they're solid?" Sarah asked.

"They feel solid to you," Mouser said.

"And if they feel solid, can't anybody get through by keeping a hand on the wall and just turning left every time there's an opening?"

"Who taught you the secret for navigating mazes?" Shadow asked, obviously impressed. "I only figured that out like two years ago."

"I just wonder what's so special about magical barriers if anybody can get past them," Sarah said.

"As soon as you enter, the maze keepers who erected the barriers will know, and if they don't want to let you in, they can seal you off," Mouser said. "It's easy enough for them to sense how many of you there are in the maze and whether you're armed for war."

"All right," Rayne said. 'Get back on board, Hercules, or do you want to drive for the river crossing? You always did the best with our Phoenician round ship."

"I'm fine driving," he said. "How many people can fit on the front bench?"

"It's a wide wagon. I'll allow four adults, or three with two children," Mouser said.

"I'm staying with Dad," Sarah announced. "He helped me with my doll." She showed the imaginary doll to Hercules and asked, "Did I get the eyes crooked?"

"They look fine, Pumpkin," Hercules said, a slight catch in his voice. "You have to stay to show me the path, Delphi."

"I'll keep jogging alongside so there's room for all of you," Shadow volunteered.

By the time the lunch hour reached an end, the wagon had safely reached the other side of the river and navigated the maze. Shadow, Rayne, and Sarah all had to return to the real world, so they called it a day.

"Are you really learning something from this, or are we just playing for real?" Delphi asked Mouser after everybody else other than Hercules left.

"I learned exactly what I wanted today, and my explanation went over without a glitch," Mouser said. He rose and went over to where he kept his outside gear. "Feel up to a little walk across the tarmac carrying a ladder, Herc?"

"Sure, but what's the mystery about Delphi's question?" Hercules asked, following Mouser to where the supplemental oxygen masks were hanging next to the door.

"I usually wouldn't tell you because it may change how you react in the future but this was sort of a one-off. It was Sarah's question about the magical barriers. I was hoping somebody would bring it up."

"You didn't feed that to her?" Delphi asked.

"No, she's just a really curious little girl," Mouser said. "Rayne could rent her out to game devs to troubleshoot magical system construction." He returned to his chair with an oxygen mask and his boots and shook off his sandals. "Could you review the latest 3D renderings while Herc and I are outside, Deli? That stuff makes me dizzy even if I'm sitting, and the description included chase scenes, which are the worst."

"Sure, I love chase scenes," Delphi said happily. "Are they from the *Time Wars* mashup with alien criminals fleeing to twenty-first-century Earth to escape justice?"

"They do seem to be the ones generating all of the chase scenes." Mouser got both of his boots on and saw that Hercules had already left and was probably waiting in the airlock. "If we aren't back in an hour, call the marines."

"What marines?"

"Good point. Just ping Rayne. Everybody is afraid of the treasurer."

Halfway across the tarmac, Mouser realized they had forgotten to bring a ladder, but Hercules reminded him that there were ladders in the maintenance dome. When they got close enough to the structure to see through the foggy lenses of their oxygen masks, Mouser saw that a step ladder was already in place right below the camera that provided the reverse angle of the target area for landings.

"I bet you somebody unplugged the data feed from the camera," Hercules said as they reached the dome.

"It's all wireless. I just hope it's been turned off and not broken."

"You couldn't fix it?"

"The cameras are all Horten tech, it may as well be magic. I don't think there are any spares in storage. It's never come up, so we'd have to scavenge one of the others that nobody monitors."

"I didn't realize there were so many outside cameras," Hercules said.

"You know aliens," Mouser said, watching the big man climb the ladder. "The more hardware, the better. Helps keep their economies churning along."

"We're in luck," Hercules called from the top of the ladder. He fiddled with the front of the camera and then seemed to be trying to shake something off of one hand.

"Be careful, you're on a ladder."

Hercules nodded and climbed down. Then he extended his arm for Mouser to see. "Some kind of black tape on the lens," he said. "Really sticky. It started out stuck to my left hand and ended up on the right when I tried to remove it."

Mouser pulled off the offending tape and then found himself transferring it from one hand to the other. "Is this stuff two-sided? I can't seem to find a part that's not sticky."

"Move it to your boot and worry about it when you're inside," Hercules advised. "I'm going to put the ladder away."

When the men were back in the workshop, Mouser pulled on a disposable glove, got the tape transferred to it, and then carefully turned the glove inside out while removing it to effectively capture the tape.

"That looked elaborate," Delphi commented from the couch. "And the 3D chase scene was great. But I have to stop and see them before our first afternoon appointment."

"Did you spot some anachronisms?" Hercules asked.

"Yeah. I double-checked against the archived version of Wikipedia while you were outside fooling around and nobody was using muzzleloaders by that time. I think an artist just fell in love with the visuals and couldn't leave them out."

Fifteen

Rayne spotted the Gem Today journalist at a table for two in the main cafeteria and went to join her. The clone was sipping from a mug of hot chocolate, and there was a second mug on the table with a saucer placed over it, presumably to keep it hot.

"Sorry I'm late," Rayne said as she took her seat. "I have the numbers you asked about on my tab. You can look at them, but I can't send you a copy. I'm sure you understand."

"This is for you," Belle said, removing the saucer from the second mug and pushing it across the table.

"Is that hot chocolate? I'm sorry, but I really shouldn't."

The Gem's head jerked back in surprise and she stared at the treasurer. "Shouldn't? Why not?"

"It's a calories thing. I'm watching my weight."

"I would run around the dome a hundred times if my choice was to meet some arbitrary weight goal or drink another hot chocolate," the clone said. "Suit yourself, more for me."

"You should know that I'm not entirely comfortable showing you this data, but Mouser told me to go ahead," Rayne said. "The bottom line is that we've spent almost ten million creds so far, with a full-time payroll that's grown to over two thousand programmers, artists, writers—"

"That comes to barely over a thousand creds per employee per month, less if you're using the same pool of funds to pay all of the subcontractors."

"We are. But Bits has always run on a royalties-based model, with workers on projects earning a future stream of payments and the tithe covering everyone's basic expenses. We've never had so much cash sloshing around."

Belle finished her hot chocolate, took the saucer off the second mug, and smiled in satisfaction at the wisps of steam that escaped. "Let me see if I understand what you're saying. The experienced game developers of Bits are working for a fraction of the going rate on the tunnel network because they're expecting future royalties that they won't receive in this case?"

"I didn't say that," Rayne hastened to tell her. "We're hoping that our client will agree to something like our standard terms going forward. For this game franchise to be a success, it's going to require a tremendous amount of ongoing work. I'm sure you've heard the rumors about Bits being on the brink of bankruptcy when this opportunity came along for us, and my first priority was to keep our heads above water."

"What water?" Belle asked, and then a stone on the bracelet she was wearing began to glow and her eyes seemed to defocus as she consulted a heads-up display. "A pirate vessel is landing. And I realize now that you were using drowning as an analogy, not referring to a present threat. May I?"

Rayne locked her tab into the view-only mode for the current spreadsheet and passed it across the table. The Gem skimmed through the pages faster than was humanly possible, nodding and occasionally clicking her tongue.

"I'll be back in a minute," the treasurer said, rising to get herself a cup of coffee. By the time she returned, the clone had set down the tab and was sipping from the second mug of hot chocolate.

"Skid plates," Belle said. "A creative use of development money, but I imagine you have a good story if your client asks."

"I thought I hid them better than that," Rayne muttered. "I must be getting out of practice."

"If anything, you aren't skimming enough, but I won't say any more on that subject. Why do you pay yourself so little?"

"It's my salary as the Rules Committee treasurer. I wasn't sure about taking it out of the game money since it's already in the Bits budget, but my mother told me I was being foolish."

"Your mother is your ethical advisor? Perhaps that's why we Gem have run into issues on that ground since overthrowing the old order."

"I don't follow," Rayne said.

"Clones, no mothers," Belle said, pointing at her own chest. "We have elder sisters, of course, but when I was brought up, we were still being discouraged from forming close personal relationships."

"I can't even imagine. My daughter is the best thing that ever happened to me."

"Then why didn't you have more? My understanding is that they're free."

"You've lost me again," Rayne said. "I mean, it doesn't cost anything to get pregnant if you can do it the natural way, but you wouldn't believe how many imported cookies a little girl can eat."

"If they're chocolate chip, I can imagine, but you're missing the point," Belle said. "Cloning is, in its essence, a manufacturing process. We knew the cost of creation per Gem down to the fraction of the cred, though swapping over to the rediscovered genetic lines has introduced some additional upfront costs."

"That's—depressing. Are you planning to reintroduce natural reproduction once you have a population of mature males?"

"Do males ever mature? I hadn't noticed, but some of them are old enough to have successfully bred. I've seen holograms of the babies and it's a bit of a shock."

"Because there are males as well as females?" Rayne asked.

"For thousands of years all Gem babies have been identical," Belle said. "Anything else would have indicated a manufacturing error. But the natural process introduces random factors such that the same male impregnating a dozen of my sisters produces babies that aren't identical to each other, much less their mothers. It's all very strange."

"Well, I don't know anything about your culture—"

"Neither do we anymore," the clone interjected.

"—but I would recommend trying motherhood at least once," Rayne completed her sentence.

"Which brings us back to my original question. Why stop at one? It's clear that Bits is underpopulated."

"I separated from my husband and it didn't seem like a good idea to have another child with him."

"Were there no other males available?" Belle asked.

Rayne sighed. "Let's talk about something else, all right? No, I'm not angry," she said, guessing at the meaning of the Gem's sudden change of posture. "I don't know the answers myself and I'd rather not dwell on the past.

We finally divorced before my ex-husband joined Flower a few years ago and I haven't been seeing anybody since."

"How about Hercules?"

"He's just a friend."

"If I was a member of your species I think I'd be tempted," the clone said. "He appears to be very well made and he looks at you with more than friendship."

"Hercules and I have known each other for a long time and I'm sure you're misreading him," Rayne said. "You don't have any additional questions about the spreadsheet?"

"My curiosity was strictly for deep background," Belle told her. "The game is a very ambitious undertaking, and your expenses, while significant, are not high by galactic standards. What really—" she cut herself off and put a finger to her temple.

"Are you all right?"

"Implant," the clone mouthed.

Rayne took back her tab, unlocked it from the spreadsheet, and checked her messages. Mouser was requesting that she come to see him as soon as possible.

"Sorry," she typed. "I'm meeting with Belle right now. Is it an emergency?"

"Bring her," Mouser responded a few seconds later.

When Rayne looked up, she saw that the clone was chugging what remained of her hot chocolate.

"I have to meet with somebody who showed up with the pirates," Belle said.

"Mouser just asked me to bring you to see him. Maybe the person you need to meet is there."

The clone nodded her agreement and the two of them took the shortest path back to Mouser's workshop. When the pair arrived, they were greeted by the sight of a young woman wearing a virtual reality visor and dancing the tango with an invisible partner. She was so graceful that neither Rayne nor Belle had any desire to interrupt, but after another minute, the unheard music ended and the dancer removed the headset.

"That was great," the new arrival to Bits proclaimed. "The visor is almost as good as holograms and it will plug right into the old hardware I brought. Hello, Belle."

"Chance," the Gem acknowledged with a slight head bob. "This is Rayne. Rayne, Chance is an artificial person from Union Station who works with EarthCent."

"You didn't have to tell her that I'm an artificial person," Chance said. "It's fun to surprise them."

"You're too beautiful to be real," Rayne told her. "I thought you were an upper cast Vergallian."

Chance managed to look even more beautiful as a pre-programmed blush blossomed on her cheeks. "Why, thank you. Mouser said that I would like you and he was right."

"Where is Mouser?"

"Outside checking the cargo."

Rayne looked puzzled and turned to the Gem. "I thought you said they were pirates."

"Part of the point of being a pirate is not following any set rules," Belle explained. "They carry cargo if the price is right and the destination is convenient."

"But who would be sending—is the shipment from our financial backers?"

"Fresh fruit and Dollnick flat-pack boxes," Chance told her. "I'm on a mission from EarthCent's president and I started out in a borrowed Sharf two-man trader. But I needed to transfer to a jump-capable ship to get to Bits, so I rendezvoused with Flower when she stopped at Alfe, the Sharf recycling orbital that the Stryx gave a connection to take of all the scrap from the tunnel network space lanes. That's where I hooked up with the pirate ship to bum a ride."

"What happened to the two-man trader?" Rayne asked.

"Oh, I left it with Flower. The owner is her third officer."

"And before Mouser returns, you had a message for me?" Belle asked.

"Is infrared okay?" Chance asked.

"I've never used it, but my implant is IR rated," the clone replied.

Chance stared at Belle for several seconds and Rayne could have sworn she caught a glimpse of something flashing in the artificial person's left eye.

"How secure is that?" Rayne wondered out loud.

"Do you have an implant that does infrared?" Chance asked.

"I don't have any implants."

"Then it's super secure. Infrared is strictly line-of-sight and it's so low power that nobody could possibly read it from outside the room. Well, maybe the Stryx."

"So we're working together," Belle said after her implant decrypted the message.

"Until Flower comes and picks me up," Chance said. "My husband had to go to an interagency conference for six weeks and those things are such a drag that I volunteered for this gig."

"You're married?" Rayne couldn't help asking.

"My husband's name is Thomas, another artificial person if you were wondering. There aren't that many of us due to the Stryx insisting that creators of artificial intelligence on the tunnel network emancipate us. You could say that we're a bad investment."

"So you know Dewey?"

"We've met," Chance said. "He's thick as thieves with Flower, and while that doesn't mean we're on opposite sides, it doesn't exactly put us on the same side either."

"I thought Flower worked for EarthCent," Rayne said.

"Do you know the old Dollnick joke about what parking orbit a Class Three sentient colony ship takes?"

"Any parking orbit it wants," Belle filled in when the treasurer failed to make a guess.

"And now that she has her confidence back, that pretty much describes Flower," Chance said. "I trust her to do what she thinks is right, which may or may not coincide with what EarthCent wants. As Thomas is fond of saying, life is a messy compromise."

Rayne finally noticed that the large display was showing a live shot of the pirate vessel unloading its cargo. "Just how many containers of fruit did Flower send?"

"Seventy-four. My understanding is that you have approximately a hundred and fifty thousand residents on Bits, and you're getting about three kilos—I heard you're on the metric system here—per head. Throw in a million or so flat-pack boxes and the shipment was around six hundred tons."

"What do we need a million flat-pack boxes for?"

"It's better to have them and not want them than want them and not have them. They hardly take up any space when they're folded."

"Any chocolate?" Belle inquired.

"There's some gourmet coffee with rich chocolate undertones but I'm just quoting the ad copy," Chance admitted. "I'm more of a grain alcohol girl myself."

"I see you've all met," Mouser said as he entered his workshop with an apple in one hand. He hung his oxygen mask over the peg next to the door, reached in the pocket of his coveralls, and tossed Rayne a pear. "I believe our backers have begun a strong push to interest us in leaving Bits." He reached in his pocket again and handed Belle a peach. "Gem are good with Earth fruits, right?"

"Everybody is good with Earth fruits," the clone said. "It's going the opposite way you have to be careful about."

"I'm sorry, but I feel like I came in at the end of a conversation," Rayne said. "What's going on?"

"From what Chance told me, the blood is in the water and the sharks are circling," Mouser said, and then took a bite of his apple. "Oh, I'd forgotten what fresh fruit tasted like," he continued after chewing and swallowing. "It seems the word is out that we're leaving Bits and Chance is here to make a recruiting pitch for Earth. They're trying to rebuild the industries that vanished in the face of competition from superior alien products and the loss of talent to tunnel network employers."

"And Flower is trying to bribe us to return to Earth with fresh fruit?"

"Flower is competing with Earth as a destination," Chance said. "Her price for arranging my transport and pickup from Bits was equal time."

"Is Dewey here to represent her?" Rayne asked.

"I'm going to represent both parties," the artificial person said. "I have excellent multitasking skills."

"Chance is going to speak at the beta testing event this weekend and will be available as a sort of ambassador of goodwill until Flower arrives," Mouser explained. "She's also an avid gamer and has volunteered to provide scaffolding for any twenty-first-century ballroom dancing scenes."

"It's my passion," Chance said.

Rayne took a bite of her pear and the juice ran down her forearm. "Are they supposed to be this messy?" she asked in dismay.

"It's ripe," Mouser said. "The Dollnick shipping containers are all date coded in order of when the fruit was harvested and I thought we better get started on the earliest batch."

"It was shipped all the way from Earth?"

"Flower grows way more produce than her population needs," Chance told them. "She started a fruitcake business just to use up the surplus because soaking everything in alcohol extends the shelf life. The brand is Harry's Fruit Cakes, and they're the only solid food that I don't mind eating."

Rayne retrieved a workshop towel from the dispenser and wrapped it around her wrist before taking another bite. "I could get used to these," she admitted. "But now I don't understand why the two of you are working together. Does Flower have an arrangement with the New Gem Empire?"

"EarthCent does," Belle told her. "Your Ambassador McAllister guided us onto the path to freedom and we consider Humans to be our closest allies on the tunnel network. We were something of a pariah before our revolution, as all of the other species disapprove of cloning."

"But I thought you were a journalist for Gem Today."

"I am, a freelancer, but I also work for Gem Intelligence."

"Did you know that?" Rayne asked Chance.

"Considering that I've been working for EarthCent Intelligence my entire professional life, I better," the artificial person said. "For what it's worth, Flower works with us as well through a sort of arms-length arrangement."

"That's the best news I've had in a month," Mouser said. "I've been worried that one of the weakest points in *A Mazing Earth* is the storyline about undercover intelligence agents from the tunnel network tracking down alien criminals hiding on twenty-first-century Earth. Nobody here has ever worked for an intelligence agency so it's all based on what they get from reading, watching immersives, and playing other games."

"I'd be happy to help," Chance said. "Thomas and I spend more time training new agents than in the field, but I've been to enough conferences to have an idea of how the other species operate."

"That would be huge. We'd welcome your help as well, Belle, if it wouldn't be a conflict of interest."

"You mean with my journalism?" the clone asked. "I don't see any issues and I'd enjoy contributing. If anything, it would help with my reporting to participate in the process."

"And I have a special request to the chairman of the Rules Committee from the president of EarthCent," Chance said. "Stephen recorded a short video in the hopes you have a public address system we can play it over."

"If you don't mind showing it to me first," Mouser said. "I don't want to give you override access and find that the president is calling upon the people of Bits to rise up and kill the Rules Committee members."

"Do I have your permission to interface with that display?" The artificial person pointed at the large screen that was still showing the pirates unloading cargo containers onto the tarmac.

"What's the video recorded on? Do you have a memory stick?"

"I'm the camera and the memory stick, and I can access the display by wireless," Chance said. The video of the tarmac was replaced by a test pattern, and then the president appeared sitting on the edge of his desk.

"You don't know me, but my name is Stephen Beyer, and I've been the Stryx-appointed president of EarthCent for the last couple of decades. Those of you who haven't been to Earth during that time won't believe all of the changes and new opportunities. I've authorized Chance to conduct preliminary negotiations for any large groups interested in repatriation, and we're willing to match any offers you get from other parties, within reason. Thanks for listening."

"That was short and sweet," Rayne said. "Do you think he was referring to Flower with that 'other parties' comment?"

"There could be more," Chance said. "While twenty-first-century programming skills aren't in demand anywhere outside of Earth and Bits, Flower has already proven that your technical people can be quickly retrained to work in anime production and other computer-related fields. If a Horten or a Drazen game developer could scoop up the lot of you, I'm sure any loss of efficiency would be made up for by the fact you work so cheap and don't live a long time."

"What does longevity have to do with it?" Mouser asked. "I would have thought that employees aging out quickly would be a negative."

"Imagine paying defined pension benefits for hundreds of years."

Rayne looked a little sick at the thought. "That never occurred to me. On average, humans last around fifteen years after retirement, and even then, our pension schemes are chronically underfunded. My mother has a pre-opening book about pension fund architecture that gave me nightmares."

"So if it's alright to broadcast the president's message, just tell me when and where," Chance said. "And if you could fill me in on when you're all planning on vacating Bits, it would help me prepare my sales pitch."

"But we aren't planning to leave Bits at all," Mouser said. "It's a rumor that took off when a Horten survey ship came and started measuring everything in sight."

"Well, that's not entirely true," Rayne said. "My mother goes to those Seniors Club meetings and she said they've broken into four armed camps."

"They've become Dollnickphiles?" Belle asked. "I've heard of that happening, but I thought it was only where your people are living on Dollnick worlds."

"Armed camp is an expression for groups of people ready to go to war with each other," Chance explained. "What are the four options?"

"Status quo, meaning, remain on Bits," Rayne ticked off an invisible list. "Emigrate to Flower and join the independent living deck. Return to Earth to retire. Move somewhere else on the tunnel network, even a Stryx station."

"I didn't realize it had gotten so bad," Mouser said. "Is everybody that concerned about our work drying up?"

"I'm not sure that has anything to do with it, other than serving as a trigger. I think there are a lot of people on Bits, more than half, who figure we had a good run and it's time to move on to something else. Even my daughter knows that we can't freeze technology in time forever. I also think that working on this game with all of the twenty-first-century imagery and data is making some people homesick."

"I wouldn't put it past Flower to have planned it that way," Chance said. "It's what I would have done."

"You know that Flower is our backer?"

"Of course. I would have spotted that by now even if Dewey and Lume hadn't briefed me."

"Are you saying Dewey is an EarthCent intelligence agent now too?" Mouser asked.

"No," the artificial person said. "I tried to recruit him but somebody else had gotten there first and second and I'm not authorized for thirds."

"This is getting to be too much for me to take in at one sitting," Rayne said. "You mentioned something about hardware to go with the virtual reality visor when we came in. I hope EarthCent warned you that our whole rationale for living on Bits is to preserve the computing culture of twenty-first-century Earth. If it's alien hardware, you won't find any takers."

"Really?" Chance asked with a non-infrared twinkle in her eye. "I heard that the whole place runs on an obsolete Frunge factory controller so I assumed second-hand alien hardware is okay."

"You're talking about the big silver cube wrapped in clear plastic sitting on a pallet?" Mouser asked. "I thought it might be an ultra-cold unit for some perishables that Flower wanted to show off."

"It is a gift from Flower, but it's not a freezer," the artificial person told him with a grin. "She recently upgraded the vector processors she uses to complement her native hardware for running LARPing studios. By a happy coincidence, the engineering school class project on her Open University campus was to build an immersive virtual reality environment using off-the-shelf components from three different species. Humanity's contribution was the headsets, but I never saw one before today."

"I've heard of being led by the nose or pushed from behind but this is getting ridiculous," Rayne said. "Does Flower really think she's going to convince us to follow the Traitors by plying us with fresh fruit and computer hardware?"

"It must be nice to be courted," Belle said wistfully. "Nobody has ever gone out of their way to get Gem to move in."

"We have," Mouser said. "We just aren't very good at it."

Sixteen

Delphi waited five minutes past the scheduled start of the beta testing session to give the kids, all in the twelve-to-fifteen age group, a chance to settle down. Then she raised a hand and nodded to Shadow's older sister, who got the attention of everybody in the room by executing a Drazen roundhouse kick that sounded painful when it impacted Delphi's palm.

"All right, settle down," Delphi told the kids. "Today was supposed to be our last youth beta-testing session for *A Mazing Earth*, but thanks to your hard work and serious gaming chops, we already finished the punch list. It's long been a tradition on Bits to reward team members for a job well done, which is why I texted you all to meet me here in the dojo rather than our usual lab."

"With the one-way mirror," a girl contributed.

"You mean there were people watching us when we were playing the game?" a fourteen-year-old boy asked in dismay. "I was cheating."

"That's all part of the beta-testing, and the use of a one-way mirror was specified in the small print," Delphi told them.

"So what's my bonus reward?" the boy asked and pointed at Lisa. "Is she going to beat me up for cheating?"

"The curtain, please," Delphi said dramatically. The hastily rigged wall of fabric behind her dropped, revealing

Shadow and Botan wearing virtual reality headsets and grasping controllers in their hands. Behind them was an enormous silver cube still on a pallet for easy moving. On top of the computer was a large screen display showing two warriors, one dressed in chainmail and carrying a heavy sword, the other in samurai armor wielding a bamboo blade.

"The knight is going to murder the little dude," one of the teenage boys said excitedly as the two fighters saluted each other.

"Go!" Lisa shouted.

Anybody capable of watching the fighters and the display at the same time would have noticed that their hand movements didn't exactly match what was happening on screen, but it wasn't enough to destroy the suspension of disbelief. Barely a minute passed before Botan found an opening in the chainmail and dealt his friend a mortal blow.

"There are headsets and controllers for all of you," Delphi spoke loudly over the clamor of kids all trying to claim the right to go next. "The system is set up to provide a limited Live Action Role Playing environment for up to sixty-four players, which happens to be just enough for everybody here. Because it works with wireless headsets and controllers instead of holograms, you can leave this room while we're playing, but the game boundaries are limited to the gym complex."

"Do we have teams?" a fifteen-year-old girl asked. "I want the cute guy with the bamboo sword."

"He's taken," Lisa informed her.

"We're going to run through a traditional LARPing scenario that's based on one of the professional league quests from last season," Delphi continued. "The first option when you power on the headset will be to choose your character. In addition to the basics, like an orc warrior or a half-elf ranger, you can pick a different tunnel network species for yourself."

"Do you mean I can be a Dollnick orc and have four arms?" a boy asked.

"Or a Vergallian elf dancer?" a girl added.

"Yes and yes," Delphi said. "The main difference between playing in a professional LARPing studio and the setup we have here is that there are no hologram-wrapped robots for non-player characters and we won't be using noodle weapons. And—" she said, raising her voice over the hubbub, "the fact that you can choose to fight each other means that there will be NO PUNCHING or dagger thrusts, anything that requires hand contact. The four of us will act as the referees and we'll disconnect anybody who gets too carried away."

"I need to check everybody's pupillary distance before we hand out visors," Lisa announced, brandishing what looked like a short plastic ruler with two slits and a notch in the middle for the nose. "There's a manual setting on the headsets to adjust for how far apart your eyes are, and I'm going to give you a number to tell Shadow, Delphi, or Botan. They'll help you get the headset on comfortably, and then we're going to spend a half-hour going through the basic calibration and demo mode before we turn you loose."

With Lisa doing all of the measuring and the referees helping the kids secure their headsets, it took about twenty minutes before everybody had the calibration and demonstration mode running. The four adults set the display to random shuffle and watched as the kids quickly chose and customized characters. There were a few minor incidents with swinging arms contacting neighbors, but on the whole, these accidents helped bring home the importance of maintaining a safe space between one another.

"Has everybody worked out the heads-up display chat?" Delphi asked, using her own hand controller to rapidly peck out the letters on a virtual keyboard. It took a minute before the replies began flowing in, and then the messages showed no sign of stopping. "All right. To save time choosing sides we're going with boys versus girls. You don't have to fight each other, the system will be generating plenty of monsters, but they don't have any physical existence, so don't try any kicks or you'll land on your butts."

"How about the audio?" somebody typed laboriously. "Can we talk to each other?"

"The headsets have a microphone pickup, but the teams are too large to use live audio unless you want to pick a faction leader and play it military style. We'll make an announcement as soon as it's enabled."

"Where's the mine complex?" another player asked.

"You're in the main antechamber, we just haven't started yet," Delphi typed back. "Just give us a minute to do a final safety check." She lifted off her visor to talk with the other referees. "Are you guys ready?"

"I went through the gym complex and chased out the people who ignored the fact we have the entire place reserved for another three hours," Lisa reported. "I locked the access doors from the inside, so barring somebody hacking their way in, we should be able to run around with the visors on and not have to worry about bumping into anybody who isn't part of the LARP."

"Shadow and I tested the collision avoidance system out in the corridor two minutes ago," Botan reported. "My visor showed him as an unknown object when he left his headset and controllers in here, so the software is continually comparing the low-resolution optical pickups to the physical map of the gym we built. Whoever did the programming knew what they were doing."

Delphi slipped her headset back on and used the controller to peck out, "Boys leave through the back exit, girls leave through the front. I want a clean game, and remember that we'll be watching." Then she felt a tap on her arm and removed the visor again.

"I've enabled the audio chat for just the four of us," Shadow said. "You can select the in-room option if you only want to talk to people within earshot. The referee map shows all of the players, but the maps the kids are using only show the players in their faction."

"Are we all going to referee everybody, or should we split into teams?" Botan asked.

"You and me will handle the boys, Shadow and Deli can have the girls," Lisa said. "Visors up. Let's get going."

"Can you hear me now?" Shadow asked after his virtual reality display showed his sister and friend had exited the dojo.

"Roger that," his sister replied. "And if you look at the map, you can see the four of us are marked in green rather than pink or blue."

Shadow switched the audio to in-room and turned to Delphi, who showed up as a halfling on his display. "Why did you go small?" he asked her.

"I'll bet I'm twice your size," she replied. "A goblin? Really?"

"I was trying to do two things at once and I clicked the wrong build," he admitted. "But then I thought it might be fun for a change."

"Your sister looked pretty cool with that tentacle. I wouldn't have thought of role-playing a Drazen playing a human."

"Yeah, she's had Drazens on the brain lately. Shouldn't we follow the girls?"

"I want to give them a little space to organize themselves. In five minutes they'll have a leader and two cliques, the bigger one for the girls who voted for the winner, and the smaller one for everybody else."

"I'll bet you the boys don't pick a raid leader unless my sister makes them," Shadow said. "Hey, I didn't have time to read through all of the history that came with the quest package because I was looking at the code. Could you fill me in on the high points?"

Delphi sighed. "We're in a mine abandoned by the dwarves after the gold vein played out. A dungeon core instantiated and it's been creating monsters ever since."

"That's it? No royal politics, no evil empires, no necromancers?"

"It's a beginner's dungeon. This is the first time any of us have ever tried role-playing with VR helmets. I'll be happy if nobody gets hurt or breaks any more equipment."

"You want to duel?" Shadow asked.

"What?"

"While we're waiting for the girls to work out their pecking order. I have my hunting sword and you have—what is that?"

"A rapier," Delphi said. "All right, but we can't get carried away because I want to go check on the girls in a few minutes."

"Look at your map," Shadow said. "They're all stopped in the corridor. Do you think they hit a locked door?"

"They're holding an election over the chat channel. I don't want to look because they're probably calling in favors and digging up old slights."

"All right. En garde!"

Shadow fared no better against Delphi than he had against Botan, mainly because the halfling enjoyed an appreciable advantage in reach over the goblin.

"This is weird," Delphi said, stepping back and sheathing her rapier. "My sword doesn't really go where my hand is sending it. I mean, it does, but not really."

"It's because of the in-character calibration we all went through," Shadow explained. "The software is matching our movements to the body of our chosen character while our controllers are wielded by the real us because we can't turn into other creatures. I bet in an hour or so it will all seem natural, and the kids may adjust even quicker than we do."

This assessment proved to be correct, and after an hour of exploring the upper level of the mine and killing all of the low-level monsters, the girls defeated the mini-boss and returned to the anteroom to teleport as a group to the next level.

"Are we ahead of the boys?" one of the girls typed out on the chat channel when she saw the referees.

"Shadow?" Delphi asked.

"One of the boys found a magic key in an urn that let them teleport to the next level before this one was cleaned out," Shadow replied, switching his vocal into the faction leader's channel so all of the girls could hear. "They did the same on the next level, so they're actually on the third now. They're taking a lot of damage and running out of healing potions if that's any consolation."

"Great," the girl who had been elected leader and was the only player in the faction with voice access replied. "They'll probably try to ambush us and steal ours."

"No boys on the second level, they can't hide from the referees on the map," Delphi assured her. "Are you ready to activate the teleportation circle?"

"Everybody get their toes inside the line," the leader ordered. "I'm going to count to ten and go, and I don't want to leave any body parts behind."

The physical layout of the second level was identical to the first, an obvious constraint of playing within a real space with walls and corridors, but the virtual reality overlay had changed. The passages were rougher, indicating that the dwarves hadn't had as much time to refine this level of the mine. There were boulders from rock falls that couldn't trip a player, but walking through them resulted in the loss of a hit point.

"Same drill as the first level," the leader ordered. "I want four teams, each supported by a healer and a spell caster with two tanks, an archer, and a rogue. Spread out, kill the remaining mobs, and we'll regroup here as soon as a new teleportation key shows up on my display."

Shadow felt a touch on his arm and removed his headset to find Delphi offering him half of an orange. "The girls can take care of themselves better than we can," she told him. "Cheryl, the leader, is the junior champion of that MMORPG with all the medieval mercenaries."

"Where did you get the orange?" he asked. "Did another ship from Flower come in?"

"I've been eating one a week. They keep pretty good in the fridge."

"My family blew through all of our fruit in three days," Shadow said ruefully. "I don't think we ate anything else."

"Fruit is really good," Delphi said. "I can't believe we grew up without any. I mean, it grows on trees, doesn't it? Why didn't our parents plant any?"

"Like a greenhouse?" Shadow shrugged. "My mom used to work in hydroponics for her day job. You wouldn't know it if you met her now because she's the hardcore gamer in the family, but she wasn't that into computers when she moved to Bits. They never planted fruit trees, but we used to grow more kinds of vegetables, not just the salad stuff we get now."

"What happened?"

"Not enough people cared to keep investing in agriculture. It was easier to just use the tithe money to order groceries from off-world like they do on mining habitats in asteroid belts and places like that. I don't get the economics, you'd have to ask Rayne for the details, but I guess it's just cheaper to grow food on a large scale somewhere with a space elevator and export it."

"That doesn't seem possible."

"Well, it has to do with the people too," Shadow said. "It's not like any gardening enthusiasts left Earth for Bits. When you consider that Bits Bakery was shut down for over a decade and people just ate frozen bread, it's pretty clear that food was never a priority with our grandparents."

"They kind of were fanatics," Delphi mused. "I didn't really think about it growing up, but our grandparents had to be a little nuts to come here. I mean, the domes are okay, but I went through all of the demos for the visor and one of them was an African safari. I never even imagined walking through grass like that and seeing all of the wildlife. The only animals we have on Bits are cats."

"Have you ever thought about, you know?"

"What?" the halfling asked, unconsciously taking a half-step back from the goblin.

"Leaving Bits," Shadow said. "I think everybody has guessed by now that *A Mazing Earth* is Flower's project and I know that most of the coders in my group are talking about moving like it's a foregone conclusion. Rayne was telling me that there's a limit to how low the population of Bits can fall before the costs for those who remain become unsustainable even if they get to keep all of the residuals coming in from old games."

"That sounds kind of like a critical mass—if there aren't enough people hanging around to sustain a chain reaction you don't have a community."

"Or it could just be about the cost of getting a cargo jump ship to bring supplies. I was listening to her talking about it with Mouser—did you know he'll be sixty-five in a few years?"

"He's pretty old," Delphi acknowledged.

"And Rayne was saying that if everybody above retirement age leaves for Earth or Flower there probably won't be enough people left to keep Bits going."

"But if they're retired, they aren't earning money."

"They're still eating, babysitting, playing games," Shadow said. "My mom said that it's the retirees working on a volunteer basis who keep the hydroponic tanks for the salad stuff going these days. They're the only ones with the time."

"I think," Delphi began, but Shadow never found out what she was going to say because the excited voice of the girl who had been elected faction head began barking orders over the raid channel.

"Surround it, but stay back. I don't want anybody getting crushed by that thing."

"Our arrows are just bouncing off!" one of the archers reported over the text chat.

"Magic dealers, spam it with all the fire you have," the leader instructed. "Don't bother with ice, trolls are resistant."

Shadow checked the map and saw all of the girls in a loose circle in the basketball court that had been repurposed in virtual reality as a giant cavern. "Let's go," he said and began running through the mine's passages to be on the scene.

"It must be the level mini-boss," Delphi's voice came from somewhere behind him. "It's not fair that the boys just island-hopped all the tough monsters."

"More fireballs, more fireballs. Tanks, keep it contained," the lead girl continued. "It may have a burst of regeneration when its hit points fall to—watch out!"

The goblin and the halfling burst into the cavern just as the troll, which had been down on one knee, suddenly seemed to catch fire and started throwing fireballs back at its tormentors.

"Hit it with the ice—now!"

"I thought trolls were resistant to ice," Shadow said to Delphi as the troll's flames were extinguished under the weight of the frost cast by four magic dealers and its hit points crashed to zero.

"Only until they do the morphing thing," Cheryl said, and the referees realized she was now part of their audio chat since they were all in the same room. "Helga, bring me the key when you loot the corpse. We have to catch up with the boys."

"They're still on the third level," Delphi told her after checking the referee's map. "They haven't moved in quite a while. Hold on a minute." She selected the broader referee's chat. "Lisa?"

"What's taking you guys so long?" Shadow's sister demanded. "We've been pinned down by orc archers for like a half an hour and the whole corridor is trapped."

"Our girls are actually cleaning out the dungeon, not jumping ahead. Is the leader of the boys proposing a truce?"

"They couldn't pick one with anything like a majority and the losers wouldn't go along. It's anarchy down here."

"Which is kind of ironic when you think about it," Botan added.

"Well, the girls just killed the mini-boss so we'll be down in a minute," Delphi said. "Anything to watch out for?"

"The traps are over the top. Those dwarves must have been worried about being attacked from behind while they worked because there are tricked-out crossbows all over the place and spears that come hurtling out of the walls. Half of the boys are hunkered down in a little fort they built from loose boulders because they don't have enough hit points left to stand another attack."

"You can move the virtual boulders?" Shadow asked. "That's pretty amazing."

"Yeah," Lisa said. "You have to hold your hand controllers near the bottom of a rock or whatever for three seconds, and then grab bars appear and you can try to pick it up. If it's too heavy for your build, the visor starts flashing red, and if you keep trying, you lose a hit point."

"Back to the teleportation circle," the leader of the girls ordered. "Same four teams when we get to the third level. The layout won't change so we'll keep the teams together and head directly for the throne room."

"Are we going to try to clean out the level?" one of the girls asked in the text chat.

"We're running out of time, and keeping the boys pinned down should distract the mobs," Cheryl replied on audio. "This is our chance to put this thing away."

As soon as the girls teleported into the third-level antechamber they could hear the sounds of distant combat drifting in from the direction of the basketball court cavern.

"Boys are so noisy," one of the girls posted to the text channel. "I think they're already in the throne room."

"Listen up," Cheryl said. "If the boys are already there, we're going to have to team up with them to kill the dungeon boss, but when it comes time to loot the corpse, I want you all to mark a boy and keep him from it."

"We're going to attack them?" a chat message asked.

"Not unless they attack us first, but we're not going to let them win after they cheated. Just keep them from the corpse until Helga can loot it for all of us. Rogues, be on the alert for traps."

Four girls headed out into the passage moving so stealthily that Shadow wouldn't have noticed them if he hadn't been a rogue himself. The high-pitched "twang" of crossbows releasing bolts and the clatter of projectiles hitting stone walls followed. A gnome with a bloody streak across her shoulder ducked back into the antechamber and motioned for the girls to follow in single file. They reached the throne room without incident, but it quickly became apparent that every remaining monster in the dungeon was between them and the throne, behind which the boys were all hunkered down.

"How did you get behind the throne?" Shadow couldn't help asking on the referee's channel.

"Secret passage," his sister replied. "Teenage boys are great at shortcuts."

"And the dungeon boss?"

"He only appears when you approach the throne from the front, probably to defend those treasure chests. Big honking rock troll, and when he reaches fifteen percent of his hit points, he regenerates and goes berserk. We got him down that far twice and then gave up."

"When you say *we*, does that mean you've been helping the boys?" Shadow asked.

"We might have gotten caught up in the action," Botan said after Lisa didn't answer. "The minions all came back to life as well."

While the girls scoped out the situation from outside the aggro radius of the orc archers who had the boys pinned down, Delphi started to sit down on a boulder in the passage, only remembering at the last moment that it was virtual.

"Watch this," she said to Shadow over the audio chat. "I'm going to try to lift it." Crouching on her heels, she held her hand controllers steady near the base of the large stone until handles appeared. Then she grabbed them and tried to lift. There was a loud click, and something shot out of an opening that suddenly appeared in the opposite wall.

The small, green goblin exploded into motion at the sound of the click and the spear transfixed his body. Delphi pulled off her visor and looked at Shadow lying on the floor, his hands clutching an invisible shaft where it had been protruding from the goblin's chest.

"Are you all right?" she asked.

"I think I hit my funny bone when I landed," he hissed between clenched teeth. "Did anybody else see?"

"I don't think so. We're behind all of the girls and they're looking the other way."

"Good," Shadow said. He rose to his knees, and then to his feet. "I forgot that as referees we have unlimited hit points. It wouldn't have killed you."

"But you took a virtual spear for me," Delphi said. "Why would—are you blushing?"

"Put your visor back on."

"But honestly. Do you like me? I never knew that you—"

"Hey, we're trying to kill a dungeon boss here and you're talking about your love life on the faction audio," the voice of the fifteen-year-old leader cut Delphi off. "You can get a room on your own time."

Seventeen

"It's getting down to the wire," Rayne said as she absent-mindedly plucked another potato chip off the coffee table where they'd spilled out of the bag. "Dewey will be back for the final review in two weeks."

Mouser looked up from the antique circuit board he was soldering. "And we finished ahead of schedule. The main coding is done, the music is recorded, and all of the basic scenery is rendered in 3D. The artists will continue working right up to the last minute, and the writers will never be happy, but that's the way it is with all games."

"Does your starting to take repairs again mean you figure everything will go back to normal?"

"I don't know what it means, I just like to keep busy. If I show up at home before supper my wife will assume I've been up to no good."

"Why doesn't Sophie ever come here?" Rayne asked.

"We keep our professional lives separate from our personal lives," Mouser said. "She's dedicated her last forty years to coming up with methodologies for creating certified bug-free code that I don't understand the first thing about."

"Come on. You're the smartest person I know on Bits."

Mouser snorted. "That says more about you than it does about me. Sophie really should have spent her career in academia. She and her colleagues in the concurrency group can spend hours discussing the value of a single variable that only has two possible states. I'm just glad I never signed up to write secure operating systems for smartphones."

The incoming-ship alarm on the workbench began to ring and Mouser silenced it with a slap.

"Aren't you going to find out who it is?" Rayne asked.

"The way things have been going around here the last six months, they've already landed, and they'll be two moves ahead of us in whatever game they're playing," Mouser said. He reluctantly reached over, keyed the microphone, and grunted, "What?"

"Porl speaking," a cultured voice with a heavy Horten accent issued from the antique radio cabinet. "I'm here to see Nir Barad."

Mouser's jaw literally dropped and he keyed the microphone again. "The Porl?"

"Just Porl," the Horten replied. "I believe Humans are the only species on the tunnel network who persist in using multiple names. Do I have permission to land?"

"Of course. It's your, I mean, your grandfather's planet."

Rayne sat bolt upright. "That Porl?" She grabbed a biodegradable trash bag from the box under the coffee table, scraped in the loose potato chips, and began scurrying around the workshop bagging everything that an alien might find offensive. "What are you doing sitting there?" she called to Mouser. "Help me. He'll probably evict us for living like pigs."

"My workshop isn't that bad," Mouser protested, but he went over to the recycling barrel in the corner that was surrounded by a field of crushed aluminum cans that had missed the mark and began tossing them in. "The dome is what it is. It's not like we can clean the whole place up in a few minutes, and I'm sure Porl got a detailed report from the surveyors his grandfather sent."

"That's it. They ratted us out."

"I know that the Hortens have a reputation for being neat freaks, but they aren't going to kick us off the planet for not tidying up our rooms. It's his being here to see Nir Barad that has me worried."

"Why?" Rayne asked. "Nir retired to Earth when Flower stopped to pick up the Traitors. It's not like we murdered him or something."

"Nir is the one who made the deal with Porl for the planet," Mouser reminded her. "How would you feel if you came hundreds of light years to see the old gaming buddy you fixed up with a planet only to find that he retired and went home?" He dunked the last soda can and looked up at the high-resolution display. "Alex. Show the landing area."

The screen lit up with the image of a Horten freighter, small enough to land on a planet, big enough to have its own jump drive. The main hatch was down and two ranks of sailors were standing respectfully at attention while a Horten wearing a cape exited and headed directly for the camera which was mounted over the dome's airlock.

"That must be Porl's son," Rayne said as she followed Mouser to meet the guest at the airlock. "He looks just like his father in that big portrait of the planetary lease signing ceremony hanging in the Rules Committee conference room."

"Have you forgotten how long the aliens all live?" Mouser chided her. "Porl was a young Horten when he met Nir at the gaming tournament and he'll still be a young Horten long after I've shuffled off my mortal coil."

"He wasn't wearing an environmental suit. I wonder if he's more used to us than most Hortens."

"I haven't been around enough of them to know."

The airlock cycled open and Porl stepped into the dome holding a gift-wrapped bottle in the crook of one arm. The cheery brown color of his face began to fade when he saw that Nir wasn't there to greet him. "Am I too late?" the Horten asked.

Mouser hesitated for a moment, then decided that the unvarnished truth was the safest bet. "Nir retired to Earth," he said. "I'm sure he'll be mortified to have missed you, but we'll send him a message with the next ship going that way."

"Ah, that's not so bad then," Porl said, and the brown returned to his cheeks. "I'm afraid that I've been so busy with the family business that I lost track of Human time. I've recently been engaged to marry, and when I told my fiancée about my experience with Nir, she reminded me of your limited lifespans and suggested I get in touch before the aid of a spiritualist is required. Perhaps we'll include Earth on our honeymoon tour."

"Please, come in," Rayne said, stepping aside when she realized that she and Mouser had been unconsciously blocking the corridor.

"May I ask who you are?"

"I'm Rayne, the Rules Committee treasurer, and he's Mouser, the chairman."

"So you're the one my grandfather is always complaining about," the Horten said, fixing his gaze on the treasurer. "We need to talk."

"I paid on time, and you can audit our books," Rayne protested. "The only—"

"Please," Porl said, glancing towards the people leaning out their office doors into the corridor. "Is there a place we can speak in private?"

Mouser led the way back to his workshop, confirmed that the Horten had no interest in imbibing soda or junk food, and then signaled to Rayne to hold her curiosity and let the alien speak first. Either she didn't see him or she had already forgotten their invented version of Phoenician sign language for traders.

"Just let me link my smartphone with the display panel and I'll take you through our payment history," she said, an unnatural note of pleading in her voice. "I know we almost missed the last deadline, but—"

"Please, don't trouble yourself," Porl said. "I'm not here to complain about the timing of your payments."

"Oh." Rayne swept away the spreadsheet that had just replaced the Horten freighter on the large monitor with a sigh of relief. "Then what seems to be troubling your grandfather? Is our Thark intermediary giving him a bad exchange rate? I thought that everybody was happy to be paid in Stryx creds."

"The issue with your payments is quantitative, not qualitative. The amounts have been steadily declining in recent years, and that puts them below twenty-five percent of my projection for this year when I originally made the deal with Nir."

"But the payments are directly linked to our population, basically a head tax," Rayne said. "Between a steady trickle of retirements to Earth and the twenty thousand people who defected to Flower a few years ago—you thought our population would have quadrupled by now?" she interrupted herself.

"My understanding of Human biology is that you can start reproducing in your teens, leaving ample time for two generations to be born on Bits," Porl said. "My grandfather hoped that you would breed rapidly and that the new generation would take an interest in terraforming work."

"Is that why he sent the surveying team?" Mouser asked. "Were all of the interior measurements they took just for cover while their drones checked the state of the terraforming work outside?"

The Horten's skin flashed grey with reddish flecks. "A survey team claiming to be from my grandfather was here?"

"They had his written authorization, complete with the seal that's on all of our official correspondence," Rayne said. She sensed the alien's skepticism and began tapping and swiping on her smartphone again. "I took a picture of it that has to be—there," and pointed up to the display where an image of an official document appeared. "Isn't that your grandfather's signature?"

Porl's skin went completely red, and for a moment, Rayne thought he was going to snatch her smartphone and smash it. Then the Horten's color shifted back to brown, and although he didn't burst out laughing, it was obvious he was holding it in.

"Yes, that's my grandfather's signature and his seal. I take it neither of you read Horten or bothered with a translation."

"But the authorization form is in English."

"You didn't notice the script below my grandfather's signature?"

"I guess I thought it was just his official title and the address of his office."

Porl put one arm behind his back and the other on his chest, one of the typical poses for a Horten giving a speech. Then he read, "Given to the winner of the three-legged sack race in honor of Eclipse Day. Draw your favorite companion animal in the space above, and with the permission of your parents, the House of Torb will acquire one for you before the Third Moon completes its next orbit."

"I don't understand," Mouser said.

"It's a traditional gift certificate given to children competing at a fair," Porl explained. "Let's see. Eclipse Day on Horten Twenty-Four, where my grandfather currently resides, took place around fifty days ago, say eighty days on the Earth calendar if I remember the conversion. I imagine somebody who wanted to get inside the domes bought the certificate from a child who won a race. It didn't seem odd to you that the surveyors needed to measure the domes when my grandfather has the blueprints for everything ever constructed on this planet?"

"Industrial spies," Mouser muttered. "The Hortens must have been here about the game."

"I find it difficult to believe that a Horten gaming concern would risk the ire of my family by sending undercover operatives here," Porl said. He gestured to Rayne's phone. "Did you save any pictures? Perhaps it was some sort of prank by somebody in our social circles and I'll recognize them."

The treasurer uploaded all of the images from the surveyor's folder to the high-resolution screen. She had taken a few dozen pictures which had seemed intrusive at the time, but now she realized that in their white environmental suits with their faces covered, she might as well have saved her energy.

"Interesting," the Horten muttered. "I expected to see a bump in the gloves for an extra thumb or the outline of a tentacle down the back, but I don't believe they were Drazens after all."

"Drazens?" Rayne asked. "No, they were Hortens. The ship was Horten, and how else could they have visited your grandfather's world and gotten the certificate?"

"We're not as xenophobic as you seem to take us for," Porl said, studying the photographs on the screen. "Definitely not Frunge, and the Vergallians would have sent face dancers before resorting to disguises. That uses up the tunnel network species who could fit in those environmental suits."

"How about the Gem?" Mouser asked.

"According to the headcount you submitted with the lease payment, there are already thousands of them living in the dome you abandoned, so they'd hardly need to go to such lengths. Hold on," he continued, focusing on a photo of one of the figures bending to adjust a tripod. "Can we get that one full screen?"

"Are you looking at the mask?" Rayne asked. "I can see in the profile that there's something strange about the nose bump compared to any species I've seen."

"Not the face, the feet," Porl said triumphantly. "I'll need copies of all of these pictures on a holo-memory chip if you don't mind."

"What's wrong with the feet?" Mouser asked before his mind could adjust to what he was seeing. "Is that a heel talon poking through the boot?"

"Not a tunnel network species," the Horten confirmed. "Well, that solves that question, but I'm afraid it still leaves us with the population problem."

"Thanks to our big project, I'm confident we can hold most of the working population together," Rayne said. "If the franchise takes off and we start actively recruiting..." She trailed off as the alien shook his head.

"I'm afraid my grandfather has received another offer and decided to accept it," Porl told them. "I was planning on breaking the news to Nir over a bottle of this single malt Scotch that he so enjoyed, but on the bright side, you have six months to make your plans."

"You mean we can't even negotiate, maybe beat the other offer?"

"They're willing to guarantee ten million heads on the ground if we bring in enough pre-fabricated domes to house them," the Horten said. "Plus they're all willing to work at the terraforming project for a modest rate plus food and housing."

Mouser stared at the ceiling, trying to think of the most critical issues to raise while Porl was present. "How about transportation? It's not like we've accumulated a huge amount of stuff, but moving ourselves and our possessions could wipe out our savings."

"More good news. My grandfather is willing to provide transportation to return you all to Earth or the tunnel network destination of your choice, providing you're all willing to go to the same place. And if you want to vacate early, he'll rebate you the prorated amount of the lease payment."

The door slid open to admit Belle, but she stopped on the threshold when she saw the Horten. "I'm sorry," she said. "Should I come back later?"

"You must be the Gem Today journalist," Porl said. "Just the clone I wanted to see."

"How did you know that Belle was here?" Rayne asked suspiciously. "Are you two working together?"

"If anything, we're on opposite sides. But it's next to impossible to keep a secret in this galaxy, especially when there's more than one species or political faction involved."

"Perhaps my Humanese isn't as fluent as I thought," Belle said, an edge to her voice neither Mouser nor Rayne had ever heard before. "Did you just imply that we're enemies?"

"Nothing so dramatic, though many species have sayings which express that the enemy of one's friend is worth keeping an eye on," the Horten replied easily. "It turns out that my family is going into business with some of your less fortunate sisters."

"The ones who refuse to let go of the Old Empire."

"Precisely. A substantial number of Gem loyalists joined predominantly Horten pirate groups after the fall of the Old Empire but it seems that the life doesn't agree with them. The Gem living here on Bits and working at getting the old terraforming plan back in motion contacted us through intermediaries in the Free Republic with a proposal to expand their presence on this planet."

"The Gem we took in suggested that you kick us out so they can take our place?" Rayne asked angrily.

"At no point did they suggest that you be evicted," Porl said. "They merely offered to take the terraforming work in hand and adhere to an aggressive schedule in return for housing, a life tenancy, and a regular supply of Earth chocolate."

"And you want me to do a story for Gem Today so you can attract even more Old Empire loyalists to come here and finish your planet?" Belle asked.

"I believe it's a situation in which everybody wins. We get the terraforming work done within a century or two, your sisters have a place to constructively live out their lives without having to see or hear about the revived bloodlines of your species, and the New Empire removes a source of friction, if not outright dissent."

"And we're homeless," Rayne added.

"I'm sorry about that, but we wouldn't have renewed the lease regardless for the reasons I already explained," Porl said. "The Gem deal was brokered by a cousin of mine who fell in with pirates at an early age and is now interested in returning to the family fold. I can't imagine how much he's going to have to spend on tattoo removal."

"My sisters won't be willing to speak with me," Belle told the Horten. "They view Gem who are bringing back male genetic lines and engaging in natural procreation with the same degree of disgust that most species see clones."

"I think you'll find that when it comes to free publicity, pragmatism is stronger than genetic orthodoxy," the Horten told her. "My understanding is that Gem Today remains the main source of information for Old Empire loyalists. Just because you hate the messenger is no reason to turn down the gift basket."

"Is that a Horten saying?" Mouser asked.

"I believe I heard it from Flower."

"Excuse me?" Rayne said, her voice rising again. "You know Flower?"

"She invited representatives from all of the major game publishers to an all-expenses paid preliminary discussion for a new gaming conference," Porl said with an elegant shrug of his shoulders. "Besides, I needed to stop somewhere with a store that stocked Earth exports to purchase this bottle." He handed it to the Rules Committee treasurer. "A consolation gift. I'll pick up another one when I get to Earth."

"And did Flower have anything to do with your Gem deal?"

"I don't think I'd be violating any confidences by saying that Flower is interested in maximizing her revenue in every way possible and transporting migrants with her excess capacity is one of her favorite money-makers. If you play your cards right, you might convince Flower to come here and pick you all up, in which case my grandfather will grant a bonus of ninety percent of what he would have spent renting a ship to move you all."

"Why not a hundred percent?" Mouser asked.

"My family wouldn't want you to think we were trying to influence your course of action by pushing you into Flower's arms," Porl said smoothly. "Speaking of the four-armed devil, if only in spirit, did I understand that she supplied you with primitive headset technology for simulating immersive environments?"

"Just how much did Flower tell you about what we're doing here with vegetable dip?" Rayne asked.

"Ah, I see your magical non-disclosure scrolls are still in effect. Flower's representative explained that she hired a Terragram mage for the job. My grandfather would be horrified, but I have to admit that Baa's Bags are a compelling accouterment for both fashion and LARPing. My fiancée was the first on her homeworld to purchase one."

Mouser retrieved a headset from his workbench and made sure it was connected to the internal network. "It's in monitor mode," he explained to Porl. "There's a beta testing round running on the hardware that Flower sent us." He glanced at the inside of the visor before handing it over. "It looks like they've stumbled into a combat scenario."

"Excellent," the Horten said, donning the headset. "How very interesting."

"Can you hear us?" Rayne asked loudly, and getting no response, turned to Belle. "You didn't know anything about this at all?"

"To be honest, a lack of trained personnel has forced my employer to emphasize efficiency," the clone replied. "I was asked to see if I could learn anything about our wayward sisters while working on getting the story about your game. I approached the Gem who live here but they rejected my advances out of hand."

"And now your documentary is going to end with our being evicted from the planet. It doesn't get much more dramatic than that."

"If I can be honest, I don't understand why you came here in the first place," Belle said. "Given your limited numbers, surely an island or other isolated situation on Earth could have served the same purpose with much less inconvenience."

"Now that I think about it, we may have been a bit hasty," Mouser said. "I had just graduated university when we made the move. We were talking about setting up a city-state for hackers in South America when Nir came back from the gaming tournament with the offer of a whole planet from the Hortens with transportation thrown in. It seemed like too good an offer to turn down, and it hasn't worked out that badly, all things considered."

"I still get the feeling that we're being jerked around by a Dollnick colony ship AI who wants us for cheap labor," Rayne said. "She probably thinks if she can get us on board for transportation to Earth she'll be able to persuade us to stay. What are you going to do, Mouser?"

"Whatever Sophie tells me, and if I had to guess, that decision will be driven by what our daughter and her husband decide. I imagine there are going to be a lot of kitchen table arguments over the next two weeks."

"Why not seven months?"

"You're the treasurer, do the math," Mouser said. "If Flower shows up with Dewey and we take passage, not only will we get a cash bonus of ninety percent of what Porl's grandfather would have spent to move us, we'll get back six months of the planetary lease payment. Nobody here has a lot of stuff, and if we need help moving, Flower can probably send bots. The Hortens have the right and the ability to end our arrangement and I don't see any point in dragging it out."

"Excellent," Porl said, removing the visor. "I'll withhold judgment until I see the final product, but I suspect that in a month's time, the House of Torb will bid to become the official Horten distributor for *A Mazing Earth*."

"I thought your family was in the planetary real estate business," Rayne said.

Porl shook his head. "I take it you never looked at the terraforming plan for Bits. The goal is to create a theme park world for our various gaming franchises as it's difficult to allow free rein for role-playing on populated planets." He handed the headset back to Mouser. "Well, I believe that's everything I needed to say. I'll just pop around to see the working Gem and get them up to date. Would you care to accompany me, Belle?"

"I suppose I might as well, but even if they cooperate in producing a mini-doc, I can't promise Gem Today will run it. I'm just a freelancer."

"I'm aware of your employment status," the Horten said, giving the clone an exaggerated wink.

As soon as the two aliens exited the workshop, Rayne began tearing the wrapping paper off of the gift Porl had brought for Nir. "That confirms it," she said, staring at the bottle.

"Confirms what?" Mouser asked.

"The Horten is serious. You don't bring somebody a blue ribbon, single cask, fifty-year-old bottle of Scotch to play a practical joke."

Eighteen

"Assuming our customer agrees to the ongoing development and service package and we all end up living in the same place, I'd like to continue these team coordination meetings on a weekly basis," Tom concluded. He looked directly at Hercules and asked, "Tomorrow? Friday? Do we have a final date for Flower's arrival?"

Hercules shook his head. "Saturday would get us to exactly six months since the project began. We haven't had any ships bringing news since Porl left so all we can do is wait."

"But I've already packed all of our family's stuff," one of the managers said. "We're basically camping out in our apartment."

"I think most of us are in the same boat, but at least it's given everybody something to do with their time," Hercules said. "It's been tough to concentrate on anything other than preparing to leave since the landlord's grandson handed us our walking papers."

"Chance is doing another question and answer thing on the Rules Committee channel starting at noon today," Delphi informed everyone. "After that, our embedded Gem Today journalist is going to screen her rough cut of the documentary. It's not anything like final, and Belle told me that the network will take all of her raw video to do their own editing, but she thought we'd want to see something while we're all still together. A sort of summing up."

"That was very thoughtful of her," an older producer at the end of the table said. "It's been a pleasure taking one last lap around the track with you all, but my husband and I will be retiring to Earth, regardless of what blandishments Flower may try on us. I just want to say that it's been a lovely experience, and I hope someday to see advertisements for an interspecies *A Mazing Earth* tournament."

The meeting broke up with most of the managers heading home to their families. Hercules saw that Delphi had made no move to rise and he remained behind as well. "Is something bothering you?"

"Are you sure you want to hear it?"

"That's what friends are for."

"All right, it's my mom," Delphi said. "Her parents retired to Earth a couple of years ago and she's already made up her mind to go directly there rather than waiting for Flower's regular stop. She's been reading the back issues of the Galactic Free Press and she found out that it's pretty cheap to rent a little ship on Flower that flies itself. From there you can go through any tunnel network connection to a Stryx station and get regular service to Earth."

"She's in that much of a hurry?" Hercules asked.

"Mom hasn't been that happy since her parents left. I mean, she has friends, and me, but she's been talking about getting the family back together the whole time, and now she doesn't see the point in waiting any longer."

"How about you?"

"She just assumes that I'll go with her," Delphi said. "But if joining Flower for a while means seeing something of the galaxy, I don't want to miss that opportunity. I'm afraid when I tell mom, she'll think I'm choosing Tom over her. I've spent my whole life in these domes and I want to see alien worlds and Stryx stations."

"This is going to sound like advice from a cereal box, but the longer you wait to tell her, the harder it will get."

Delphi nodded glumly. "It's just that there's been so much happening. What are you going to do?"

"I promised to remain available for character scaffolding so I'll be sticking with the *A Mazing Earth* development group if we get approved to continue working," Hercules said. "We'll start with living on Flower, and then take a vote when we get to Earth on whether or not to stay on board."

"Shadow's sister also does character scaffolding so I guess she'll stay. I don't know about his parents, they aren't old enough to retire yet, but some of the work Shadow's doing would probably be easier on Earth."

"Don't forget that Flower primarily visits tunnel network worlds, and I've heard she's got a Stryxnet connection that works from almost anywhere."

"He kind of asked me to be his girlfriend," Delphi blurted out.

"Shadow? It's about time."

"You should talk. The way your friends tell it, you've been carrying a torch for Rayne since you were my age."

"I took a decade off for her marriage," Hercules said quietly. "If I've learned one thing in that time, it's that you can't make somebody love you, especially if they haven't moved on from their last relationship."

"You think she's still in love with Gorgeous George?"

"They broke up and got back together so often that you could set your clock by it. She's never dated anybody else that I'm aware of."

"I guess that's why she's in such a bad mood all the time," Delphi said, and then frowned. "But it's not fair to you. Are you going to waste the rest of your life waiting?"

"I don't think I've wasted any of my life, I just haven't gotten married yet," Hercules said. "And what did you tell Shadow?"

"I sort of froze, and then I told him I'd think about it. He's a year younger than me so it's kind of weird."

Hercules broke into a wide grin and couldn't keep himself from barking a short laugh. "Sorry, but didn't you just turn twenty? It's not like there's some vast gap between you."

"But there is," Delphi protested. "Everybody knows that girls mature faster than boys, and if you don't count childhood, he's only like seventy-five percent of my age."

"You'll have to explain that one to me."

"You can't figure we're grown up until, say, sixteen, so age differences matter a lot for a few years right after that. Like an eighteen-year-old has been an adult twice as long as a seventeen-year-old. By the time you're in your thirties, the differences don't matter as much."

"I'm not buying it," Hercules said, getting up from the table. "I will say that I'm impressed with how you've made room for your father in your life. I had a couple of friends in similar situations when I was your age and they didn't deal with it half as well."

"Tom's great, and mom seems okay with it as long as I don't talk about my half-sister's mother. But if she thinks I'm staying on Flower to be with them? I don't know."

"Talk about it with her today," Hercules counseled as he stood aside to let her leave first. "Are you going to watch Chance's propaganda show?"

"I still can't believe she's an artificial intelligence. She's so much more natural than Dewey."

"That's because she's been at it longer than either of us have been alive while Dewey is really a child in terms of years. It's easy to forget because he has an encyclopedic memory, and I guess not sleeping gives him a few extra months a year of experience. I hope he's not letting Flower lead him by the nose."

"It didn't seem that way to me," Delphi said as she stepped onto the moving walk. "I'm going to go to The Cave to watch Chance and the rough cut of the documentary. Want to come along?"

"You're ten years too young for me," Hercules deadpanned. "Besides, I promised Sarah I'd come over and help them pack. Her grandmother has a lot of old-fashioned paper books and she doesn't want her mother lifting the boxes."

"Sounds to me like Sarah's matchmaking," Delphi said under her breath, but only after the sidewalk carried her out of earshot.

Hercules glanced after her, swiped his smartphone to life, and tapped out the text, "She's going to The Cave."

Shadow removed his visor, blinked a few times to adjust his focal distance, and congratulated himself for figuring out how to patch his smartphone into the headset's ancient Bluetooth, a feat that had required all of his hacking skills.

"Did you just go offline?" his sister asked, removing her own headset.

"I'm going to The Cave. Hercules texted me that Delphi is on her way."

"I never thought I'd have a stalker for a brother."

"It's not stalking until she rejects me," Shadow protested. "Want to be my wingman?"

Lisa looked over at their parents, both of whom were sitting on the couch with virtual reality headsets and controllers and oblivious to the fact that their children had dropped out of the race. "There's something deeply wrong with them," she observed. "Sure, I'll go. Just let me change and text Botan."

Shadow grimaced. "You're going to dress all girly for him?"

"Hey, if you've got it, flaunt it," Lisa said. "You and Delphi could learn a lot from us."

As it turned out, Botan had gone to The Cave early to get away from his parents and grandparents arguing over whether to give Flower a chance or move directly to Earth. He texted Shadow when Delphi arrived before Lisa had finished changing. By the time the siblings got there, Chance was just wrapping up her dueling presentations for Flower and EarthCent's president on The Cave's big display. The Gem Today journalist, who was waiting to show her documentary after the Q&A, volunteered to read off the questions that people texted to the Rules Committee channel.

"Will EarthCent give us our own city?" Belle read the first question.

"If I haven't made it clear, EarthCent isn't Earth's government," Chance replied. "They're responsible for human-alien relations on the tunnel network and for working with non-humans who come to Earth. They can grant the alien businesses and diplomatic missions extraterritorial status, but the president's office is so small that they sublet space from a software company. EarthCent can't give you a city because they don't have any to give."

"Did anybody really think we were going to get our own city?" Shadow asked.

"My grandparents do," Botan said. "I guess there are some completely empty ones in Japan, but I don't get what the advantage is supposed to be of moving somewhere without people."

"Look at Belle's expression," Lisa said, pointing at the screen. "I'm guessing that most of the questions she's getting aren't suitable for broadcast."

Eventually, the clone found a text she was comfortable reading out loud and asked, "Does Flower offer free food to everybody or just the retirees?"

"Flower doesn't offer anybody free food unless they're ship-wrecked," Chance said. "It's strictly pay-for-play, but her prices are as low as you're going to pay on Earth, and she offers work to anybody who can't find employment on their own."

"I still can't get over that fruit," Shadow said, glancing towards the counter to see if their food was ready.

"Ask for a job on an ag deck when we get there," Delphi suggested. "I've heard they let you eat all you want on the first day because after that you'll be sick of the stuff."

"Food's up," Botan announced. "I'll get it."

"I'll come with," Lisa said, winking at her brother.

"Will our royalty income be taxed if we move to Earth or Flower?" Belle read the next question.

"My understanding from your Rules Committee treasurer is that the tithe will continue as long as you remain a community," Chance answered. "As far as Earth goes, taxes are a matter for the local governments, primarily city-states, and with modern technology replacing old-fashioned public infrastructure, it's common for the less populated areas to offer limited government services and collect no income tax. Flower doesn't tax anything, but she has four thumbs in every pie. so you won't have to worry that you're not paying your fair share."

"Rayne told me that Bits never established break-up rules for what happens to royalty payments if we stop working together," Delphi told Shadow. "There's just some language about the treasurer making a fair arrangement."

"Sounds like she's got a lot of power," Shadow said. "Maybe that's why she never got together with Hercules."

"What do you mean?"

"My sister made me read a book about relationships and the author said that most men are intimidated by professional women with higher status jobs than their own."

"That's nonsense," Delphi said, but she didn't sound as sure of herself as usual. "Really?"

"Really. There were lots of statistics but I didn't look at them that carefully," Shadow admitted. "I just remember that the author's advice to ambitious women was to form a relationship early, ideally with a younger, supportive man."

"You're full of—she's got one."

Belle looked back up at the camera and read, "Can we use our smartphones on Flower?"

Chance nodded energetically. "Yes. There are only three places in the universe that maintain a compatible cellular network for Earth's phone technology and Flower is one of them. Bits is the third, but I imagine the Gem will shut the equipment down after you leave. It's a service that Flower recently added to make it easier for people to contact family when she stops at Earth, but my understanding is that most people on board, including emigrants from Bits, prefer to use modern tabs."

"Figures," Delphi said to Shadow. "Are you going to keep using your smartphone, or are you going to ditch it for Dollnick technology?"

"That depends on you," Shadow said with a grin. "See how supportive I am?"

"Some people would call that needy."

"For all we know, Flower could show up this evening. In the rush to get everybody moved on board and settled it may be weeks before I see you again. I really care about you, Delphi, and I don't want to wake up in a month and find that you went off with your mother and I never even told you how I feel."

"Any more questions suitable for all ages?" Chance asked the Gem on the big screen.

"I guess you've already covered most of the serious ones at your previous presentations and public meetings," Belle said. "The best thing I can say about the texts I'm ignoring is that they're universally complimentary of your physical appearance."

"I get a lot of that," Chance said with a happy smile. "As to the rest of it—sorry kids, I'm taken."

"Oh, wait. Here's one. Why don't we all move to a Stryx station?"

"All right. Considering that I choose to live on Union Station that's a tough one for me to answer. I think the first point is cost. Living space on Flower is much cheaper because of demand and capacity considerations, and the Stryx aren't going to set aside an entire deck for Bits or rearrange any current tenants so you can live in a contiguous space. And Flower can offer you all employment in anime or gaming."

"Did Belle just imply that all the adolescent boys on Bits are propositioning Chance, even though she's an artificial person?" Delphi asked Shadow.

"Maybe, but there are probably a bunch of conspiracy theory texts as well," he replied. "I was talking with Rayne yesterday, and her mother stopped going to the extra meetings the seniors club has been putting on in recent weeks because it's all crazy talk. I mean, I understand that some of the older people have decent savings because there's just not much to spend money on here, but there's no way Flower and EarthCent are conspiring to cheat them."

"They think that Flower and EarthCent are teaming up to defraud them of their savings?"

"Not all of them, but that's what Rayne said. I guess some retired people got scammed a few years back when Flower first started taking humans and it was a big deal in the Galactic Free Press."

"Here's another one," Belle said after scrolling through more questions. "Can you demonstrate how to assemble a flat-pack box? We picked up our allotment, but they're paper thin, and we don't see how they can hold anything."

"I'm glad you asked that question because I forgot to bring it up myself," Chance said. She issued a silent command for the camera to zoom out so that half of the conference room table was now showing. "I brought examples of both the medium and small boxes with me—the large size wouldn't fit through your doors once they're popped up. We'll start with the small one," she continued, holding up what appeared to be a thin sheet of paper about the size of a pillowcase that had been cut open and laid flat. "Would you help me, Belle?"

The clone took the other end of the flat-pack and the two of them flicked their wrists, almost like people might do with wet laundry to get the wrinkles out before hanging. The action caused the flat pack to spring into box form, something large enough for a small child to hide in. The lid was hinged rather than being a separate piece.

"Easy peasy," Chance said, and placing the box on the floor, proceeded to jump up on top of it. The lid bowed in a little but held. "I'm not going to tell any of you how much I weigh because then I'd have to kill you, but Dollnick flat-pack boxes are the gold standard for movers around the tunnel network."

Belle glanced at the screen for incoming texts and grimaced. "They didn't see," she said. "There are a hundred requests to do it again, but slower."

"It's more obvious with the medium size." Chance took up one end of the flimsy paper that was perhaps as large as half a bed sheet, and Belle took the other end. They flicked their wrists and a box the size of a card table suddenly appeared.

"Still too fast," the Gem reported after checking the texts.

"Doesn't this planet have slow-motion replay?" Chance asked.

"Head slap," Belle read off the next text. "What does that mean?"

"It's an Earth expression meaning, of course, they have slow motion replay," Chance said. "And don't forget to write your name and your current apartment and dome number on the boxes. Flower will send bots to move your stuff, and boarding will go much faster if you only take your personal belongings in bags that can fit the shuttle's overhead compartments or beneath the seat in front of you."

"You look different," Lisa said to Delphi as she set the tray with drinks on the table. "Kind of confused about life and love."

"Don't push her," Shadow said. "I think I'm making progress."

"They were out of fresh bread and substituted frozen," Botan reported, setting Shadow's sandwich in front of him. "You should have ordered salad like the rest of us."

"I can't tell the difference with the bread once it's toasted," Shadow said.

"He's not a picky eater if you're thinking ahead," Lisa told Delphi and received an elbow in the ribs from Botan.

"All right already, I'll give him a beta test, but I'm not promising anything long-term," Delphi said, watching Shadow out of the corner of her eye.

"Does this mean I can finally call you Deli?" he asked.

"Not yet. You're on evaluation."

"The documentary is starting," Botan said, pointing at the big display. "Hey. That's us in a telephoto shot."

"Belle was recording video the first time we met her?" Lisa asked. "I don't remember her having a camera with her."

"The Gem are the tunnel network's leaders in nanotechnology," Delphi said. "I heard Belle discussing cameras with some of the techs, and she said the Gem can get usable video from cameras that are almost invisible to the human eye."

"Why did she think it was important to include video of the first time she met us here?" Shadow asked.

"Shhh," his sister said. "I can't hear the voiceover."

"—addition to having nearly unlimited access to chocolate, young Humans typically form relationships with a variety of potential mates," Belle was saying. "But their genes are so different that they can have trouble communicating even when it's obvious to a complete alien that they like each other."

"Did I just get Gemsplained in front of all of Bits?" Delphi sputtered and turned to Shadow. "Did you put her up to this?"

Shadow shook his head vigorously. "If you had shot me down everybody on Bits would have known about it. I never said a thing to her."

"How do you know she wasn't talking about us?" Lisa said, spearing an olive from Botan's salad. "We were all in that framing shot."

Botan's phone began reporting incoming messages, and if he hadn't put it on vibrate before entering the café, they would have been interrupted by every obnoxious text tone from Delphi's collection.

"Aren't you going to answer?" Shadow asked his friend.

"It's my mom," Botan replied, and took another forkful of salad.

"All of the texts?"

"Dad, older sister, two grandmothers," he said, glancing at the list.

"You still haven't told your family that you're dating me," Lisa said accusingly, and then laughed. "Busted."

Nineteen

"Do you know something we don't know?" Delphi asked as she took her accustomed place on the couch in Mouser's workshop.

"What do you mean?" the gamemaster asked from his overstuffed chair.

"Everybody is expecting Flower any minute and you want to start a game that goes on for hours."

"I was getting in my wife's hair and I figured it might be the same with the rest of you."

"I hit the gym this morning and cleaned out my locker, so Flower better get here today," Hercules said. "Everything has ground to a complete halt. I stopped by Bits Bakery and the sign on the door said they were closed forever."

"Six months ago we would have had a revolution on our hands if we suggested leaving Bits," Rayne said. "Today we'd have a revolution if we told people they have to stay."

"Where's Shadow?" Mouser asked.

"Late as usual," Delphi said. "Sometimes I think he does it just to annoy me."

"Sorry, sorry," Shadow said as he entered the workshop. "Lisa and I stayed up late last night packing everything. When we got up this morning, my parents had the game system back out and were sitting on the couch playing *Moon Racer* like nothing has changed."

"Maybe they have a point," Mouser said. "Even if Flower gets here in five minutes she can't load all of us and our stuff in one day."

"Chance said Flower operates four large shuttles that seat a thousand each with plenty of cargo room," Delphi said. "How long will it take them to go back and forth?"

"The real issue is loading, unloading, and timing the departures so the shuttles don't have to chase halfway around Bits to catch her in orbit," Hercules said.

"Can't Flower just come to a complete halt above the atmosphere?" Shadow asked. "I thought those Dollnick colony ships were so overpowered that they can hold their positions on gravity drive and ignore all the astrophysics."

Mouser shook his head. "If Flower came to a complete stop, she'd be subject to the planet's gravity. Orbit creates radial acceleration that cancels it out."

"But if she has the power—"

"It doesn't matter," Mouser interrupted. "A colony ship like Flower is always spinning to create weight. In an external gravitational field without orbital acceleration to cancel it out, everybody on board would feel like they were on an amusement park ride. A bad one."

"And there would be water all over the place," Hercules said. "Didn't you read the electronic brochures Chance sent everybody? Flower's whole outer deck is a reservoir and the spin keeps the water pressed up against the hull."

"So what happens when the ship accelerates to go somewhere?" Shadow asked.

"Read the brochure," Hercules told him. "She never accelerates hard enough that you'd feel yourself leaning, it's just enough to navigate through tunnels or do orbital insertions after jumps. And you've heard of atmosphere retention fields?"

"I'm not a complete idiot."

"The Dollnicks have the same thing for water that keeps the reservoir from sloshing to the end of the cylinder."

"I think it's called the stern," Delphi said.

"Are you guys going to spend the day talking about Dollnick engineering or are we going to play?" Rayne asked. "I could use something to keep my mind off of the move."

"How's Sarah taking it?" Delphi asked.

"Oh, she's thrilled, and so is my mom."

"All right," Mouser said, looking down at the plastic trifold on his lap that was designed to stand free on a table. "You awaken in a forest to the sound of birds greeting the rising sun, but you can't see more than a few paces because a heavy fog covers the ground. As you rise to your feet, a figure begins to form in the mist, and a voice says—"

"Glad to see you're all packed," Dewey announced his presence from the doorway. "You didn't answer our hails and Flower was worried that you decided to stay after all."

"I didn't answer because I boxed all my communications gear up last night," Mouser explained. "Nobody who landed here ever did what I told them in any case."

"That's it?" Delphi asked, jumping to her feet. "We're going? I better run home and tell mom."

"Flower pushed her schedule around enough to gain seven days so there's no hurry," Dewey informed them. "We're planning six round trips a day with each of the four shuttles, so twenty-four thousand people a day with room for error. If you'll give me your official permission to use the public address system—you didn't break that down, did you?"

"No, it belongs to the Hortens," Mouser said. "It was already installed in the domes when we arrived."

"Good. I made a copy of the residential directory last time I was here and we worked out a loading plan. I'm going to inform the first thousand people to queue up on the right side of the corridor and the shuttle will extend an atmosphere retention field so they don't have to fool around with oxygen masks."

"What about all of their stuff?" Rayne asked.

"We're going to cheat and use bots," Dewey said. "The first shuttle will go without luggage, and after that, each one will be carrying the possessions the bots remove from the apartments of those who already left. Flower's bots can carry an amazing amount in their four arms and they'll be much faster than people once you're out of the way. They can move a household in the time it takes you to move yourselves."

"All of that traffic is going to be rushing back and forth through a single corridor?" Mouser asked skeptically.

"The bots will use the emergency exits from all of the domes," the artificial person explained. "Flower has transported hundreds of thousands of colonists to Earth Two in the past year. We've built up a lot of expertise at moving, and you don't even have barns or livestock."

"Are any of us on the first shuttle?" Hercules asked.

"None of you or your families are even on the first day. We have to do the final product review, after all."

"Are you serious?" Rayne asked. "I was so sure that the whole game development was just Flower's ploy to get us to move on board that I've been taking bets."

"I'm sorry to inform you that you lost those bets," Dewey said. "*A Mazing Earth* represents a major investment on

Flower's part. Certainly the largest she's made since getting involved with EarthCent."

"Was she in the game business before that?"

"Flower had a rough couple thousand years before taking her current position, but she doesn't like to talk about that now. Do you mind if I invite Belle and Chance to join us?"

Mouser glanced around at the others, and seeing no objection, said, "Go ahead. Are they going to participate in the review?"

"They've already done it, I just need to hear their final report," Dewey said.

"What?" Rayne croaked. "Flower hired a Gem and an artificial person—no offense intended—to make the final decision about the most involved game we've ever created on Bits?"

"Belle is an expert, even if game journalism is only a sideline, and Chance loaded up on personality overlays from QuickU while she was on Earth." The artificial person noted their blank looks and nodded to himself. "QuickU is the software company that sublets space to the president's office. They specialize in personality overlays for artificial people that have even had some success beyond the human-derived AI market. That means Chance was able to test your game while emulating a dozen different types of personalities."

"I thought she was a bit buggy when I saw her playing with a beta testing group," Shadow said. "She was acting like an old man but I didn't want to say anything."

"While we're waiting for them to arrive, do you mind if I ask what you've decided for your own futures?"

"You can tell Flower that the independent living commercials won my mom over," Rayne said. "And I'd like for

Sarah to have the experience of attending a real school. I doubt I could afford one on Earth."

"Flower has schools for kids?" Shadow asked. "My sister said something about an Open University campus, but I assumed that other than people traveling between stops, it would be all adults on board."

"He didn't read the brochure," Delphi told Dewey.

"Even with the independent living deck, Flower's population demographics skew younger than the average extraterrestrial human community. In addition to the children who live on board with their parents, she runs a boarding school for kids from some of the mining habitats we stop at," Dewey explained. "If you enjoy working with children, there are lots of volunteer opportunities in the schools to meet your mandatory requirement."

"My what?" Shadow asked.

"It's just a couple of hours a week," Hercules told him. "From what I've heard, people who hate following rules have more trouble with the morning exercises than the volunteering."

"I couldn't stop laughing when Sarah told me her father had to get up in the morning and stretch or Flower would blast Dollnick opera over his cabin's sound system," Rayne said. "George hated getting up in the morning."

"And you?" the artificial person asked Delphi.

"I'm in at least until we stop at Earth," the girl said. "My mom is planning to go on ahead of me but she understands my wanting to see something of the galaxy after a lifetime cooped up in the domes. She made me promise to take some classes at the Open University and to visit her as soon as we get to Earth."

"If Flower is really going to build *A Mazing Earth* into a franchise, I have to stay available for character scaffolding," Hercules said. "Some of the other game developers have promised to give me dialogue, and I guess I've caught the acting bug."

"We all like a challenge," the artificial person said. "Mouser?"

"Whatever my wife decides," Mouser said. "Our daughter seems sold on giving Flower's schools a shot for the grandkids, so I imagine we'll be joining you."

Belle and Chance entered together, and for the few seconds the door was open, a queue of people lining up in the corridor with backpacks and rollaway bags was visible.

"It's a madhouse out there," Chance said. "People kept accusing us of trying to jump the line. I explained that everybody who was notified has a guaranteed seat on the shuttle and that they're all going to arrive at the same time. Some people are just so competitive."

"It's an occupational hazard with gamers," Belle said. "Even in the Old Empire, the sisters who were addicted to playing Cloner had shorter fuses than the rest of us."

"Correlation doesn't equal causation," Mouser objected. "All of our research shows that role players have superior social skills."

"Given the source, I'd like to check your experimental criteria for confirmation bias," Dewey said. "And did the two of you write up your reports?"

"I've never been much for paperwork," Chance admitted. "Can't I make an oral report?"

"Belle?"

"Do you read Gem handwriting?" the clone asked. "I took notes on my smartphone with a stylus. The operating system is from Bits and it can't tell my writing from line drawings."

"Something tells me that Chance has been a bad influence on you," Dewey said. "Fine. Give me your oral reports."

"The game has good bones, and as is, it will probably do well with the Hortens and Drazens," Belle said. "But to engage the attention of the advanced species, it will need more complexity of plot, as opposed to being so heavy on the action and graphics."

"Getting the story right was sort of my department," Mouser said. "Are you saying it's juvenile?"

"Not necessarily, just that the storylines develop too quickly for species used to the slow burn of a Vergallian drama, or a Verlock historical epic game based on real probabilities. The version with the traders and maze-runner guides will come closest to the mark for the older species, but the commercial aspects are underemphasized at the expense of moving between the city-states with their magical barrier maze. The whole economic system was oversimplified."

"The developers didn't want to make it so wonky that we'd lose the human market. I suppose it would be possible to build species-specific versions with some help from alien consultants but I'm not sure the cost could be justified."

"There are roughly ten billion humans in the galaxy and they have limited buying power compared to any of the other tunnel network species," Dewey pointed out. "There are over a trillion Vergallians alone, and if you add in the others, you can more than triple that number."

"Why didn't you say anything about this earlier?" Rayne asked. "We knew Flower wanted a cross-species game, but nobody said she was interested in versions that would be over our heads."

"I'm just responding to Mouser's objection to Belle's critique. If Drazens and Hortens will play the game with just minor alterations, that's better than Flower or myself expected."

"What about the Gem?" Delphi asked.

"With apologies to our mutual friend, the New Empire is pouring all of its resources into rebuilding a population that can be sustained without cloning, so they don't have the cash for in-game purchases," Dewey said. "Chance, I'm counting on you for an unbiased assessment of the game's suitability for the human market. What did you conclude?"

"It's a bit too complicated in parts, especially the whole business with hacking networks to establish false identities for alien undercover agents, but that's easy enough to fix with cheat codes," Chance said. "The artwork is phenomenal, and when I played with the personality overlay of Earth expatriates, it evoked a sense of nostalgia that will make it stand out in the marketplace."

"And what did you think of the spell-casting abilities?" Mouser asked.

"Pretty cool, and I think they'll work even better in LARPing studios where magic is real."

"How does a LARPing studio make magic real?" Shadow asked. "I thought it was just a bunch of bots wrapped in holograms playing NPCs."

Chance shook her head pityingly. "You should get into one of Flower's LARPing studios as soon as possible. I'll go with you if I haven't left for Union Station yet."

"So, the bottom line is that you're approving us for further development?" Rayne asked.

"I don't think it was ever really in doubt," Dewey said. "You're all professionals, and Lume and I were impressed with how much progress you made in the initial month. He told me then that *A Mazing Earth* won't stand much of a chance in the Dollnick market unless you crank up the engineering aspects, but the truth is, they aren't big gamers, even with their own products."

Belle touched the side of her head, the New Empire method of telling whoever she was with that she was using her implant, and nodded.

"The first thousand of my sisters have exited the shuttle and Flower wants me to lead them around to their dome," the clone said. "I hope they're in a good mood."

"And I'm on traffic cop duty," Dewey said. "If you want to watch how the loading goes, come along."

"Don't you need an oxygen mask if you're going outside of the atmosphere retention field?" Mouser asked Belle.

"Our homeworld has lower oxygen content than yours so we can stay outside indefinitely on Bits," the clone said. "It's one of the factors that make us so well suited for terraforming work here at the current stage."

"Hey, get in line," a number of voices called out when Mouser and his group followed Dewey into the corridor and turned for the airlock.

"We're working," Rayne retorted. "The Gem just finished unloading so the line should start moving any minute."

Outside, it was clear that Flower's shuttle crew needed no help with the loading process. Dewey and Chance positioned themselves at the front of the queue and sent family groups to one of four ramps so they could be seated together. A team of people dressed in what might have been homespun clothing stood at the top of the ramps directing traffic, and the first thousand emigrants disappeared into the shuttle at regular walking speed.

"How come they didn't pile up in the aisles?" Rayne asked Dewey.

"Because the aisles are wide enough for larger species, and there's enough space between the rows of seats for people to exchange places without climbing all over each other," the artificial person replied. "I have a friend who was a money courier for the drug syndicate on Earth and it's beyond me how she put up with travelling around there."

"I'm sure the job had greater downsides."

The artificial person shrugged as the shuttle's ramps began to rise back into the hull. "Perhaps, but I can put myself into standby mode if I'm trapped in a small space for an extended time. I don't believe you have that option."

"This is the way the world ends," Hercules said, craning his neck as the shuttle silently lifted into the sky at a steadily increasing velocity. "Not with a bang but a whimper."

"Did you just make that up?" Shadow asked.

"It's from a poem by T. S. Elliot. Rayne's mother gave me the book for helping them pack and suggested that reading poetry out loud would be good practice for acting."

"I think I'm going to cry," Delphi said. "I was looking forward to going, but now it just seems so final."

Shadow snuck an arm around her shoulder, and to his surprise, she leaned against him rather than jerking away.

"We'll still be together on Flower, and I bet before the week is out, the domes and the vending machine food will be a bad memory," Rayne said.

"And here comes the next one," Hercules said, still staring up at the sky through the slight distorting shimmer of the atmosphere retention field. "Hey, how come we still have enough air after the shuttle lifted off?"

"The crew left the atmosphere retention field generator behind for the duration," Dewey said.

"Shouldn't we go back inside so it doesn't land on top of us?" Delphi asked.

"Flower can land her shuttles with pinpoint accuracy and I'm feeding her a location beacon as a backup," the artificial person said. "Just keep behind me."

"Why is it taking so long?" Shadow asked two minutes later. "If Flower is so great at navigation, why didn't the second shuttle land right after the first one took off?"

"It's not an emergency so she's leaving a larger safety margin than necessary. Slow deceleration is also more comfortable for the passengers."

"How did it go with your sisters?" Chance asked Belle as the clone returned just in time to see the shuttle complete its vertical landing.

"Dewey was right. They're willing to talk to me in return for publicizing Bits as the new rallying point for the Old Empire. I'm not sure if it's the right thing to do but that's above my pay grade. I'll send the video in and the higher-ups can decide whether or not to broadcast it on Gem Today."

Four ramps lowered to the tarmac and columns of clones, all dressed identically and carrying the same duffle bags, began trooping off. Belle moved away to make room for a mustering area, and in less than five minutes, a group of a thousand Gem was formed up in front of her.

"You can say what you will about clones, but if you're in the transportation business, Gem are the most efficient passengers," Dewey observed.

Twenty

Mouser blinked when the overhead lighting in his workshop came on at full brightness. He returned the soldering iron to its holder, placed the antique circuit board in a silvery antistatic bag, and swiveled on his faux-antique workbench stool to see who had entered.

"Dewey," he greeted the artificial person. "Did I forget to tell you we moved the game to Sunday afternoon? Shadow and Delphi signed up for a Saturday dance class to meet their team sport requirement and it's the only time everybody had free."

"You texted and I replied that it worked for me," Dewey said. "I'm looking forward to getting back to playing a tabletop game. Strangely enough, I find role-playing with you as the gamemaster more immersive than the LARPing studios. I suppose it's because I see right through the holograms if I'm not careful about my refresh rates."

"So what brings you by?"

"Hiring. Flower understands that you don't want the responsibility of creative control for a large project at this point in your life but she's looking for technical talent to help her maintain the internal cellular network. She thought that after a month or two on board you would all give in and exchange your phones for Dollnick tabs, but you're proving more stubborn than the first group she recruited from Bits."

"That's not surprising," Mouser said. "You have to take into account that the group Flower recruited from Bits three years ago were already looking to modernize. The rest of us only left because we lost the option to stay."

"Are you unhappy with the move?" Dewey asked.

Mouser snorted. "I'm unhappy about being manipulated into doing what's good for me at my age, but other than that, it's the smartest move I've ever made. Sophie picked up an adjunct professorship at the Open University, my grandchildren are going to real schools with space for playgrounds, and my daughter has discovered that given the ingredients, she loves to cook. If it wasn't for the required exercise and the team sport, my belly would be out to here," he concluded, holding his arms out in a hoop.

"What did you take for your team sport?"

"Water aerobics," Mouser said. "Tell Flower that she doesn't have to offer me a make-work job maintaining the cellular network to keep me on board for a while. I'm getting more repairs than I can handle from the legacy electronics sellers at the bazaar. I guess they buy container loads of old game consoles and kitchen widgets by weight when we visit Earth and then sort out what works and what doesn't when they have time."

"Flower will be disappointed to hear that," Dewey said. "It's true that she can maintain everything on board with her bots, but the advanced species try to minimize the use of automation wherever possible. Let me know if you change your mind."

"Will do. See you on Sunday, and don't forget to come in character. Sarah is looking forward to meeting the twenty-first century's most famous spy."

"Shaken," the artificial person said with a reasonable Scottish burr. "Not stirred."

.....

"How was your day at school?" June asked when her granddaughter came into the kitchen.

"Great, like always," Sarah replied. "How come you don't want to live with us anymore?"

"Why do you ask me the same question every day? You see me just as much as you did on Bits, and if you want to come to my place, it's only a lift tube ride away."

"Flower's Paradise is all old people. They look at me funny."

"They look at you wistfully because they're wishing that their own grandchildren were living on Flower," June said. "Not that many people on the independent living deck have their whole family on board, though I understand the number is growing."

"Are you making me a snack?" Sarah asked, standing on her tiptoes to see into the mixing bowl. "Oh, it's cookies."

"You sound disappointed. I thought you'd enjoy a change from fruit salad."

"I *like* fruit salad. And it's healthy. M793qK says so."

"Isn't he the alien doctor who all of my friends in Flower's Paradise talk about? I thought he was a geriatric specialist."

"Em told me he's actually a large mammal veterinarian, but I don't really know what that means," Sarah said. "Flower substituted for our teacher today and she invited M793qK to come and talk to us about nutrition."

"What did you learn?" June asked.

"Not to eat anything that comes in a package unless it's from Flower Foods. He said all of those Earth cookies I used to like were full of preservatives and artificial flavors to fool my taste buds into thinking my body needed them. Next time Flower sends a bot to substitute, we're going on a field trip to an ag deck to learn where dairy food comes from."

"Well, these are healthy cookies, except for maybe the sugar. I made them from natural ingredients that I bought at the ag deck market."

"Then it's okay," Sarah said happily. "M793qK suggested keeping refined sugar to one snack a day."

"Didn't your teacher miss a day last week, and the week before as well?" June asked as she spooned the cookie dough out onto the baking sheet. "I hope there's nothing wrong with her."

"Em told me that Flower locks Miss Chalmers in her cabin, or pretends there's a lift tube malfunction and sends Miss Chalmers to the wrong deck. Flower *likes* substitute teaching."

"I see." June placed the cookie sheet in the preheated oven and poured herself a cup of tea from the pot that had been set to steep. "It's going to be a while before the cookies are baked and cooled. Do you want a piece of fruit?"

Sarah thought for a moment and then shook her head. "I want to save room because Hercules is taking me out for dinner."

"Just you?"

"Me and Mom." The girl caught her grandmother's look and giggled. "I was teasing. I know that he's taking mom on a date and they're only bringing me along because I asked."

"That's okay sometimes, but you should also give them time alone if you want to give Hercules a chance to woo her," June said. "You can always come have dinner with me."

"Woo?"

"Win her heart. Woo, wooing, wooed."

"I only asked to go because it's that café that Em told me about where all the food is alien," Sarah said.

"You seem to be learning a lot from Em."

"She's the captain's daughter and she knows *everything* about Flower. She even said that her mother named her after M793qK."

"How interesting," June said, not quite ready to believe this last bit. "But I didn't know we could eat any alien food, aside from Vergallian Vegan, and supposedly it's terrible."

"We have Vergallian Vegan for lunch once a week and it's good," Sarah said. "And the Blue Tea Café isn't *real* alien food, it's—I forgot the word. But a real alien *owns* the café."

"Then I hope you have a good time," June said. She gazed fondly at her granddaughter, who seemed to be growing by the day. "Is there anything about living on Flower that disappoints you?"

Sarah thought again for a moment. "Only that magic isn't real. Chance joined the final session of our children's beta testing group for *A Mazing Earth* before we left Bits and she said that in Flower's LARPing studios magic was real."

"And it looks fake?"

"No, it *looks* real, but it's not real. It's Flower making the holograms do stuff because she's super smart. Maybe there isn't any real magic after all, but I pretend to believe when we're playing Mouser's game and Hercules tries to teach me."

.....

"It's just baby oil," the assistant make-up artist told Hercules. "If you feel awkward putting it on, I could do it for you."

"It's not that," Hercules said, reluctantly taking up the squeeze bottle. "When they offered me a featured part in the video game I thought I would be getting some good lines. This script just has me standing around and flexing."

"That's only for today. They don't shoot the scenes in order, you know. The first week is always for easy-to-do background stuff so the other production teams have something to start working around. I'm sure that a featured part means you'll get plenty of dialogue."

"Hey, Herc," Lisa called, peeking into the dressing room. "Nice deltoids. Are you oiling up?"

"Under protest," Hercules said. "How come you're not all shiny? We're both in the same basic roles."

"I promised Botan that if anybody got to slather me with baby oil it would be him."

"What did his family decide to do in the end?"

"You mean after his grandparents offered me money to dump him?" Lisa asked.

"Your boyfriend's family tried to buy you off?" the makeup artist asked. "That's just like a Vergallian drama."

"I don't blame them. If I had a son and he started dating somebody like me, I'd pay her to go away. Especially if she was three years older than he was and could beat him up with both of her hands tied behind her back."

"Maybe you shouldn't bring that up so often," Hercules observed. "Either that or start teaching him how to protect himself outside of LARPing studios."

"I'm doing better than that," Lisa said. "It turns out that martial arts counts as a team sport so I talked Botan into signing up with me at a dojo run by a Drazen. Now I'm saving up for a prosthetic tentacle."

"But is Botan's family staying or leaving when Flower stops at Earth?"

"Oh, they're still arguing about it. I'm beginning to think they just like to argue. Botan has practically moved into me and Shadow's cabin to get away from it."

Hercules tried to hand the baby oil bottle back to the makeup artist but it slipped out of his hand. "Sorry," he said, crouching to pick it up, but she waved him off.

"You'll only get more oil on it," she said, using a towel to pick up the bottle. "Don't touch anything until your shoot is over."

"Hey," Hercules said to Shadow's sister. "Did you get any lines?"

"Not today. They just had me flexing and doing katas."

"At least you didn't have to oil up."

Lisa sighed and loosened her robe to show the string bikini she was wearing. "Want to trade?"

"Never mind," Hercules said. "It's going to be hard enough explaining to Rayne why I smell like baby oil."

"We've got special soap for that," the makeup artist told him brightly.

.....

"Hi," Flower's executive assistant said, sticking her head into Rayne's office. "Do you have a minute?"

"Of course, Julie," Rayne said. "How can I help you?"

"One of my jobs is doing wellness checks on recent executive hires just to make sure you're settled in and everything is going well. You've been working for us for eight weeks now. Does everything meet your expectations?"

"Well, it's not what I thought it would be like and my head is still spinning. When you offered me the job working as a comptroller for Flower Entertainment, I thought it was going to be for *A Mazing Earth,* not for all of your anime production and cons as well."

"Is it too much work?" Julie asked.

"No, it just came as a surprise. As the Rules Committee treasurer I was already used to checking the books for all of the business groups on Bits to keep everybody honest about the tithe. This has been easier since you already have everything so well organized."

"It's the Princely Standards bookkeeping system. Flower tried to make me learn it but I played dumb." The young woman shot a nervous look at the desk speaker when she realized what she'd just admitted out loud. "If it's not enough work for you, there's Flower Foods, Flower Shipyards, Flower—"

"It's enough for the moment," Rayne interrupted with a smile. "And I'm still getting used to working out of an office after a lifetime of having my desk in my bedroom. I can't believe how much space you gave me."

"Flower likes big offices because they keep the ship from feeling empty," Julie said. "We're still way under capacity." She moved closer to examine the small hologram of Sarah on the corner of the desk. "Did you have that taken at the new Horten booth in the Bazaar?"

"Yes. I couldn't believe how inexpensive it was for a single-purpose projector with a lifetime guarantee."

"I think we're the only species that get a lifetime—for everybody else, it's a hundred years. Is your daughter happy with her new school?"

"Ecstatic, I'm surprised she hasn't decided to live there," Rayne said with a laugh. "The only fault she's found with life on Flower so far is that she still can't do magic."

"It could be coming," Julie said. "I hear through friends that there's a girl around my age on Union Station who can do real magic, though she's just an apprentice for the time being. But if you think about it, Flower does magic too."

"Do you mean the spinning around to create gravity? That's just physics."

"I think the real magic is how she gets more and more people to move on board and builds an economy out of nothing to keep us all employed."

"I wouldn't call a colony ship that took an advanced species hundreds of years and trillions of creds to build 'nothing,'" Rayne said.

"Without the inhabitants, I'm just alone in a big empty cylinder," Flower interjected herself into the conversation through the desk speaker. "You can't build an economy trading goods and services with yourself—believe me, I tried it. And there's a survey course in advanced accounting systems starting at the Open University next semester covering Princely Standards, Consortium Scales, and Verlock Quadruple Entry Bookkeeping. I've reserved spots for both of you."

.....

"What are you going to take?" Delphi asked Shadow.

"I haven't decided yet," the young man replied, studying the course schedule on his smartphone. "Flower Gaming is paying our tuition, and according to the employee handbook, we can take time off during the work day to attend classes."

"You read the employee handbook? That must be a first."

"I thought I better skim it, and then when I saw it was mainly perks, I went back through it slow. I can't believe the retirement package."

"You're nineteen years old. Don't you think it's a little early to be worrying about retirement?"

"It pays to plan ahead," Shadow said. "Flower Gaming allows double-dipping, so we could put in twenty-five years while the kids are growing up, and then do whatever we wanted with the second half of our lives."

"Kids?" Delphi squawked. "Where did that come from?"

"I had a question about the annuity so I tried asking out loud and Flower answered me. It turned out that she knew about our dating—I guess she kind of eavesdrops a lot—and she reeled off a bunch of statistics about how we're both the best age to have children."

Delphi scowled at the speaker on her desk. "Sometimes I think my mother was right to move directly to Earth."

"You wouldn't like the weather half of the time and there are creepy-crawlies everywhere," the Dollnick artificial intelligence joined the conversation. "I keep all of my pollinating insects and worms on the ag decks where they belong."

"If you're so great, why aren't there any advanced music composition classes at your university? I've been asked to help with a choral arrangement for the Drazen version of *A Mazing Earth* but I don't know a thing about composing for voices."

"I have a tutor for you. Her name is Rinka and she's a certified Drazen choral mistress. You can start tomorrow."

"Will Deli get Open University credit?" Shadow asked.

"Consider it done," Flower said.

Delphi looked from the speaker to Shadow, and back to the speaker again. "And what is this tutoring going to cost me?"

"Not a single cred. I have an arrangement with Rinka in cases like this and we do each other favors. It seems to work out well."

"If that's settled, can we get something to eat?" Shadow asked. "Trying to pick courses has made me hungry."

"I almost forgot we were meeting for lunch," Delphi said, getting up from her desk. "Where do you want to eat?"

"How about the Open University cafeteria? If I'm going to take courses there I better check out the food."

"You mean the pizza."

"We've already tried every lunch counter in the food court, including the one run by the Dollnick guy who came to Bits with Dewey," Shadow said. "There's something weird about the way he dices vegetables that makes me nervous."

"You're just biased against aliens with four arms," Delphi said. "Lume's salads are my favorite quick meals."

.....

"And this is Harry," the Dollnick introduced Belle to a man in his late sixties who was bringing a tray out of the kitchen. "He's a baker by trade, but he and Bill prepare the communal meal we take here."

"Pleased to meet you," Harry said to the clone as he placed the vegetable platter on the table. "Is there anything in particular that you'd like me to prepare for you?"

"Chocolate," Belle responded enthusiastically. "Hot chocolate, chocolate bars, chocolate cake, chocolate pudding, chocolate-covered truffles—"

"You'll have to fight Avisia for those," the baker interrupted. "Bill occasionally gets a batch of them to certify for the All Species Cookbook but they always go missing." He suddenly noticed that Lume had disappeared and had to turn completely around to spot the Dollnick at the minibar making a drink. "At this time in the morning?"

"It's only morning on your clock," Lume replied, throwing a stalk of celery in the blender. "I've been up for three Human-days straight, so for me, it's late afternoon. Are we out of lemon juice?"

"There's a bottle of concentrate in the fridge door, next to the Worcestershire sauce." Harry shook his head in mock dismay and turned back to Belle. "I'm planning on potato pancakes for lunch because they're the only kind your Frunge colleague will eat. Do you have any experience with human food other than chocolate?"

"I spent several months on Bits before returning to Gem Prime for a few weeks to take care of loose ends before accepting this assignment," Belle said. "While all of the food on Bits was better than the nutrition drink I grew up with, it didn't come close to what I ate during an earlier visit to Earth."

"Are you alright with dairy? Potato pancakes are filling, but it's the sour cream and apple sauce that makes them a meal."

"Dairy won't hurt me, though I need an enzyme pill to get the nutritional benefit. I stopped at Union Station for a briefing from EarthCent Intelligence on my way here and I was pleased when they told me about the collegial relations of intelligence professionals on Flower. Have you worked with Lume and the others for long?"

"Oh, I'm not a spy," Harry said with a laugh. "Just a semi-retired baker. My assistant, Bill, seems to have been drawn into your game, though he's not always certain of what side he's on."

"Nice boy, we raised him from a pup," Lume said, handing the Gem a Bloody Mary. "I hope I got the Worcestershire sauce right. I've only made these for the captain's wife and she always says I don't put in enough salt. I've seen her medical charts and she doesn't need it."

Belle took a sip of the drink and couldn't help smiling. "It seems you've done your homework on me as well."

"Just your basic likes and dislikes, professional history, and current enemies. As the only Dollnick intelligence officer on board, I'm Flower's right hands when it comes to hosting."

"My understanding was that Flower works for EarthCent."

"Yes, well, we all do what we can to make ends meet," Lume said with an amused whistle. "Come, I'll take you to the bridge to meet the captain."

.....

"So you're saying that seventy-four percent of our passengers from Bits plan to remain with Flower when we stop at Earth?" Captain Pyun asked Dewey. "EarthCent's president will be disappointed."

"That's the risk of working through proxies," the artificial person said. "Chance made a good case for returning to Earth when we were on Bits, but then she had to get back to Union Station, and Flower has already had eight weeks to tempt people into staying on board."

"I doubt it would have made much difference if Chance had stayed," the captain said. "Flower does a good job of selling herself and she's getting better at it all the time. The people leaving when we get to Earth must be the ones who had their hearts set on returning home or who just can't stand her pushiness."

"Pushy works," Flower informed them via an overhead speaker grille. "And I still have time to convince the remaining twenty-six percent that they're making a mistake. We're talking almost forty thousand people."

"It must be strange for you, Dewey," Captain Pyun said. "You left Bits years ago to find yourself as an artificial person and here it's almost as if Bits is returning to you."

"It's exactly like Bits is returning to me," Dewey said. "Those domes could have been on any planet in the galaxy with similar gravity and it wouldn't have made a difference to their culture. It will be interesting to see how much of it they can retain now that they're plunging into mainstream society."

"Lume is on his way here with our new intelligence agent from the Gem Empire," Flower told them. "They just entered the lift tube."

"Does she have a cover job?" the captain asked.

"A games journalist for Gem Today," Dewey told him.

Woojin sighed and adjusted his three-cornered captain's hat in preparation to meet the latest addition to the group of alien intelligence agents traveling on board. "I hope you know what you're doing, Flower. If somebody had told me ten years ago that my retirement job would be playing figurehead captain on an alien colony ship I would have laughed in their face."

"M793qK says that laughter is the second best medicine," Dewey said.

"Then what's the first?"

"Do you really have to ask?"

.....

"I don't like it," Krey said to the Farling doctor. "Too many personalities involved."

"Flower is doing her best to emulate one of the most manipulative sentients in the galaxy," M793qK said, handing the Human Empire's Cayl mentor an elaborate cocktail that he'd just completed mixing from what a visitor to his clinic would have assumed were medical supplies. "Even the best plans don't come without risk. The galaxy wouldn't be very interesting if they did."

"Are you sure you can't do anything about their lifespans? If we just had a few hundred years to work with them, it would make things much simpler."

The alien doctor, who resembled a giant beetle standing on its hind set of limbs, rubbed out a chuckle on his speaking legs.

"If life was simple, I'd have taken over as the head of the Farling Hierarchy centuries ago and we never would have met. Speaking of co-conspirators, are you with us, Flower?"

"I've got two groups in LARPing studios and I'm introducing the captain to the latest intelligence agent to join us," the Dollnick AI replied immediately. "Between running the ship and turning the lights on and off for a million Humans who think I'm a voice-activated switch, I'm a bit busy at the moment. But I think I can declare that we've achieved over ninety-five percent of our Phase One goals and we can proceed to Phase Two immediately."

From the Author

The next two EarthCent books are a bit of an experiment as they both take place on Flower with overlapping timelines. I originally intended to release them within a week or two of each other, but it's important to read them in order so I might stretch it to the usual three months. The first will be **Double Living**, the sixth book in **EarthCent Universe**, and the second is tentatively titled **Bits of Flower**, the second in **EarthCent Metaverse**. If you're new to the EarthCent books, you can start back at the beginning with **Union Station 1, 2, 3**, a discounted three-book bundle.

For notifications of new releases, sign up for the mailing list at www.ifitbreaks.com. I also post new releases to facebook.com/E.M.Foner/ and respond to all temperate e-mail sent to e_foner@yahoo.com

Also by the author in reading order:

Destiny: Union Station

Date Night on Union Station

Alien Night on Union Station

High Priest on Union Station

Spy Night on Union Station

Carnival on Union Station

Wanderers on Union Station

Vacation on Union Station

Guest Night on Union Station

Word Night on Union Station

Party Night on Union Station

Review Night on Union Station

Family Night on Union Station

Book Night on Union Station

LARP Night on Union Station

Career Night on Union Station

Last Night on Union Station

Independent Living

Soup Night on Union Station

Assisted Living

Freelance on the Galactic Tunnel Network

Con Living

Empire Night on Union Station

Space Living

Traders on the Galactic Tunnel Network

Orphans on the Galactic Tunnel Network

Swap Night on Union Station

Slow Living

Artists on the Galactic Tunnel Network

History Night on Union Station

Printed in Great Britain
by Amazon

16052403R00173